Life is sweet with

Jenny
COLGAN

Jenny
COLGAN

Christmas
at the
Cupcake
Cafe

sphere

SPHERE

First published in Great Britain in 2012 by Sphere
Reprinted 2012

Copyright © Jenny Colgan 2012
'Baking your first cupcake' piece,
copyright © The Caked Crusader 2011

The moral right of the author has been asserted.

A CIP catalogue record for this book
is available from the British Library.

ISBN 978-0-7515-4922-5

Typeset in Caslon by M Rules
Printed and bound in Great Britain by
Clays Ltd, St Ives plc

Papers used by Sphere are from well-managed forests
and other responsible sources.

MIX
Paper from
responsible sources
FSC
www.fsc.org   FSC® C104740

To anyone who still leaves a mince pie out for Santa
(and a carrot for the reindeer).

A Word From Jenny

Hello! Even though *Meet Me at the Cupcake Café* was my thirteenth novel, I found it was a harder one to leave behind than some of the others. Maybe because it was the longest book I'd ever written, I really felt that I'd grown fond of the characters. I found myself going into Christmas mode after it came out – I love Christmas – and starting to make my Christmas cake and some mince pies and thinking – I know this makes me sound totally ridiculous, by the way – I wonder how Issy would do them? So I figured I'd better just write them down. Plus, if you enjoy the recipes, it's nice to have a few together just for this time of year. We've also reprinted (so when you see it, don't think SWIZZ!), the Caked Crusader's brilliant introductory guide to baking cupcakes from the last book, in case you're just starting out.

It's weird, because although I like reading sequels,

I've never written one before. There are a couple of things I sometimes don't like about them, though, so I have tried to avoid paragraphs like: 'Jane walked into the room. "Hello, Jane!" said Peter. "How are you ever since you were abandoned in that shipwreck and had to take part in human cannibalism then a dolphin picked you up and gave you a ride home where you married your true love who turned out not to be your brother after all?" "Fine," said Jane.'

I have also tried to avoid the opposite, where you have to remember everything yourself (come on, we're all busy), like: '"This is worse than Bermuda," spat Jane, hurling her prosthetic leg across the room.'

So. Instead of having to shoehorn everyone in, here's a quick rundown (and also, welcome if you're new!).

Issy Randall lost her job in an estate agency, and threw her redundancy money into opening the Cupcake Café in Stoke Newington, which is a mixed, villagey area of London (her grandad, **Joe**, had been a baker in Manchester and she had always loved to bake and decided to turn it into a career).

She employed **Pearl McGregor**, who is bringing up **Louis** mostly single-handedly, although his dad, **Benjamin Kmbota**, swings by from time to time; and **Caroline**, who is in the process of divorcing her rich husband. And Issy broke up from her estate agent boyfriend Graeme, who was horrible, and has started dating **Austin Tyler**, the local bank manager, who is raising his brother,

Darny, after their parents died. Austin was offered a new job overseas, but that got delayed – it's now over a year since the last book, if that makes sense. Well, anyway, Louis is four now, and in reception, Darny is eleven and in his first year of secondary school, and Issy's best friend **Helena**, a nurse, has had a baby with her doctor boyfriend **Ashok**.

So hopefully we're all up to speed!

With grateful thanks to BBC Books and Delia Smith for allowing me to use her recipe. And another thanks to The Little Loaf for the recipe in Chapter fifteen. For more recipes go to http://thelittleloaf.wordpress.com

Let us know at www.facebook.com/jennycolganbooks or @jennycolgan on twitter if you try any of the recipes, and may I wish you the merriest of Christmases.

Very warmest wishes,

Jenny

Author's Note

All these recipes have been successfully tested by me, many repeatedly and greedily. If you have time to do the Christmas cake a good four weeks in advance, it really helps!

NB: altitude cookies are very, very sweet indeed at ground level.

Sitting under the mistletoe
(Pale-green, fairy mistletoe),
One last candle burning low,
All the sleepy dancers gone,
Just one candle burning on,
Shadows lurking everywhere:
Some one came, and kissed me there,

Walter de la Mare, 'Mistletoe'

Chapter One

Gingerbread

This is not for gingerbread men, which is more of a cookie recipe as it has to stay hard and crunchy. And it is not for gingerbread houses, unless you have endless time on your hands and (let's say it quietly) are a bit of a show-off who would rather their cakes were admired than devoured. No, this is old-fashioned soft, sticky gingerbread. It doesn't take long to make, but you'll be glad you did.

NB Oil the container before you fill it with treacle. Otherwise you and your dishwasher are going to fall out really badly.

50g white sugar

50g brown sugar
120g butter

1 egg

180ml treacle

300g self-raising flour

1 tsp baking powder

1 tbsp powdered cinnamon

1 tbsp powdered ginger (or a little more if you like)

½ tsp ground cloves (I just threw in a 'lucky' clove)

½ tsp salt

60ml hot water

Preheat oven to 175°C/gas mark 3. Grease a loaf tin or square baking tin.

Cream sugar and butter together (you can do this entire thing in the mixer), then add the egg and the treacle.

Mix the spices, baking powder, flour and salt. Fold in to wet mixture. Add the water, then pour into baking tin and bake for 45 minutes.

You can sprinkle icing sugar on the top, or make an icing glaze, or just slice it like it is – proper yummy, sticky Christmas gingerbread. Serve liberally to people you like.

☕

The scent of cinnamon, orange peel and ginger perfumed the air, with a strong undercurrent of coffee. Outside the rain was battering against the large windows of the eau-de-nil-painted exterior of the Cupcake Café, tucked into a little grey stone close next to an ironmonger's and a fenced-in tree that looked chilled and bare in the freezing afternoon.

Issy, putting out fresh chestnut-purée cupcakes decorated with tiny green leaves, took a deep breath of happiness and wondered if it was too early to start playing her *Silver Bells* CD. The weather had been uncharacteristically mild for much of November, but now winter was truly kicking in.

Customers arrived looking beaten and battered by the gale, disgorging umbrellas into the basket by the front door (so many got left behind, Pearl had commented that if they ran into financial difficulties, they could always start a second-hand umbrella business), then would pause halfway through wrestling with their jackets as the warm scent reached their nostrils. And Issy could see it come over them: their shoulders, hunched against the rain, would slowly start to unfurl in the cosy atmosphere of the café; their tense, anxious London faces would relax, and a smile would play around their lips as they approached the old-fashioned glass-fronted cabinet which hosted the daily array of goodies: cupcakes piled high with the best butter icing, changing every week depending on Issy's whim, or whether she'd just received a tip-off about the best vanilla pods, or a special on rose hips, or had the urge to go a bit mad with hazelnut meringue. The huge banging orange coffee machine (the colour clashed completely with the pale greens and greys and florals of the café itself, but they'd had to get it on the cheap, and it worked like an absolute charm) was fizzing in the background, the little fire was lit and cheery-looking (Issy would have preferred wood, but it was banned, so they had gas flames); there were newspapers on poles and books on the bookshelves; wifi, and cosy nooks and corners in which to hide oneself, as well as a long open table where mums could sit with their buggies and not block everybody else's way.

Smiling, people would take a while to make up their minds. Issy liked to go through the various things they had on offer, explain what went into each one: how she crushed the strawberries then left them in syrup for the little strawberry tarts they did in the summer; or the whole blueberries she liked to use in the middle of the summer fruits cupcake; or, as now, making customers smell her new batch of fresh cloves. Pearl simply let people choose. They had to make sure Caroline had had enough sleep or she tended to get slightly impatient and make remarks about the number of calories in each treat. This made Issy very cross.

'The "c" word is banned in this shop,' she'd said. 'People don't come in here looking to feel guilty. They're looking to relax, take a break, sit down with their friends. They don't need you snorting away about saturated fats.'

'I'm just trying to be helpful,' said Caroline. 'The

economy is in trouble. I know how much tax avoidance my ex-husband does. There's not going to be the money to pay for cardiac units, that's all I'm saying.'

Pearl came up from the basement kitchen with a new tray of gingerbread men. The first had been snapped up in moments by the children coming in after school, delighted by their little bow ties and fearful expressions. She saw Issy standing there looking a bit dreamy as she served up two cinnamon rolls with a steaming latte to a man with a large tummy, a red coat and a white beard.

'Don't even think it,' she said.

'Think what?' said Issy guiltily.

'About starting up the entire Christmas shebang. That isn't Santa.'

'I might be Santa,' protested the old man. 'How would you know?'

'Because this would be your busy season,' said Pearl, turning her focus back to her boss.

Issy's eyes strayed reluctantly to the glass jar of candy canes that had somehow found their way to being beside the cash till.

'It's *November*!' said Pearl. 'We've just finished selling our Guy Fawkes cupcakes, remember? And don't make me remind you how long it took me to get all that spiderwebbing down from Hallowe'en.'

'Maybe we should have left it up there for fake snow,' wondered Issy.

'No,' said Pearl. 'It's ridiculous. These holidays take up such a long time and everyone gets sick of them and they're totally over the top and inappropriate.'

'Bah humbug,' said Issy. But Pearl would not be jarred out of her bad mood.

'And it's a difficult year for everyone,' said Caroline. 'I've told Hermia the pony may have to go if her father doesn't buck up his ideas.'

'Go where?' said Pearl.

'To the happy hunting grounds,' said Caroline promptly. 'Meanwhile he's going to Antigua. Antigua! Did he ever take me to Antigua? No. You know what Antigua's like,' she said to Pearl.

'Why would I?' said Pearl.

Issy leapt into action. Caroline was a good, efficient worker, but she definitely lacked a sensitivity chip since her husband left her, and now he was trying to cut her maintenance. Caroline had never really known anything other than a very comfortable life. Working for a living and mixing with normal people she still tended to treat as something of a hilarious novelty.

'Well, it is nearly the last week of November,' said Issy. 'Everyone else is doing red cups and Santa hats and jingle bells. Frankly, London is not the place to be if you want to escape Christmas. It does the most wonderful Christmas in the world, and I want us to be a part of it.'

'Ho ho ho,' said the fat man with the white beard. They looked at him, then at each other.

'Stop it,' said Pearl.

'No, don't!' said Issy. She was so excited about Christmas this year; there was so much to celebrate. The Cupcake Café wasn't exactly going to make them rich, but they were keeping their heads above water. Her best friend Helena and her partner Ashok were going to join them with their bouncing (and she was very bouncing indeed) one-year-old Chadani Imelda, and Issy's mother might come too. The last time Issy had heard from Marian, in September, she'd been on a Greek island where she was currently making rather a good living teaching yoga to women who were pretending they were in *Mamma Mia*. Marian was a free spirit, which was supposed to make her romantic, but didn't always make her very reliable, mother-wise.

And then of course there was Austin, Issy's gorgeous, distracted boyfriend with the mismatched socks and the intense expression. Austin was curly-haired and green-eyed, with horn-rimmed spectacles he tended to take on and off again a lot when he was thinking, and Issy's heart bounced in her chest every time she thought of him.

The door pinged again, unleashing another torrent of customers: young women in to have a sit-down after some early Christmas shopping. Their bags overflowed with tinsel and hand-made ornaments from the little independent shops on the pretty local high street, and their flushed cheeks and wet hair meant they brought the cold in with them in a riot of shaken anoraks and unwrapped scarves. Perhaps just a quick chain of fairy lights above the coffee machine, thought Issy. Christmas in London. Best in the world.

Christmas in New York, thought Austin, looking up and around him, dazzled. It really was something else; as dramatic as people said. Early snow was falling, and every shop window was lit up with over-the-top displays and luxury goods. Radio City Music Hall had a tree several storeys high and something called the Rockettes playing – he felt as though he had fallen through time and emerged in a movie from the fifties.

He adored it, he couldn't help it. New York made him feel like a child, even though he was supposed to be here very much as a grown-up. It was so exciting. His bank had sent him here on an 'ideas-sharing exercise' after the American office had apparently requested somebody calm and 'not a bullshit artist'. It appeared New York had tired of its crazed, risk-taking bankers and now desperately needed anyone with a reasonably level head to hold things together. Austin was disorganised and a little impatient with paperwork, but he rarely made loans that went bad, and was very good at spotting who was worth taking a risk on (Issy had most definitely been one of those) and who came in spouting pipe dreams and the latest management jargon. He was a safe pair of hands in a financial world that, increasingly, appeared to have gone completely crazy.

Issy had helped him pack, as otherwise he couldn't be trusted to keep hold of matching socks. She'd kissed him on the forehead.

'So you'll come back full of amazing New York know-how and everyone will have to bend and scrape before you and they'll make you king of the bank.'

'I don't think they have kings. Maybe they do. I haven't climbed up to those esteemed heights yet. I want a gigantic crown if they do.'

'And one of those pole things. For whacking.'

'Is that what those are for?'

'I don't know what the point is of being a king if you can't do whacking,' pointed out Issy.

'You're right about everything,' said Austin. 'I will also ask for fake ermine.'

She had gently pinged his nose.

'What a wise and gracious king you are. Look at me!' she said. 'I can't believe I'm balling socks for you. I feel like I'm sending you to boarding school.'

'Ooh, will you be my very firm matron?' said Austin teasingly.

'Are you obsessed with whacking today, or what?

Have I just had to wait all this time for your disgusting perv side to come out?'

'You started it, perv-o.'

She had driven him to the airport. 'And then you'll come back and it'll be nearly Christmas!'

Austin smiled. 'Do you really not mind doing it the same way as last year? Truly?'

'Truly?' said Issy. 'Truly, last year was the best Christmas I've ever had.'

And she had meant it. The first time Issy's mother had left – or the first time she remembered clearly, without it getting muddled in her head – she was seven, and writing out a letter to Santa, being very careful with the spelling.

Her mother had glanced over her shoulder. She was going through one of her rougher patches, which usually corresponded with a lot of complaining about the Manchester weather and the dark evenings and the sodding leaves. Joe, Issy's grampa, and Issy had exchanged looks as Marian paced up and down like a tiger in a cage, then stopped to look at Issy's list.

'My own piper? Why would you want a piper? We're not even Scottish.'

'No,' explained Issy patiently. Her mother had no interest in baking and relatively little in food, unless it was mung beans, or tofu – neither of which were readily available in 1980s Manchester – or some other fad she'd read about in one of the badly mimeographed pamphlets about alterative lifestyles she subscribed to.

'An icing piper. Gramps won't let me use his.'

'It's too big and you kept ripping it,' grumbled Grampa Joe, then winked at Issy to show that he wasn't really cross. 'That butterscotch icing you made was pretty good, though, my girl.'

Issy beamed with pride.

Marian glanced downwards. 'My Little Pony oven gloves ... My darling, I don't think they do those.'

'They should,' said Issy.

'Pink mixing bowl ... Girl's World ... what's that?'

'It's a doll's head. You put make-up on it.' Issy had heard the other girls in her class talking about it. That was what they were all getting. She hadn't heard anyone wanting a mixing bowl. So she'd decided she'd better join in with them.

'You put make-up on a plastic head?' said Marian, who had perfect skin and had never worn make-up in her life. 'For what, to make her look like a tramp?'

Issy shook her head, blushing a bit.

'Women don't need make-up,' said Marian. 'That's just to please men. You are perfectly fine as you are, do you understand? It's what's in here that counts.' She rapped Issy sharply on the temple. 'God, this bloody country. Imagine selling make-up to small children.'

'I don't see too much harm in it,' said Grampa Joe mildly. 'At least it's a toy. The others are all work tools.'

'Oh Lord, it's so much stuff,' said Marian. 'The commercialisation of Christmas is disgusting. It drives me mad. Everyone stuffing themselves and making themselves ill and trying to pretend they've got these perfect bloody nuclear families when everybody knows it's all a total lie and we're living under the Thatcher jackboot and the bomb could go off at any moment . . .'

Grampa Joe shot her a warning look. Issy got very upset when Marian started talking about the bomb, or made noises about taking her to Greenham Common, or forced her to wear her CND badge to school. Then he went on calmly buttering the bread they were having with their turnip soup. (Marian insisted on very plain vegetables; Grampa Joe provided sugar and carbohydrates. It was a balanced diet, if you included both extremes.)

Issy didn't bother sending the letter after all, didn't even sign her name, which at that point had a big loveheart above the 'I' because all her friends did the same.

Two days later Marian had gone, leaving behind a letter.

Darling, I need some sun on my face or I can't breathe.
I wanted to take you with me, but Joe says you need
schooling more than you need sunshine. Given that I
left school at fourteen I can't really see the point
myself but best do what he says for now. Have a very
lovely Christmas my darling and I will see you soon.

Next to the card was a brand-new, unwrapped, shiny-boxed Girl's World.

Issy became aware, later in life, that it must have cost her mother something to buy it – something more than money – but it didn't feel like that at the time. Despite her grandad's efforts to interest her in it, she left the box unopened in the corner of her bedroom, unplayed with.

They both woke early on Christmas morning, Joe from long habit, Issy from excitement of a kind, although she was aware that other children she knew would be waking up with their mummies and probably their daddies too. It broke Joe's heart to see how she tried so hard not to mind, and as she unwrapped her new mixing bowl, and her lovely little whisk, all child-sized, and the tiniest patty pans he could find, and they made pancakes together before walking to church on Christmas morning, saying hello to their many friends and neighbours, it broke his heart all over again to see that some of her truly didn't mind; that even as a small child she was already used to being let down by the person who ought to be there for her the most.

She'd looked up at him, eyes shining as she flipped over a pancake.

'Merry Christmas, my darling,' he had said, kissing her gently on the head. 'Merry Christmas.'

Austin had his own reasons for hating Christmas. He'd never really bothered since that first one after their parents died, when a tiny Darny hadn't cried, hadn't yelled, hadn't moaned, had simply sat in silence, staring bewildered at the ridiculous number of presents from everyone he had ever met cluttering up the corner of the room. He hadn't wanted to open a single one. Austin hadn't blamed him. In the end, they'd unplugged the phone from the wall (after Austin had turned down endless invites, everyone rang to coo pitying noises at them, and it was unbearable) and gone back to bed to watch *Transformers* on the computer whilst eating crisps. Somehow, watching ludicrous gigantic machine robots smashing lumps out of everything was as close to their mood as they could get, and they'd done something similar every year since.

But last year, he and Issy had been so new together, so wrapped up in one another, and it had been thrilling. He'd thought for ever about what presents to get her, and she had been utterly delighted: a going-out dress from her favourite little Stoke Newington vintage shop, and a fancy pair of shoes that she couldn't walk in. Oddly, it wasn't the fact that he'd bought them so much as what they represented: nights out, and fun, which could be hard to come by when you were working all hours.

'I thought you'd get me a pinny,' she'd said, trying on the blue dress, which made her eyes a vivid bluey-green and fitted her perfectly. 'Or a mixer or something. Everyone else always does! If I get one more cupcake jar, I'm going to start selling them on the side.'

And in the bottom of the bag, bought with his bonus – he had been the only person in the entire bank to get a bonus that year, he seemed to recall – a small, but immaculately cut, pair of diamond earrings. Her eyes had gone all big and wide and she had been completely unable to speak.

She had worn them every single day since.

And they had spoiled Darny horribly with games (Austin) and books (Issy), and watched telly in their pyjamas and had smoked salmon and champagne at eleven, and the weather was too disgusting outside for anyone to mention a walk, and Issy had cooked an amazing lunch ... Issy had ... she had made it all right again. She had made it fun; made it their own Christmas. She hadn't tried to gussy it up, or push them into party games or silly hats or church or long walks, like the aunties would have done. She understood and respected entirely their right to watch *Transformers* all day in their pyjamas and had sweetly been there with them whilst they did so.

'I can't wait till Christmas,' said Austin at the airport. 'But I wish you were coming to New York.'

'One day,' said Issy, who longed to visit more than almost anything. 'Go and be clever and impressive and wow them all, and then come straight back home to us.'

And now here he was in the middle of Manhattan, Darny back in London with Issy. A year ago, the idea of leaving his headstrong, hyper-intelligent, super-cunning eleven-year-old brother with anyone other than an armed response team and a team of vets with tranquilliser guns would have seemed utter madness. Darny had bounced from school to school and run rings around his elder brother since their parents' death in an accident. Austin had immediately given up his college course and taken a banking job in order to keep a roof over their heads and prevent his brother being taken away by social services, or any number of well-meaning aunties. Darny had not repaid this by being particularly grateful.

Yet somehow, after being frankly abominable to all Austin's other girlfriends – girls who had cooed over Darny and gone all mushy-eyed at tall, handsome Austin, which made Darny want to vomit – he had really taken to Issy. Indeed, the fact that Darny had liked her so much had been one of the first things that had attracted Austin to her in the first place – along with her large eyes, generous mouth and easy laugh. Now when he thought of them together in the little house that had been, frankly, a bit of a midden when it was just the two boys together, but that under Issy's auspices had become cosy and welcoming, he got the sudden urge to ring her. He was on his way to a meeting and, not trusting himself to make his way around the subway system, had decided to walk. He checked his watch: 11 a.m. That meant 4 p.m. in London. Worth a shot.

'Hey.'

"Hey,' said Issy, struggling up the stairs with five kilo bags of finest milled Ethiopian blend. People were queuing for their afternoon pick-me-ups, or their post-school treats, but she was still delighted to hear from him. 'Wassup?'

'Are you stuffing plum pudding in your gob, by any chance?' teased Austin. 'You want to watch for wastage.'

'I am *not*,' said Issy, outraged, letting the coffee drop on the counter. 'Yes, hello, can I help you?'

'Do you have any Christmas cake?'

Issy arched her eyebrows at Pearl. 'Not yet,' she said. 'Apparently the little baby Jesus starts to cry if we start celebrating ten seconds before the official beginning of Advent.'

'That's a shame.'

'It *is*.'

'Don't disrespect my beliefs,' sniffed Pearl.

'So, anyway, here I am, hanging on the unbelievably expensive mobile phone from New York,' said Austin.

'Sorry, my love,' said Issy as the customer pointed, slightly disappointed, to a cherry-topped cupcake instead. They wouldn't be, Issy thought, when they got to the glacé cherries hidden inside. 'How is it?'

'Oh, it's amazing!' said Austin. 'I mean, just fantastic. The lights everywhere, and they're skating down at the Rockefeller Center ... that's this huge building with an ice rink outside it, and it's full of skaters and they're really good, and there's music playing around the street corners, and Central Park is all lit up with these amazing lights, and you can take a horse and cart ride through it with a blanket and mistletoe and … well, it's just fantastic and amazing and wow.'

'Ooh, really. Bugger. Argh, I wish I was there so much. Stop having such a good time without me!'

A thought struck her.

'Is it super-brilliant? Are they all being dead nice to you? They're not going to offer you a job, are they?'

She felt a sudden clutch of panic in her breast that he was going to up sticks and move away, an idea that would make her best friend Helena stop breastfeeding for ninety seconds and snort that that was ridiculous, which was all right for Helena, who was sitting there with Ashok dashing about trying to fulfil her every need, constantly glowing with the joy of winning such a magnificent prize as H, with her wild long red hair and triumphant bosom; her way of sweeping through life felling lesser mortals as she went. Issy just wasn't that confident a personality.

'Nah,' said Austin. 'They're just showing me round, swapping ideas, blah blah.'

He thought it was best not to mention to Issy that someone in the back office had asked him if it was true they were shutting half the London branches. There was more spurious gossip in banking than there was in the Cupcake Café Stitch 'n' Bitch, and that was saying something.

Issy tried to stop her mind from racing overtime. What

if they wanted him? What would she do about the café? She couldn't leave it. She couldn't just leave and dump everything she'd worked so hard for. But if Austin was in love with amazing, fantastic New York, and she was in love with Austin … well. It was a pickle. No. She was being stupid.

She thought back to their parting at the airport. It had been rather a thrill – Heathrow had no compunction about when Christmas started, and had decorated its huge high-ceilinged terminal with long hangings of purple tinsel and gigantic silver trees.

'This is like that film,' she'd whispered to Austin, who was looking rather dashing in a smart green scarf she'd bought him.

'It isn't,' Austin had said. 'All the children in that film are cute.'

Darny was standing to one side and scowling. His hair stuck up in exactly the same place as his big brother's.

'Don't do that thing. It's disgusting.'

'What, this thing?' Austin had said, nuzzling Issy's neck till she squealed.

'Yes, that thing,' said Darny. 'It's having a terrible effect on my development. I am basically scarred for life.'

Austin glanced at Issy. 'Worth it, though,' he said, and she had grinned with happiness. She'd watched his tall figure disappear into the crowds at passport control, turning at the last moment to give them a cheery wave before he disappeared. She wanted to shout it to the world:

'That's my man! Over there! That's him! He's mine! He loves me and everything!'

She'd turned to Darny. 'Just you and me for a week,' she said cheerily. It had been unorthodox, falling in love with a man who already had someone else in his life , but she and Darny rubbed along pretty well.

'I'm very sad,' said Darny, not sounding or looking in the least perturbed. 'Can you buy me a muffin?'

'I am *far*,' said Issy, 'too fond of you to let you eat air-port muffins. Come on home, I'll make you something.'

'Can I use the mixer?'

'Yes,' said Issy. Then, after a pause, 'You mean to make cakes, right?'

Darny tutted.

Somehow, Issy supposed, she'd expected Austin to be desperate to get back home. Anyway, in New York they were all shouty and fast-paced and yelled 'buy buy sell sell' all day, didn't they? That wouldn't suit Austin at all, she was sure of it. He was so laid-back. He would check a few things out, meet some people, then they'd all go along as before. They'd threatened to send him overseas a year ago, but with the economy being how it was, it hadn't transpired, and that was just fine by Issy. So she was a little put out to hear him so cheerful.

'That sounds great,' she said, a tad unenthusiastically. 'London looks amazing too. Everywhere is all dolled up with lights and decorations and windows. Well, every-where except for here.'

Pearl coughed, unabashed.

'Oh yeah,' said Austin. 'Oh, but wow, you have to see it. The skyscrapers put special red lights in their win-dows, and there's snow on the streets . . . it's just magical.'

Issy picked up a stack of chocolate-stained plates and cups that had just landed on the countertop next to her.

'Magical,' she said.

Austin frowned after hanging up the phone. Issy hadn't been quite her normal ebullient self. He supposed it was hard when there was a time difference. Everyone was at sixes and sevens with one another. He'd have to call again later anyway, to talk to Darny, even though Darny was entering adolescence and was thus quite likely either to answer every question with a grunt or, even worse, an invisible shrug, or to start castigating his brother for being in the finance industry and therefore, as far as Darny was concerned, responsible for bringing about the end of the world, massive apocalyptic catastrophe and general evil. Austin deeply regretted letting him read *The Hunger Games*.

Explaining that Austin's job was necessary to put the enormous amount of food Darny got through on the table and buy him new trainers for his gigantic boat-like feet didn't seem to cut him any slack whatsoever. Darny only muttered about how come Issy managed to buy Fairtrade coffee, which somehow made her one of the nice capitalists. Issy would wink at Austin and try and explain to Darny that she couldn't have opened the shop without Austin's help, whereupon Darny would end the conversation by tutting loudly and slouching off, his thin shoulders hunched. It was going to be, Austin sometimes thought, a tricky next seven years.

The café bell rang and in rushed Louis, Pearl's four-year-old, with his best friend, Big Louis. Big Louis was substantially smaller than Louis but had been at the school first, and there was another Louis, smaller than both of them, so that was how it worked. Louis had explained this in painstaking detail to Pearl one night, and it had taken him almost the entire length of the number 73 bus trip to do so.

Pearl had tried to move from her south London estate up to north London to be nearer work and Louis' excellent, difficult-to-get-into school (they'd used the café address, which she'd told her vicar made her feel uneasy and he had patted her hand and told her that the Lord worked in mysterious ways and he'd heard William Patten was a wonderful school), but it was difficult: her mother, who lived with them, hated leaving the house, and Ben, Louis' dad, didn't live with them but popped in regularly, and she really didn't want that to stop. So it made for a long commute, but she couldn't think of a better plan right at the moment.

Big Louis' mum picked the boys up every day from reception, a massive favour she was repaid for in coffee and buns. Pearl left the counter and crouched down so Louis could launch himself into her arms. It was bad for her knees, but, she told herself sternly, there would come a day, who knew when, when he would no longer want to rush to her and give her a huge cuddle and a big wet kiss on the cheek and tell her all about his day and generally behave as if she was the best person in the world; which to him, of course, she was. She never grew tired of it.

'Hello, sweetheart,' she said. Although Big Louis' mum probably felt exactly the same way about her own little boy (there was, in fact, no probably about it), Pearl could never help but feel that the curve of Louis' smooth cheeks, his long black eyelashes, his soft tight curls, his round little tummy and ready smile were possibly the most beautiful things she had ever seen. And even to dis-interested observers, he was an appealing-looking child.

'MUMMY!' Louis had a worried look on his face as he pulled a picture out of his *Cars* rucksack. It was a large butterfly, roughly painted in splurges with silver paper on its head and wired antennae. 'BUFLYS ARE BUGS! DID YOU KNOW THAT?'

'Well, yes, I suppose I did know that. Don't you remember the book about how hungry he is?'

'They are caterpillars. Caterpillars are bugs with legs

23

but they are also butterflies. Like toast,' he added reflectively.

'What do you mean, like toast?' said Pearl.

'There is bread, and there is toast. But one is bread and then it is toast and is different. I hungry,' said Louis.

'I HUNGRY,' barked Big Louis, suddenly anxious in case he was missing out.

'Here you go, you two,' said Issy, appearing with some toasted fruit bread and two cups of milk. Being let loose in a cake shop every day wasn't very good for four-year-olds, so they all made sure they kept an eye on the boys, particularly Louis, whose body shape echoed his mother's, and who liked nothing better than settling down for a chat about diggers with a customer – anyone would do, although he particularly liked Doti, the postman – with a large wodge of icing in his chubby fingers.

'Mamma?' said Louis. 'Is it Christmas?'

'Not yet,' said Pearl. 'When it's Advent, and we start opening all the little doors up till Jesus comes. That's Christmas.'

'Everyone at school says it's Christmas. We have a big tree in our classroom and Miss Sangita says that it's a good time for everyone to slebate.'

'Slebate?'

'Yes.'

'Well, it *is* a good time to celebrate. In its own time. This is still November. Fireworks and Hallowe'en just finished, remember? Scary costumes and loud noises?'

Louis looked down at the floor and bit his lip. 'I'm not afraid of fireworks,' he said quietly. He had been, undeniably, very very scared of the fireworks. And although he had enjoyed getting the sweeties at Hallowe'en, he had found running into ghosts and ghouls – particularly the big boys off the estate in their Scream masks, charging about shouting on their bicycles – rather off-putting too, if they were being honest about it. Miss Sangita had told Pearl that Louis was a little sensitive, and Pearl had sniffed and said that what she meant was not a total lout like the rest of the children, and Miss Sangita had smiled nicely and said she didn't think that attitude was really necessary, and Pearl had felt cowed again, and remembered that this was a nice school and she had to stop panicking about her boy.

She thought about it too as they rode the bus home together, Louis helpfully pointing out every Christmas tree and decoration in every house they passed – and there were many. When they reached the centre of town to change buses, his eyes grew huge and round as he looked at the window displays of the famous department stores: Hamleys, with its feast of magical moving animals in a woodland scene; the great cascade of lights down Regent Street; John Lewis, its windows seeming to brim with every form of bounty imaginable. The pavements were full of excited shoppers looking for bargains and soaking up the atmosphere, and already pubs and restaurants, festooned with gaudy garlands and turkey menus, were packed full of revellers. Pearl sighed. She couldn't deny it. Christmas was definitely coming.

It was just, it had been such a hard year. Not for her – the shop was doing well, and Issy had been more than kind, making her a manager, paying her as much as she was able, as well as being flexible for Louis' sake. Pearl had even, for the first time in her life, been able to put a bit by; to begin, possibly, to think about a future; moving closer to the shop and Louis' school and away from the estate. Not that it was a bad estate, she thought loyally. Not the worst, by any means. But to move into a little place that wasn't exactly like everyone else's, where she could decorate how she wanted and have an extra room for her mum. That would be nice. That would be very nice indeed. And it had looked, briefly, like it might be possible.

That was before the economic downturn had taken its terrible toll on Benjamin.

If Pearl had had a Facebook page – which she didn't, as she didn't have an internet connection – her heart status with Benjamin would have been 'it's complicated'. Ben was absolutely gorgeous, and they'd dated and she'd got pregnant, and whilst obviously she wouldn't swap Louis for the world – he was the best thing that had ever happened to her – nonetheless, Ben had never lived with them and came and went in their lives far more than she would have liked. The problem was that Louis absolutely worshipped him; thought his tall, handsome, muscular dad was a superhero, swooping in on the family from time to time in between top-secret missions. And Pearl couldn't bear to burst his happy bubble; his cries of joy when Ben came round, and it felt, for a while, like they were a proper family. So she was stuck. She couldn't move on. It wasn't fair to Louis. Things had been starting to get better for Ben too, the work coming in more steadily . . . until the last six months.

The building site jobs had dried up, just like that. He'd got some work up at the Olympics park, but it felt like every contractor in the whole of Europe had bowled up there, and the competition was fierce. Elsewhere, there wasn't much either. People were putting off moving or building extensions or finishing renovations or expanding their premises till they found out how the cards would fall; whether they would lose their jobs, or have their hours cut or see their incomes fall; whether their pensions would flatline and their savings would become worthless against inflation. Pearl struggled with the one bedroom; sometimes, she thought, looking out at the rain, she had no idea how people managed to heat larger properties at all. Keeping her power key charged up was a job in itself.

It wasn't Benjamin's fault, it really wasn't. He was looking for work, trying everything, but there just wasn't anything for him, and he'd had a few problems with the benefit office in the past, so he got the absolute bare legal minimum.

She knew him so well. He was easily led, but he was a proud man. A hard worker when he had work, but if he didn't ... Well. He had a lot of friends who dabbled in things she didn't want Louis' daddy anywhere near.

So she'd been helping him out, here and there, and more and more, and she didn't know where it would end. Benjamin hated taking the money too, hated having to ask and beg like a dog from a woman. Which meant that their rare nights out, the odd meal, the odd staying over – it killed her to admit it, but he was still the best-looking man she had ever seen in her life – became less frequent. It was no fun taking your woman out to dinner when she had to pick up the tab.

Pearl was really feeling the pinch. But oh, Benjamin was so good with their boy. He played with Louis for hours, was genuinely impressed by his daubings and scrawlings from school; would kick a ball round the waste ground or discuss diggers and cranes till the cows came home. Pearl would starve before she deprived her son of that.

It wasn't going to come to that. But Christmas was going to be tight, that was all, and she hated being reminded of that fact in every decorated window and expectant-looking face.

Chapter Two

Christmas Cherry Chocolate Biscuit Slice

This is a no-cook cake that is utterly delicious. You can add a slug of rum if you want to be extra seasonal, but bear in mind it won't burn off in the cooking. ☺

275g butter (I used about 200g unsalted)
150ml golden syrup (2 very generous tablespoons)
225g good-quality dark chocolate
200g digestive biscuits (roughly crushed)
200g Rich Tea biscuits (roughly crushed)
125g mixed nuts (walnuts, brazils, almonds) (optional)
125g glacé cherries
1 packet of Maltesers (plus if you have any other
    sweeties – Rolos, Munchies, etc. – lying around,
    they can go in too)

Line a 15cm round cake tin or a 2lb loaf tin with a double layer of greaseproof paper. (I used a silicone loaf mould. There is no need to line the silicone mould.)

Melt the butter, syrup and chocolate in a pan over a low heat. This took some time as I used the lowest setting on the hob. Make sure that the pot is large enough to take all the crushed biscuits, etc. Stir to mix the ingredients thoroughly.

Add the biscuits, Maltesers and fruit and nuts (if used). Stir well. Make sure to break the biscuits relatively small as they will not fit in the mould/tin otherwise.

Transfer to prepared tin. Level it on top and press down well to avoid air gaps. Allow to get cold and hard. It needs about two hours in the fridge or about 45 minutes in the freezer. The longer the better. It tasted much better on Saturday. Wrap completely in greaseproof paper and store in a fridge.

Decorate with holly. Do NOT count calories. This is a time of joy.

🧁

Helena picked up Chadani Imelda and gave a grim smile of satisfaction that denoted the size of her achievement. Even though Chadani had hollered unwaveringly, she was now dressed in frilly knickers, a frilled shirt, a ballet skirt and a pompom coat, plus lacy tights with small pom-poms at the back, baby-pink Ugg boots with tiny stars and a pink pompom hat with long dangling ribbons. Her fierce red hair clashed outlandishly with all the pink, but Chadani was a girl, Helena thought determinedly, and therefore needed to be identified as such.

'Don't you look pretty?' she cooed.

Chadani gave her mother a ferocious look and tugged mutinously at the hat. To no avail; Helena had already tied it up for safe keeping. A one-year-old's hands were no match for the strapping power of a registered accident and emergency nurse. And she was still a nurse, she kept telling everyone. She was going back to it. Just as soon as she found the right person or nursery to take care of Chadani Imelda. So far, there had not been one to meet her standards.

Issy at first had thought Helena must be joking about being overprotective. Helena herself was so strong and confident and independent; how could it even be possible? And it might have taken Helena herself by surprise. Nonetheless, from the first squalling breath Chadani Imelda had taken, sunk deep into Helena's remarkable bosom, after a quick and utterly straightforward labour Issy felt would do nothing to help Helena's empathetic skills with the sick – she had marched into hospital under her own steam and popped the baby out in under ninety minutes without even an aspirin – Helena's entire life had become the Chadani Project.

Ashok's adoring family, once they'd got over the shock of him fathering a child out of wedlock to a rather staggering and distinctly larger-than-life redhead, did nothing to deflect Helena from Operation C. Ashok was the youngest of six, four of them female, all of them noisy (one of the reasons why he had been totally unworried about taking on a strong woman), and all of them very keen to kick in with help, advice and gifts for the new baby, their own children grown up.

So Chadani never left the house without a couple of extra layers just in case, or an extra feeding bottle here and there so she didn't go hungry; every toy in the catalogue now subsumed Issy's old flat, which Helena and Ashok had bought. Once small and cosy, it was now small, cosy and completely hidden under vast amounts of plastic, drying babygros and a large sign on the wall that said 'Princess'.

Issy had narrowed her eyes at that.

'She'll have high self-esteem,' Helena had insisted. 'I don't want anyone pushing her around.'

'No one pushes you around,' pointed out Issy. 'I'm sure she'll inherit that from you anyway.'

'You can't be too sure,' said Helena, leaving Issy to clear a space on her own old red velvet sofa, now piled high with very small designer knitwear.

'Helena, this says "dry clean only",' said Issy sternly. 'Now, I may not be a parent, but ...'

Helena looked slightly shamefaced. 'I know, I know.

But she does look so amazing in it. I'm surprised no one has stolen her, I really am.'

Issy made a nodding face, like she often did around Chadani Imelda. It wasn't that she wasn't a lovely baby – she was, of course; the daughter of her dearest friend. But she was very noisy and squally and demanding, and Issy did sometimes feel that she would be more comfortable out of all those clothes; and perhaps if she didn't have Helena, Ashok and at least four other relatives jumping to attention every time she squeaked, she might do a little better.

'So,' said Helena, importantly. 'Let me know what you think. Here are the outfits I was planning for Christmas Day. Look at this little reindeer hat, isn't it *darling*? To die for.'

Chadani picked up the corner of the reindeer antlers and started biting it, angrily.

'Then I thought red velvet for church.'

'Since when do you go to church?'

'I think everyone at church might like to see a lovely baby at Christmas time. That's the whole point,' said Helena.

'Well, yes, the baby Jesus, symbol of light and hope for the world. Not just a random baby ...' Helena's face stiffened. 'Even though she's obviously a very, very special baby. And she's a year old now anyway. Does she still qualify as a baby?'

Chadani had cruised over to the television and was

pulling Baby Einstein DVDs out of the rack and throwing them on the floor. Helena was completely ignoring it.

'Of course!'

'And Ashok's a Sikh,' Issy added, unnecessarily.

'We'll go to temple for Diwali as well,' said Helena. 'Now for that you need to *really* dress up.'

Issy smiled. She wanted to open a bottle of wine, but remembered that she couldn't because Helena wasn't drinking because she was still breastfeeding on demand, and at this rate looked likely to be doing so till about 2025.

'So anyway,' said Helena, 'Chadani is ... ' and she launched into a list of Chadani Imelda's latest accomplishments, which may or may not have included 'scatter all the Baby Einstein DVDs'.

Suddenly Issy had slightly lost the urge to confide in her friend. Normally they could chat about anything, but since Chadani had arrived, Issy had felt them drifting apart in a way she couldn't quite put her finger on. Helena had met a load of new, pushy mums through North London Mummy Connexshins, which she presided over by virtue of having the most natural birth and breastfeeding the longest, and their endless, stupefying discussions about baby-led weaning and sleeping through the night left Issy completely cold. Even when she tried to join in by bringing up Darny's latest misadventures (all the children had to be either perfect or awful, it seemed, there was no middle way; likewise, when you'd given birth you had to have either hardly noticed, or nearly died and required fifteen pints of emergency blood transfusions), Helena had looked at her patronisingly and said it would be different when she had her own. Starting a conversation about missing her boyfriend seemed a bit . . .

'I miss Austin,' said Issy, suddenly. She was going to at least give it a shot. 'In New York. I wish he was hating it.'

Helena looked at her. 'Ashok's on call,' she said. 'I've been getting up four times every single night, then he comes in and wants me to keep the baby quiet all day. In this tiny, crappy apartment! I ask you.'

Issy loved the flat, and still felt very proprietorial about it.

'Oh dear,' she said tentatively, then ventured, feeling cut off from her own feeble complaint, 'Should Chadani still be waking up at night?'

'Yes,' snapped Helena. 'She's very sensitive.'

As if in answer to this, Chadani toddled over to the large pile of freshly washed clothes on the sofa and upturned her beaker of supplementary milk all over them.

'No!' howled Helena. 'NO! Don't! I just . . . Chadani! That is behaviour of which I am critical! Not that I am criticising you as a person and as a goddess. It is because this behaviour at this time . . . '

Chadani stared at Helena, continuing to hold the beaker upside down, as if conducting an experiment.

Issy decided not to press the boyfriend matter any further.

'I'll just head out . . . ' she said.

As she went, she could hear Helena saying, 'Now, I would be very happy if you would give me that cup now, Chadani Imelda. Very happy. Make Mummy happy now and give me the cup. Give me the cup now, Chadani. Give Mummy the cup.'

Chapter Three

Whatever Pearl thought, Issy decided when she got home, it was time to start the Christmas cakes. She gathered together the huge bags of sultanas, raisins and currants – wondering, as she passingly did once a year, and once a year only, what the difference between them was again – along with the glacé cherries and candied peel. If she didn't start them now, she wouldn't have enough time to feed them and they wouldn't be good and strong and delicious in time.

Darny thumped through to the kitchen as soon as he got in from homework club. As he marched through the door, Issy jumped; he sounded like a grown man already, even though he was only eleven. And of course he'd had his own set of keys since he was six years old.

'Hey,' he shouted. Normally he swung straight past her up the stairs to his bedroom to play on his Xbox – unless, of course, she was making something good to eat.

The house Austin and Darny had inherited from their parents was a rather pretty red-brick terrace, with a large knocked-through downstairs sitting room and a back kitchen, and upstairs three little bedrooms. There was a patch of garden out the back which was in no way large enough to play football, rugby, handball, volleyball or Robin Hood, not that it had stopped the boys trying over the years. Five years of just two chaps there, one small and one overworked and dreamy, had left the place in a very unpleasant state, even though they had a despondent cleaner. Issy was, gradually, trying to do up bits of it: a coat of paint here; a new flagstone floor there. The bones of the house were reasserting themselves, though Issy had kept intact a little square of the skirting board that had a long procession of racing cars drawn on in indelible ink in the hand of a five-year-old.

'Why didn't you stop him?' she'd asked Austin.

'Well, I rather liked it,' he'd said mildly. 'He's good at drawing; look, he's got all the wheels in the right positions and everything.'

Issy looked and decided it was sweet. She cleaned up the rest of the paintwork and kept the cars. The rest she was trying to make over.

She couldn't help it. She never felt she needed to see a therapist to confirm that it was because of her insecure childhood – her mother a restless spirit; her father a traveller she'd never known. The only constant in her life had been her beloved Grampa Joe, whose bakery had always been a warm and cosy haven for her. Ever since then, she'd tried to reproduce that cosy, comfortable feeling wherever she went.

Pre-Austin, Helena had said once that she was a people-pleaser. Issy had asked what was wrong with that exactly, and Helena had pointed out that all her boyfriends had been really horrible users. But Issy could never march through life like Helena did, doing what she felt like doing and damning the consequences. Meeting Austin, who liked the fact that she liked to please him ... well, the boys had complained at first about the house – who really needed curtains anyway, Darny had said; they were just bourgeois (a word he clearly had no concept of the meaning of), about shame and a fake privacy the state didn't even let you have – but Issy had persisted, and gradually, as the windows were cleaned, and a new kitchen table brought in (they let Darny keep the old one, covered in ink spills and old glue and that part where they'd played the knife-throwing game that time, as a desk upstairs) with a comfortable wall bench covered in cushions, and all Issy's kitchen appliances, which she bought like other women bought shoes; lamps in the corner of the room rather than bare bulbs (Austin had complained he couldn't see a thing until Issy had told him it was romantic and would make romantic things happen, which changed his outlook somewhat), and even cushions (which were constantly being secreted upstairs for Darny to use as target practice), the house was beginning to look really rather cosy. More like a home, Issy had pointed out, like normal people had, and not a holding pen for delinquent zebras.

Austin might have grumbled cheerfully – because, on the whole, it was expected of him, and also because it was exactly what all his interfering aunts had been saying for years, that the place needed a woman's touch. In the past there had been plenty of women who'd promised to supply that and tried to inveigle their way in. Austin and Darny had even had a name for them: the Awws, because of the concerned expression they got on their faces and the way they said 'awww' when they looked at Darny like he was an abandoned puppy. Austin hated it when someone said 'awww'. It meant that Darny was about to do or say something unspeakable.

But somehow with Issy it was different. Issy didn't say 'awww'. She listened. And she made them both feel that coming home to somewhere cosy and warm every evening might actually be rather pleasant, even if it did require them to start making their own beds and remembering to put the rubbish out and eating with cutlery and having fruit and stuff. Yes, there were more soft furnishings and bits and bobs about, but that was just the price you paid, Austin reckoned, for all the lovely stuff too; for something that felt not a million miles away from happiness.

Darny took off his winter jacket and rucksack, scattering school books, hats, scarves, Moshi Monster cards and random small pieces of plastic everywhere.

'Hello Darny,' said Issy. He padded through into the kitchen.

'What are you doing?' he said. 'I'm starving.'

'You're always starving,' said Issy. 'You can't eat this, though.'

He gazed into the huge pans. 'What are you doing?'

'Oh, this is the easy bit. Just marinating the fruit.'

Darny took a sniff of the bottle she was applying liberally to the mix. 'Phew. What's that?'

'It's brandy.'

'Can I—'

'Nope,' said Issy without hesitating.

'Come on, just a taste. In France they let the kids drink wine with their meals.'

'And they eat horses and have mistresses. When we decide to be French, Darny, I'll be sure to let you know.'

Darny scowled. 'What is there to eat, then?'

'Have a couple of bananas, and I made you some fruit toast,' said Issy. 'And there's a lasagne in the oven.'

'Fruit toast? I can't believe you run a cake shop and all I get is fruit toast.'

'Well, learn to bake your own cakes then.'

'Yeah, not likely,' said Darny. 'That's for girls.'

'Scared?' said Issy.

'No!'

'My grandfather baked hundreds of cream horns a day till he was seventy years old.'

Darny snorted.

'What's funny?'

'Cream horns. It's rude.'

Issy thought about it for a while. 'It is a bit rude,' she allowed eventually. 'Men make wonderful bakers, though. Or they can do.'

Darny had already scarfed the fruit toast and was peeling a banana. He glanced at the phone.

'I'm expecting him,' said Issy. 'Any minute.'

'I don't care,' said Darny instantly. 'He's probably in stupid meetings anyway.'

He looked out of the back French windows that led on to the dark patio. He could see their reflections in the glass. The house looked cosy and warm. He wouldn't admit it, but he did like having Issy there. It was nice. Not that she was ... she wasn't his mum or anything like that. That would totally NEVER happen. But compared with the drippy women Austin had brought home over the years, she was probably all right he supposed. And now she was here, well, it was almost like they had a nice house like his friends did, and everything was kind of all right when it really hadn't been all right for a really long time. So why was his stupid brother in stupid America?

'You know the schools in America, right?' he asked, faux-casually, trying to steal some raisins from the mixing bowl. Issy smacked his hand lightly with the wooden spoon.

'Yes,' she said. Issy had, in fact, never been to America, which made it a bit difficult to calm Darny's fears.

'Do they have … do they have a LOT of guns at school and things?' he asked, finally.

'No,' said Issy, wishing she could be more sure. 'I'm sure they don't. Absolutely not.'

Darny's mouth curled in contempt. 'And do they sing all the time?'

'I don't know,' said Issy. 'I just don't know.'

The phone rang.

'Sorry,' said Austin. 'The meeting ran on. They wanted me to meet a few more people and pop into their board meeting …'

'Wow,' said Issy. 'They're obviously impressed by you.'

'I don't know about that,' said Austin. 'I think they just like hearing me talk.'

'Don't be modest,' said Issy, cheerful, but with a slight wobble in her voice. 'Of course they love you. Why wouldn't they love you? You're amazing.'

Austin heard the emotional tone in her voice and cursed internally. He hadn't wanted to think, hadn't wanted to even consider, what it meant if he was offered a job here – and it seemed to be shaping up to be more than that. Not just a job; a real career; an amazing opportunity. Given the state of banking at the moment, he was lucky to have a job at all, never mind a career that was going places. And the idea of making some real money for once, instead of just bobbing along ... Issy had the café, of course, but it was hardly a big earner, and it would be nice for the two of them to do some lovely things ... take a nice holiday ... maybe even ... well. He didn't want to think about the next step. That was a bit too far in the future. But still. It would make sense, he told himself firmly. For whatever lay ahead. It would make sense to have a nest egg, to have a cushion beneath them. To be secure. Together.

'Well, they have been very nice ...' he conceded. 'How's Darny doing at school?'

Issy didn't want to say that she'd seen him in the playground in the company of a teacher being marched quickly to the gate. She tried not to get too involved in the school, even though she worried about Darny, the smallest kid in the year, and the only one without even one parent, almost as much as Austin did.

'Hmm,' she said.

'What are you doing?'

'Making Christmas cake. It smells amazing!'

'It smells foul,' said Darny down the speaker phone. 'And she won't let me taste it.'

'Because you said it smells foul,' said Issy, unarguably.

'And it's about twenty per cent proof, so you can't have it anyway.'

'Austin would let me have it.'

'No I wouldn't,' came the voice down the phone.

'When we have proportional representation,' said Darny, 'I'll have more of a say around here.'

'If you get on to teen voting rights, I'm hanging up,' warned Austin.

'No, don't . . . ' said Issy.

There was a silence as Darny gave the phone a rude gesture, then, muttering darkly about how things would change around here when teens got the vote, he grabbed a bunch of bananas and disappeared upstairs.

'Has he gone?' said Austin eventually.

'Yup,' said Issy. 'He seems in a pretty good mood tonight, actually. Maybe school wasn't as bad as all that.'

'Oh good,' said Austin. 'Thanks, Issy. I didn't really think puberty was going to kick in till a bit later.'

'Oh, it's not too bad yet,' said Issy. 'He's still talking to us. I think that goes altogether soon. Although his trainers . . . '

'I know,' said Austin, wrinkling his nose. 'I'd kind of stopped noticing the smell before you came along.'

'Hmm,' said Issy. There was another pause. This wasn't like them at all. Normally there was no end to the conversation. He would tell her what was up at the bank; she would mention funny clients or whatever it was Pearl and Caroline had had their latest fight about.

But what she was doing was the same as always. For him, life seemed to be becoming very different.

Issy racked her brains to try and think of something to talk to him about, but came up short – compared to New York, her day had been the usual: talking to sugar suppliers and trying to convince Pearl to let her hang some tinsel. And the rest of the time ... well, she couldn't say this, because it felt like it would be unfair on him, that she was blaming him for being away, or turning into one of those awful clingy women she didn't want to be, always moaning at their other halves. So she couldn't tell him that pretty much all she'd been thinking of, all that was filling her head, was how much she missed him and wanted him home and how much she was dreading him uprooting their lives just as, for the first time in years, she felt she was coming into safe harbour.

So she didn't say anything at all.

'So what's up?' said Austin, confused. Getting Issy to talk was rarely a problem. Getting her to not talk when the cricket was on was usually far trickier.

'Oh, nothing really. Same old.'

Issy felt her face grow hot as the silence drew out between them. Austin, however, was waiting to cross a four-lane highway without being entirely sure of which way the traffic was coming, and was blind to minor emotional nuance. He thought she was cross with him for leaving Darny with her.

'Look, Aunt Jessica said she'd be happy to take Darny ...'

'What?' said Issy, exasperated. 'There's nothing wrong with me and Darny. He's fine. Don't worry about us.'

'I'm not worried,' said Austin, as a yellow taxi cab honked loudly at him for having the temerity to pause before crossing the road. 'I was just saying. You know. It's an option.'

'I'm coming home every night after a full day's work and managing to check his homework and make his supper. I think it's fine. I don't think I need options, do you?'

'No, no, you're doing brilliantly.'

Austin wondered just when this conversation had started to drift out of his grasp so badly.

'Sorry,' he said. 'I didn't mean to ...'

His phone was beeping. Another call was coming in.

'Listen, I have to go,' he said. 'I'll call you later.'

'I'll be in bed,' said Issy, sounding more huffy than she meant to. 'We can speak tomorrow.'

'OK ... all right.'

Issy felt alarmingly frustrated when she hung up the phone. They hadn't managed to talk at all, not about anything proper, and she'd no idea what he was up to or how it was going, apart from the definite sense she'd got from talking to him that he was having a really good time.

She told herself she was being stupid; this was a big fuss about nothing. She was getting all wound up for no reason. Her last boyfriend had been very emotionally distant, and had treated her like dirt, so she was finding her new relationship sometimes very difficult to manage. With Graeme, she couldn't say anything at all or he would coldly close up; she knew Austin was very very different, but wasn't sure exactly how far she could go. Men – no, not just men, everybody – shied away from neediness. She didn't want to look needy. She wanted to be warm, casual, breezy, reminding him that they were building a loving home, not defensive and shrewlike.

Issy sighed and looked back down at the fruit she was mixing.

'No,' she said, feeling a bit self-conscious and daft. 'You can't have negative thoughts when you're making the Christmas cake. It's unlucky. DARNY!' she hollered up the stairs. 'Do you want to come and drop twenty pees in the cake mix?'

'Can it be two-pound coins?'

'NO!'

Austin sighed. He didn't want to worry Issy, but sometimes it was easy to do. He'd been called in just before he left. Kirsty Dubose, the primary headmistress, had always been very soft on Darny in the past, knowing his background. Plus, unbeknown to Austin, she had had the most enormous crush on him. Mrs Baedeker, Darny's new head at secondary, had absolutely no such qualms. And Darny's behaviour really was appalling.

'We're looking at what you might call a last-chance situation,' Mrs Baedeker had barked at Austin, who sometimes found it difficult in school situations to remember he was meant to be a grown-up.

'For answering back?' protested Austin.

'For persistent class-disrupting insubordination,' Mrs Baedeker said.

Austin's lips had twitched.

'It's not funny,' she added. 'It's stopping others from learning. And let me tell you this. Darny Tyler might be clever and sharp and well-read and all the rest of it, and he may well turn out noisy and fine and all right.' She hit the desk with her palm to make her point. 'But there are a lot of kids at this school who don't have what Darny's got, and do need good teaching and organised lessons and proper discipline, and he's stopping that process from happening and it's not right and not welcome in my school.'

That had shut Austin up very quickly indeed. He'd put Mrs Baedeker's argument forcibly to Darny that evening, and Darny had argued back, equally forcibly, that formal examinations were a total waste of everybody's time so it hardly mattered either way, that those kids kept trying to set him on fire at playtime so it was righteous vengeance, and surely critical thinking was an important part of education. Issy had hidden in the kitchen and made a smoked haddock quiche. But Austin found it hard to worry about Issy and Darny at the same time, and his thoughts at that moment were with his brother, even as Issy was thinking endlessly of him.

Chapter Four

Perfect Christmas Cake

I make no apologies for this, wrote Issy in her recipe book for the extra staff she liked to think she would employ one day. It was a tradition her grampa had started, and she was determined to continue with it; she had kept all his hand-written recipes and her friends had bound them for her into a book. She never, ever let herself think about perhaps one day having a daughter to pass it on to. That would never do. And anyway, she thought, if she did have a daughter, she'd probably be just like Marian and only eat mung beans and run off travelling and send mysterious postcards and interrupt crackly Skype conversations with long, involved stories about people Issy didn't know. Regardless.

Most recipes I tend to tweak and move around to suit what I like, in the hope that my customers will like them too. I'm not fond of anything too fiddly, or overly fancy, and if I'm looking at American recipes I know they'll probably be too sweet for British people, while French recipes probably won't be sweet enough. So all of that is fine, but this is different. This is one of those occasions where a recipe has been written that can't be bettered. Some people may do fancy things with whole oranges or surprises or various bits of malarkey, but this, as it stands, is one of the best, most reliable recipes ever written. It doesn't matter if you've never baked before in your life. You can make a wonderful, wonderful Christmas cake, and it's by St Delia Smith.

Although Delia isn't officially a saint quite yet, and fortunately for everyone still alive and well, it will, one day, be a mere formality down at the Vatican. No one has made cooking so clear, and no one is quite as successful. Whilst we all know – naming no names – famous chefs who say their dinner takes half an hour when it takes all afternoon and some crying, or who leave ingredients out altogether because they are too busy tossing their hair, Delia can always be relied upon, and rarely more so than here. Do what she says – exactly what she says, neither more nor less – and a lovely Christmas cake will be yours. Not to mention the smell of your kitchen as you make it. You should do it ideally by the end of November to give it a few weeks to ripen, and if I were to make one change it would be to add a little more brandy, but that is completely up to you.

The Classic Christmas Cake
By Delia Smith

This, with no apologies, is a Christmas cake that has been in print since 1978, has been made and loved by thousands and is, along with the Traditional Christmas Pudding, one of the most popular recipes I've produced. It is rich, dark and quite moist, so will not suit those who like a crumblier texture. Recently we took some of these cakes along to book-signing sessions up and down the country and were quite amazed to see so many people take a mouthful and then buy a book!

1lb (450g) currants
6oz (175g) sultanas
6oz (175g) raisins
2oz (50g) glacé cherries, rinsed, dried and finely
    chopped
2oz (50g) mixed candied peel, finely chopped

3 tablespoons brandy, plus extra for 'feeding'

8oz (225g) plain flour

½ level teaspoon salt

¼ level teaspoon freshly grated nutmeg

½ level teaspoon ground mixed spice

8oz (225g) unsalted butter

8oz (225g) soft brown sugar

4 large eggs

2oz (50g) almonds, chopped (the skins can be left on)

1 level dessertspoon black treacle

grated zest 1 lemon

grated zest 1 orange

4oz (110g) whole blanched almonds (only if you don't intend to ice the cake

You will also need an 8 inch (20cm) round cake tin or a 7 inch (18cm) square tin, greased and lined with silicone paper (baking parchment). Tie a band of brown paper round the outside of the tin for extra protection.

You need to begin this cake the night before you want to bake it. All you do is weigh out the dried fruit and mixed peel, place it in a mixing bowl and mix in the brandy as evenly and thoroughly as possible. Cover the bowl with a clean tea cloth and leave the fruit aside to absorb the brandy for 12 hours.

Next day pre-heat the oven to gas mark 1, 275°F (140°C). Then measure out all the rest of the ingredients, ticking them off to make quite sure they're all there. The treacle will be easier to measure if you remove the lid and place the tin in a small pan of barely simmering water. Now begin the cake by sifting the flour, salt and spices into a large mixing bowl, lifting the sieve up high to give the flour a good airing. Next, in a separate large mixing bowl, whisk the butter and sugar together until it's light, pale and fluffy. Now beat the eggs in a separate bowl and add them to the creamed mixture a tablespoonful at a time; keep the whisk running until all the egg is incorporated. If you add the eggs slowly by degrees like this the mixture won't curdle. If it does, don't worry, any cake full of such beautiful things can't fail to taste good!

When all the egg has been added, fold in the flour and spices, using gentle, folding movements and not beating at all (this is to keep all that precious air in). Now fold in the fruit, peel, chopped nuts and treacle and finally the grated lemon and orange zests. Next, using a large kitchen spoon, transfer the cake mixture into the prepared tin, spread it out evenly with the back of a spoon and, if you don't intend to ice the cake, lightly drop the whole blanched almonds in circles or squares all over the surface. Finally cover the top of the cake with a double square of silicone paper with a 50p-size hole in the centre (this gives extra protection during the long slow cooking).

Bake the cake on the lowest shelf of the oven for $4\frac{1}{2}$–$4\frac{3}{4}$ hours. Sometimes it can take up to $\frac{1}{2}$–$\frac{3}{4}$ hour longer than this, but in any case don't look till at least 4 hours have passed. Cool the cake for 30 minutes in the tin, then remove it to a wire rack to finish cooling. When it's cold, 'feed' it – make small holes in the top and base of the cake with a cocktail stick or small skewer, then spoon over a few teaspoons of brandy, wrap it in double silicone paper secured with an elastic band and either wrap again in foil or store in an airtight container. You can now feed it at odd intervals until you need to ice or eat it.

Pearl looked at Issy. 'You're doing this on purpose,' she said.

'I am not,' said Issy. 'It needs time to sit.'

Everyone who had walked through the door had raised their noses and sniffed appreciatively and smiled.

'You know, you can buy this smell in a scented candle,' said Caroline. 'It's only fifty pounds.'

The others looked at her.

'Fifty pounds for a candle?' said Pearl. 'My church sells them for thirty pence.'

'Well, they're for gifts.'

'People give candles as gifts?'

'Smart people do,' said Caroline.

'Smart people give gifts that say, here, take this, I think your house smells really terrible and you need this stinky candle to make it better?'

'Hush, you two,' said Issy, putting on the noisy coffee machine to stop them bickering. She glanced over at the fireplace, where she had hung a small red stocking for Louis. Pearl followed her gaze.

'Are you *smuggling in* Christmas decorations?'

'No,' said Issy hastily. 'It's just leftover laundry.'

'That is the most Christmassy smell I've ever come across,' said the young customer Caroline was serving. The child next to her shot her a wide-eyed, beaming glance.

'SANTY IS COMING,' she said.

'Ssh,' said Issy. 'I know, but don't tell everyone.'

The child smiled with her mouth closed, as if they shared a secret. Pearl rolled her eyes.

'Fine. Fine. Drape the place in tinsel that will gather dust and make a total mess for me to clean up and start those stupid Christmas songs until if I have to listen to "Stop the Cavalry" one more time I'll want to punch something. Do you want me to wear a Santa hat for five weeks? Maybe I'll tie some bells round my waist and I can jingle solidly for a month and a half. Will that suit you?'

'Pearl!' said Issy. 'It's just a bit of fun.'

'I'm having all-white decorations this year,' mused Caroline. 'Hand-made by the Inuit. They don't sparkle or light up, but they're sustainable. The children complain, but I explain to them how a stylish Christmas is a better Christmas.'

Issy was watching Pearl closely. She didn't normally take offence.

'Seriously, are you all right?' said Issy. She was worried she'd been too wrapped up in her worries about Austin to notice that Pearl was feeling the pressure of her own.

'I'll be fine,' said Pearl, looking shamefaced. 'Sorry. It's just, it happens so fast and there's so much to do . . . '

Issy nodded. 'But it will be lovely, won't it? Louis is at just the right age for it.'

'But it's expensive,' said Pearl. 'Getting him all those toys.'

'Louis is the least demanding child I've ever met,' said Issy. 'He isn't going to demand toys.'

'Benjamin keeps going on about him getting a new garage and everything he sees on TV and football kit and stuff,' said Pearl. 'But I don't even . . . '

Issy looked at her. 'Pearl McGregor, you are the most sensible woman I've ever met in my life. I can't believe you're talking like this. Craig the builder asked Louis who his favourite football team was last week and he said Rainbow United.'

Pearl let out a smile.

'He means Brazil.'

'He doesn't know what he means! He's four! Don't worry about it! *And*,' added Issy as an inspired incentive, 'the more Christmassy and lovely we do things, the more we're going to sell so the bigger bonus you can have. Hmm?'

Pearl shrugged.

'I still think people forget why we celebrate this time of year.'

'Would you like me to make a gingerbread nativity?' asked Issy, assuming that Pearl would laugh off the suggestion. It was a fiddly job and would take absolutely ages.

Instead Pearl said, 'I think that would be lovely. Could we put it in the window?'

Caroline wasn't looking forward to Christmas either. It was Richard, her ex-husband's turn to have the children. Well, she had told everyone, that was just fine by her. She was going to spend the day pampering, using her day spa bathroom and detoxing early, avoiding all that awful bloat everyone got at Christmas time.

She knew she was being miserable – and so snappy and sarcastic – and she was aware that Pearl and Issy were about the only two people on earth who could put up with her at the moment, but she didn't seem to be able to help it. Richard had originally left her for a woman at work, but now he'd apparently moved on, and she couldn't for the life of her find out where he was staying or who he was with. He was only contacting her through lawyers. Had he met someone else? Was he going to fall in love and have thousands of babies with another woman and spend Hermia and Achilles' inheritance? And the house cost a lot to run, *and* City bonuses were way down, everybody knew that. It was getting impossible to live in London.

Deep down the fear gnawed away at her, and she took it out on almost anyone. Pearl and Issy understood and tried their hardest to be good about it. Pearl had said out loud several times that putting up with Caroline was going to guarantee her place in heaven. Issy liked to think in her dreamier moments that if she and Austin had daughters, this was what the teenage years would be like.

'How's that hot boyfriend of yours doing in New York?' Caroline asked her as they handled the lunchtime rush together – Pearl had let Issy change the sandwich order to include turkey, stuffing and cranberry sauce, and they were flying off the shelves as fast as they could load them.

'He's fine,' said Issy, in a tone of voice that Pearl and Caroline realised immediately meant anything but.

'Oh well, you know New York,' said Caroline in a superior tone.

'No, I don't,' said Issy. 'Not at all really. I've never been.'

'You've never been?'

'Neither have I,' said Pearl. 'And I haven't injected poison in my face either. Isn't it amazing what people haven't done?'

Caroline ignored her. 'Oh well, it is full of the most incredible-looking women, really beautiful, and all totally desperate for a man. What they'll do for a tall, handsome banker with an English accent . . . they'll be all over him like vultures.'

Issy looked shocked.

'Is this something you know for a fact?' asked Pearl heavily. 'Or is it just something you've made up from watching television programmes?'

'Oh no, darlings, I've been there. The women there make *me* feel ugly.' Caroline let out a tinkly laugh that was presumably meant to sound self-deprecating and charming but failed utterly.

'He's coming home soon,' said Issy.

'I wouldn't count on that,' said Caroline. 'They'll snap him up in no time.'

This didn't improve Issy's mood in the slightest, even when the latest batch of Christmas cake in the big industrial oven started to perfume the entire street and brought over a crowd of scaffolders from across the road. They were from Ukraine, and could normally only ever spare the money to share a cake. Somehow, every single member of staff, without telling the others, always managed to slip them an extra bit of something.

Austin couldn't deny that this was proving an eye-opener.

Merv Ferani, vice president of Kingall Lowestein, one of the largest Wall Street banks still standing, was manoeuvring him through the tables of the oak-panelled dining room, following the shapely form of the most beautiful waitress Austin had ever seen. Well, maybe she wasn't a waitress. She had been standing at the front desk, checking names off on a list and being very rude to the people in front of her, but when Merv had marched in – he was very short, very fat and wore flamboyant bow ties – she had come over all smiles and gushing and eyed Austin up in a very forward way he found completely unnerving. He wasn't used to very beautiful people being nice to him. He was used to quite normal-looking people asking him to please take his son off the bus.

They threaded their way through the tables, all of which were filled with affluent-looking people: men in expensive suits with pointed shoes; beautiful women, sometimes with much older, much less beautiful men. Merv stopped often to shake hands, exchange witticisms Austin didn't understand and clasp people on the shoulder. To one or two he introduced Austin – 'he's just come over from London' – and they would nod and ask if he knew so-and-so at Goldman Sachs or someone at Barclays and he'd have to shake his head and try not to blurt out that he was in charge of small business loans at a very small branch on Stoke Newington High Street.

Finally they reached their table. Two more waiters came dashing up to pull out their seats and pour them some water. Merv glanced in passing at the heavy embossed menu, then tossed it to one side.

'Ah, what the hell. It's getting towards that time of year. I love Christmas food. Let's see if they do anything Christmassy. And a bottle of claret, the 2007 if they have it. Same for you?'

He cocked an eyebrow at Austin, whose stomach still thought it was night-time and was therefore more than happy to oblige. He did wonder, though, what would have happened if he'd asked for a green salad. He'd certainly have failed a test in some way.

The dinner plates were the size of heads. Austin wondered how much he was going to have to eat.

'So, Austin,' said Merv, starting in on the bread basket. Austin supposed that when you hit a certain level of wealth and success, you were just allowed to eat however you wanted. Manners were for little people.

It had happened very suddenly the previous afternoon. Austin had been in the offices of KL, feeling rather anxious about everything. The place was full of sharp-looking young men who must have been about his age but looked rather more groomed, worked out, somehow smooth; perfectly shaved with weirdly shiny skin and buffed fingernails, in expensive suits and shined shoes. (The only time Austin had ever been in a gym had been to pick Darny up from Scouts, and that had only lasted till Darny insisted that it was against his human rights to be sent to a quasi-paramilitary organisation.) And that was before you even got to the women. The women in New York were the most terrifying specimens Austin had ever seen. They didn't even seem vaguely on the same planet as everyone else. They had incredibly muscular legs that ended in really sharp stiletto heels, and pointy elbows and pointy faces and they moved fast, like giant insects. They were beautiful, of course, Austin couldn't deny that. They just seemed somehow other-worldly. Still, they had all looked over at him when he came in and had been very friendly. Austin wasn't used to being scrutinised by women who looked like they could be models when they were finished with their banking careers. It was unnerving.

Another Brit, Kelvin, had walked him round. Austin knew Kelvin a little from before, from various courses they'd taken together when the bank was still stubbornly trying to promote Austin and Austin was still stubbornly trying to resist it. Back when he thought working in the bank was some kind of temporary manoeuvre.

Austin was impressed to see that Kelvin had lost weight, smartened up and generally seemed different.

He'd even adopted a strange kind of transatlantic accent. Austin thought this made him sound a bit like Lulu, but didn't want to mention it.

'So you're liking it here, then?'

Kelvin smiled broadly. 'Well, the hours are a bit of a killer. But the lifestyle ... amazing. The women, the bars, the parties ... it's like Christmas all year, man.'

Austin really didn't want to say 'man' at the end of his sentences.

'Okay. Um. Kelvin.'

Kelvin lowered his voice. 'They're short on men here, you know. As soon as they hear the accent and you lay it on a bit thick and pretend you know Prince William, they're all over you.'

Austin frowned. 'Kelvin, you were born in Hackney Marshes.'

'Still London, isn't it?'

They rounded the corner into the main trading floor. Austin looked around carefully.

'Where the magic happens, bro.'

Austin only had one bro, who was almost as annoying as Kelvin.

'Hmm,' he said.

Kelvin winked broadly at one of the girls on the floor, who was tapping ferociously on her computer whilst on the telephone, but still managed to find the time to shake back her beautiful long black hair that looked like something out of a shampoo advert. The huge open-plan room was a hive of frenzied, scurrying activity: men standing up and shouting into phones, a ticker running overhead on an LCD display, people dashing about with files and looking busy.

'Yup, here's where the magic happens.'

'Hmm,' said Austin again.

'What's the matter? You're not impressed?'

'Not really,' said Austin, a bit glumly. This was only a finding-out visit, and it was already obvious to him that he wouldn't fit in here in a hundred years, so he might as well say what he thought. 'I can't believe you're still pulling all this bullshit like it's 2007.'

He pointed at a flashily-dressed trader bellowing into a telephone. 'Come on! We've tried all this shouting bollocks before and it didn't work then. This is a total waste of time. I bet no one in here really understands what a derivative is or why it's such a terrible idea, except three quants in a back office taking five minutes off playing World of Warcraft. Banks have spent years pulling the wool over their own eyes. It's not sustainable, and we know it now. Why isn't the money flowing properly? To help real businesses, real people grow and build and make things? Because that castle-in-the-air stuff fell right down. Still, nice suit, Kelvin.'

Austin turned round and got ready to go. That was when he saw the little man with the large bow tie who had been standing in the middle of the trading floor with an unlit cigar, watching them intensely.

'You,' he said, stabbing a stubby finger at Austin. 'You're having lunch with me.'

And now here he was, sitting in front of six different types of bread that were being explained to him by a ludicrously handsome young man. Austin wondered vaguely where all those fat Americans you heard about were. Maybe Manhattan's skinny buildings and tiny living spaces simply discouraged it.

'Two olive, one rye, but not if it's warm,' ordered Merv, and settled himself down to look at Austin. His eyes were small and curious.

'London tells us you're a bit of a curveball. Young, on the up, incorruptible ... might be ready to jump from clearing while you still can.'

'Um,' said Austin. 'That was very nice of them.'

'They also said you were the only person in the entire company whose loans had never lost money.'

Austin smiled at this. It was a nice compliment to get. He loaned on his gut instincts for people; how hard he thought they could work, how much they wanted it. When Issy had walked into his office nearly two years ago, Austin could see beyond the nerves and anxiety and the frankly total lack of preparation to the person beneath; she had more steel in her than you would think by looking at her. Well, an unusual upbringing could do that to you, as he knew only too well.

'Do you know how much my bond traders lost me last year? Those klutzes in the trading room?'

Austin shook his head politely.

'About seventeen billion dollars.'

Austin wasn't entirely sure whether this was, in context, a lot of money or not.

'We have to get back to basics, Austin.' Merv refilled their glasses with claret. 'We need decent, honest brokers with no blotted copybooks. We need transparency. We need to do something before the public decide we should all be in jail, capisce?'

Austin nodded.

'Guys like you ... making smaller loans, more cautious investments. Not behaving like drunk fucking beavers at the wheel of a 747, you know what I'm saying? Not acting like coked-up weasels who exist simply to spunk cash down the panties of cocktail waitresses and buy themselves fucking indoor fucking trampolines.'

Austin was slightly lost, but he smiled gamely nonetheless.

'Sustainable banking?' he tried. This was a phrase that had gone down well at head office.

'Yeah,' said Merv. 'Exactly. You married?'

'No ...' Austin was confused by the curveball question.

'Kids?'

'Uh, I look after my brother.'

'Why, what's up with him?'

'He's eleven.'

Merv nodded. 'Oh yeah, one of my kids is eleven. From Mrs Ferani number two. Doesn't know if he's coming or going. Half of him wants to play *Star Wars*, half of him wants to race in the Indy 500 ... '

'Is that like Formula 1?'

' ... so I said to him, "Well, fine, you can have the damn car, but don't drive it off the ranch."'

The waiter came over and started to explain the enormously complicated list of daily specials, in such a friendly way that Austin wondered for a few moments if they'd been at school together, but Merv waved him away.

'It's Christmas, isn't it? Bring us something with turkey. And cranberry sauce and the rest of that bullshit. And some more claret.'

Austin, his body clock slightly messed up, and having drunk some very good but rather rich claret at lunch, lurched out of the restaurant at 4 p.m. A black town car appeared silently out of seemingly nowhere to pick up Merv, who seemed to be suffering no ill effects at all and offered Austin a lift. He declined. The New York city air was absolutely freezing in his throat, but he wanted to clear his head a little and think things over.

'Sure thing,' Merv said. 'But you're one of my men now, OK?'

They shook hands and Merv pulled him into a large bear hug. It was extremely unsettling.

Austin found himself just by the Plaza Hotel at the south-east end of Central Park. Long rows of horses and carriages lined up opposite, with jingling bells and icy breath. The horses wore blankets, and Austin went to take a picture of them on his phone before remembering that Darny would probably think this was infringing the rights of horses or something, so decided against it. Opposite the park was FAO Schwarz, the massive toy shop. Even Darny, Austin suspected, would have liked a peek in there. He headed on to Fifth Avenue, among the crowds of excited shoppers hopping in and out of Barneys and Saks and the other great department stores that lined the sidewalk. The lights and window displays were almost overwhelming, and snow was starting to fall. Wrapped up in warmth and the excitement of new people and new places . . . it was enervating.

A whole new world? Really?

He hadn't told Issy because he didn't want to worry her, but there was every chance the Stoke Newington branch wouldn't make it through the next round of cuts. And to make the dizzying leap from local to global banking . . . it was almost unheard of. The bank had only ever been meant as a stopgap. He'd known he was capable of more, but life was so complicated, and providing stability for a terrified and confused four-year-old had been paramount at the time.

Now, though . . . maybe it was time for him to reclaim some ambition for himself?

He thought of Issy. She'd often said how much she'd love to go to New York. She could come . . . she'd love it, wouldn't she? Would she? He thought with a sinking heart of how happy she was in the Cupcake Café; how she'd worked so hard to build it into a lovely cosy place for people to come and sit for a while; how she'd got to know the locals and the regulars and how the café had taken its place in Stoke Newington like it had always been there. It gave him an ominous feeling.

But she could do it again! Maybe get her green card, start up something wonderful. Americans had invented the cupcake, surely? Two very tall women pushed past him to get into the Chanel store, talking loudly about their dates. Austin buried the thought that Issy wouldn't feel at all at home here. That she possibly wasn't tough enough and sharp enough for New York. He decided to buy her a present. Something lovely to show her how magical the city would be.

In his slightly fuddled state, he couldn't believe it. The smell. He'd just been thinking about Issy, and suddenly, out of nowhere, he'd smelled her. He followed his nose off down a side street. And sure enough, right there on the corner was the most adorable, charming, perfect little cupcake café he'd ever seen in his life.

Outside, the little corner building was painted pink. It was completely covered top to toe in little white fairy lights, with more lights strung inside visible through the windows. Mismatched dark-coloured sofas – greens and burgundies – were dotted around, covered in tartan rugs, and the walls and the floor were dark mahogany. The smell of coffee and baking cakes made Austin nearly tearful with homesickness. He pushed open the door, and it clanged just like Issy's did.

'Well, hello there,' said a friendly voice from behind the counter. The back wall was entirely lined with red and green twisted candy canes. 'What can I get you today?'

Chapter Five

Polar Bear Cupcakes

These little cakes are irresistible. Cut the liquorice into tiny eyes and a little nose, and use white buttons for the ears. Or if, like me, you hate liquorice, use chocolate chips. Try not to feel too sad when you bite into them; let's face it, anyone who can eat a jelly baby can eat a coconut baby polar bear.

125g unsalted butter, at room temperature
125g caster sugar
2 large eggs, at room temperature
125g sifted self-raising flour
2 tsp vanilla extract
2 tsp milk

For this recipe you need two different sizes of cupcake tin, one smaller than the other.

Preheat oven to 190°C/gas mark 5, and put paper cases in the tins.

Beat butter and sugar together, then add eggs, flour, vanilla and milk and beat until the mix drops slowly off the spoon (add more milk if it won't).

Spoon into paper cases, put in oven. Check with a toothpick after 12 minutes – if it comes out clean, we're ready.

For the topping

125g unsalted butter
250g icing sugar, sifted
1tsp coconut extract (you can also use Malibu, if
     you're feeling frisky!)
splash of milk
desiccated coconut
chocolate chips, large and small
white chocolate buttons

Beat the butter and add the icing sugar, then add the coconut extract and the milk until you have a light frosting.

Spread the frosting all over one small and one large cupcake, then stick them together so the little cake makes the polar bear's head. Carefully roll the bear in the desiccated coconut.

Add chocolate chips to make the eyes and the nose, and the white chocolate buttons to make the ears – and voilà! Polar bear cupcakes!!!!

Merry Christmas!

'So we're going full Christmas,' said Pearl in a resigned tone of voice.

'They're polar bears,' said Issy. 'Polar bears are for life, Pearl, not just Christmas. Anyway,' she added, 'it's the first of December today! It's Advent! It's all official! Ta-dah!'

She unveiled her *pièce de résistance* from her shoulder bag: a huge Advent calendar. It was in the shape of a traditional snow-coloured village, and the brightly coloured windows of the houses formed the numbers of the calendar.

'First child every morning gets to open a door. Except for Louis.'

Louis looked up from where he was sitting engrossed in a book about frogs.

'Do you have your own calendar?' she asked.

Louis nodded gravely.

'Grammy did give me one. It has sweeties. I get chocolate every day! And Daddy gave me one too.'

Issy looked at Pearl.

'Don't look at me,' said Pearl, who had some trouble watching Louis' weight. 'I told them both,' she said. 'I took one of them away.'

'For the poor children,' said Louis gravely. 'Poor, poor children. I kept Grammy's because I ate that first.'

'OK, good,' said Issy. 'Don't open this one, if you don't mind. You can open the big doors on Christmas Eve.'

Louis studied it carefully. 'Issy!' he said urgently. 'It has no chocolate left, Issy!'

'Not all Advent calendars have chocolate, Louis.'

'Yes! They do!' said Louis. 'I think a robber came.'

'Well, I'm glad I'm not going to have too much trouble keeping you away from it,' said Issy.

She unfolded the calendar on top of the fireplace. It looked lovely, but wouldn't stay up.

'Hmm, I wonder what would keep that up?' she said. 'Oh, I know. Perhaps this long rope of holly I just happen to have in my bag.'

Pearl snorted. 'Yeah, all right,' she said. 'You've made your point.'

'Did you know who started with the holly and the ivy?' said Issy cheerfully.

'Baby Jesus!' hollered Louis.

'Well, yes,' said Issy. 'But also the Romans. And mistletoe is from even further back, from the Druids, their midwinter festival.'

Pearl sold another six polar bear cakes and didn't say anything. Caroline turned up to let Issy get back downstairs to the baking. Her face fell when she saw the holly on the fireplace.

'Oh,' she said. 'You've decided to go with red and green, have you?'

'At Christmas?' said Issy. 'Well. Yes, funnily enough.'

'But there's so many more chic ways to do it!' said Caroline. 'I was thinking maybe an all-silver motif, or those clear plastic trees they do in the Conran shop? So stylish.'

'If I wanted to be stylish, I wouldn't wear clothes from a catalogue,' said Issy. 'I want it to be nice and cosy and comfortable, not scary like those posh places where they make you sit on jaggedy chairs and everyone is blonde and skinny and wears leather trousers . . . '

Realising she was exactly describing Caroline, Issy fell silent. Fortunately Caroline, despite having zero body fat, managed to be very thick-skinned.

'We'll never make it into the *Super Secret London Guide*,' she said. 'They choose the most select hidden shops of the year and run a special issue. There's a prize for the most stylishly decorated.'

'We will not,' said Issy. 'I will try and get through it as stoically as I can.'

Caroline pouted. 'Don't you want to at least make the effort? They run a special supplement in January.'

'The problem is,' said Pearl, 'if we were in it, we'd fill the shop with other people who looked like you. And people that look like you are bad for turnover. Don't eat enough cakes.'

'Yes, but we take up less room,' pleaded Caroline. 'So

you can fit more of us in. And let's face it, we'll pay almost anything for a smoothie, especially if it's green.'

Issy smiled. 'Well, even so. We wouldn't win and I don't want to spend a lot of time doing stupid stuff.'

'You might,' said Caroline. 'And it might bump you up the ladder a bit. It's time you were expanding anyway. That's how the Bastard grew his business. Well, I think. He used to talk about it, but I didn't really listen, obviously – very boring.'

'I will never understand why you two split up,' murmured Pearl.

'At least I was a married mother,' sniffed Caroline.

Thankfully, the bell tinged, and Helena entered, carrying Chadani. She had a gigantic buggy that had cost about as much as a small car, with personally commissioned muff, hood, foot cosy and car seat in pink and purple tiger stripes, so that from a distance it looked, as Austin had pointed out (quietly), like a small monster that had just eaten a baby, then exploded. It didn't fit up the stairwell of their apartment, through the doorway of most shops or in the boot of their Fiat, so Helena regularly left it in the middle of the pavement, which managed to make it look even more like a monster, and meant it got in absolutely everybody's way. This didn't stop her from recommending it as the very best in buggies to everyone she met. Issy was rather grateful it didn't fit inside, but she'd had to insist that Helena chain it to the little tree that grew in their courtyard, after she kept leaving it outside the door and it tripped up four people in one morning (it had an extra, malevolent wheel that jutted out the front, and was used mostly to jar people's heels at pelican crossings).

'Hello!' said Issy cheerily, glad she wouldn't have to break up Pearl and Caroline. 'Hello, Chadani!'

Chadani yelled and contorted her face.

Issy looked at Helena.

'Tell me that isn't real fur.' Chadani was practically buried in a huge fur coat with a matching bonnet and her pale pink Uggs.

'No!' said Helena. 'But doesn't she look so CUU-UUTE? Ashok's great-aunt wants to pierce her ears.'

Issy didn't say anything to this, but kissed Chadani on her little button nose. Once you got past all the fluff and nonsense, she was a very endearing baby.

Chadani smiled cheerfully and pointed at the largest cake on the stand, winter raspberry with pink icing confection that Issy, in whimsical mood, had covered in sparkly stars. They were very pretty and shiny, she conceded.

'WAAAH!' shouted Chadani.

'Will I get one for you to share?' said Issy, firing up a cappuccino for Helena.

'Oh, Chadani doesn't really like to share,' said Helena. 'She's a bit young to be forced into that, don't you think?'

'It's a very big cake,' said Issy.

'Yes,' said Helena. 'You really shouldn't have made them so large. You have to think about children too.'

Issy decided not to roll her eyes, and put another batch of bear cakes into the oven. Then she decided to take a quick break – Pearl and Caroline weren't talking to one another, which made them both work really quickly and efficiently in a gigantic huff – and sat down next to Helena, who was looking at toys in the Argos catalogue whilst Chadani made shorter work of a gigantic cupcake than Issy would have believed a one-year-old capable of.

'Hey,' said Issy.

'Do you know,' said Helena, flicking through the catalogue, 'Chadani has every single one of these, just about. They really need to invent some new toys.'

'You love having a daughter, don't you?' said Issy, suddenly.

Helena beamed. 'Well,' she said, 'yes. Yes, I do. I mean, obviously we got a very special child, not everyone gets that. But yes. In general. I mean, obviously, it can be ...' She stopped herself. 'Yes. It's wonderful. So when are you and Austin going to get to it, then?'

Issy bit her lip. Ever since they'd got together ... well, everyone had just seemed to think that it was the end to a fairy tale, a happy ever after; there was Austin and Issy, and wasn't it funny, she fell in love with her bank manager, ha ha, bet she'll never be short of a few bob, ha, well, you can guess where he's putting his deposits ... oh, she'd heard all the jokes. And now it was more than a year ago, and everyone was expecting some kind of announcement, or at least for something to happen. But Austin's work had gone on and on and she'd got caught up in the shop and moving, and, well . . .

Something in her expression penetrated Helena's baby haze.

'You two are all right, aren't you? There's nothing wrong? I refuse to believe there's anything wrong. After all the goat's arseholes you've dated, I won't let anything bad happen to you. Don't you dare. I mean it. I'll march Austin round at gunpoint. I will put him in a wrestling hold. I will remove his horn-rimmed glasses and stuff them up his—'

'I'm sure it's nothing,' said Issy hastily. 'I'm sure he's just . . . you know, a bit caught up in New York and a bit excited. That's all. Nothing bad.'

The doorbell rang. Issy looked up. It was a delivery service. She wasn't expecting anything.

'Issy Randall?' the man in the uniform said.

Issy signed for the box, noticing with excitement that it was from Austin.

'AHA!' she said. 'Look! I shouldn't have mentioned anything! Look! He's sent me a present from New York!'

Helena beamed as Issy cut through the brown tape. 'Hurrah! Now never think badly of him again! You need a relationship like Ashok and me.'

'What, where you tell him what to do and he lies down and kisses the ground you walk on? Hmmm,' said Issy, but she was smiling with happiness.

Inside was a bright green box, wrapped with a paler, pistachio-coloured ribbon.

🧁

The girl in the New York cupcake shop was called Kelly-Lee. She was very pretty, with a snub nose and wide grey eyes and a few light freckles that looked as though they were dusted on like icing sugar. Her hair was thick and auburn, in a high ponytail, and she wore the pink polo shirt uniform of the shop in a way that was pert but not too sexy.

She'd been so excited to move to New York – Queens, to be precise – to finish her masters, but she was finding it hard to make ends meet. Everything was so expensive, and she'd hoped to find a good job – like Ugly Betty – on a cool magazine, or in an art gallery or with a photographer. She'd been a bit shocked to find out that those jobs didn't actually pay any money; you were expected to work for free – how you paid for food didn't seem to come into it – which clearly meant that any of the cooler jobs were only open to really rich people, which seemed unbelievably wrong and had opened up a distinct glow of unfairness in a life that up to now had been nicely skewed in her favour, as she was pretty and clever and had grown up in a happy Wisconsin family.

So she had taken this stopgap job to make ends meet, but now it had dragged on for three years and none of the other cool stuff seemed to be happening, and frankly she was getting tired of it. That was before she even got to the New York men. She'd been asked out, of course, and had been wined and dined by handsome guys, sexy guys, crazy guys, nice guys, and every single one of them had asked her at the end of the evening if she wouldn't mind remaining non-exclusive, and every single time Kelly-Lee had said no. She was worth more than that. She was sure of it. But it was getting a bit tiring waiting around. Her roommate Alesha thought she was a buttoned-up idiot, but then Kelly-Lee had noticed Alesha get home several times early in the morning with her silver dress still on from the night before, so she was trying not to pay too much attention to what Alesha thought. Then, after two years she'd changed her mind on that one too. Sure enough, the guys that said they were going to call called her about the same as before – i.e., not at all. But at least she occasionally woke up with someone in her bed. Alesha had smiled unpleasantly and made remarks about Little Miss Snooty being brought down a peg or two, and how you had to kiss a lot of frogs. Then Alesha had moved out with someone that she'd met, and Kelly-Lee felt more alone than ever.

You didn't meet many men in the cupcake shop, though. Well, you did, but not very useful ones. Some fat, some gay, some buying for their wives or girlfriends. (That was the worst, if they were nice. Imagine having a husband who also bought you cakes. Kelly-Lee some-times had trouble finding a guy who would buy her a drink, even if they'd only just met.) And some obviously feeling sorry for something they'd done and hoping the cupcakes would make up for it, which, in the case of a woman, very much depended on whether they were on a diet or not. Kelly-Lee was always on a diet. She had to try the new cupcake recipes at the beginning of every month, but she always made sure she restricted each one to a mouthful, and spent an extra ten minutes at Aquabike Extreme.

Her mother wanted her to go back to Wisconsin for Christmas. It would be about ten degrees below zero, snowed up to the windows, and her relatives would spend the entire time banging on and on about her amazing life in the Big Apple and was it really like what they saw on TV, and then they'd all fall out about gay marriage and her mom would say something that was meant to be conciliatory, like how she knew Kelly-Lee wasn't quite married yet, but if she wanted to bring a boy home, they could probably overlook the sleeping arrangements, and Kelly-Lee would look at her prom queen picture (truly, her proudest moment at the time) and want to scream. She sighed. Then the doorbell had rung and she'd hopped up to her perky best.

'What can I get you today?'

Foreigner, she thought. Cute, but a bit rumpled-looking.

'Uhm, hello,' said Austin, blinking and taking off his glasses.

Ah, thought Kelly-Lee. English. So probably drunk. Still cute, though. She checked his finger automatically. No ring.

'Are you looking for something sweet?' she asked, cheekily. She liked Englishmen, you could have a laugh with them. Not like American men; they always took you seriously, then carried on talking about themselves anyway.

Austin smiled. 'I just liked the smell.'

'Have you been in New York long?'

'About two days,' said Austin. 'It's been a long two days though.'

'It's confusing at first, isn't it?' said Kelly-Lee. 'When I first got here, I just stared upwards all the time. I nearly fell down a manhole.'

'Oh no,' said Austin. 'Well, it could have been worse. A giant anvil could have fallen from the sky.'

'Are you looking for some cakes?'

'Yes,' he said. 'My girlfriend runs a cake shop.'

Kelly-Lee liked the word girlfriend. It could mean anything. It could mean girl I just met, someone I know in passing, near ex. It didn't mean fiancée or wife.

'Which one?' she asked happily.

'Oh no, you wouldn't know it. It's in London. London, England,' he clarified needlessly. She smiled.

Better and better, thought Kelly-Lee.

'Oh no,' she said. 'So you're all the way over here and she's over there? Are you going to be separated for long?'

'Hmm,' said Austin. 'I'm not sure. I hope not. You know how things go.'

Kelly-Lee did.

'Coffee?'

Austin did want a coffee, to clear his head a bit. 'Yes,' he said.

'So do you like running a cupcake café here?'

Kelly-Lee had learned long ago that moaning was not considered very attractive in a woman. Men liked perkiness and happy girls.

'I LOVE it,' she said. 'It's amazing! The smell of cinnamon in the morning! The first cup of coffee! Trying out all the new amazing flavours.'

'Do you bake them yourself?' Austin asked.

Kelly-Lee frowned. She had always considered it the hallmark of a sophisticated New Yorker to be unable to turn on her own oven.

'Well, kinda,' she said. 'The van drops them off, you know, half mixed? Then I just kinda heat them up. Like Mac and cheese.'

'But you like baking?'

'Love it,' smiled Kelly-Lee. 'Hey, you know, we deliver.'

'To London?'

'Sure! We've got a sister shop there. I can call them right away, they'll be there in half an hour.'

'Really?' This struck Austin as a fantastic idea. And it seemed there was absolutely nothing to stop Issy coming over here and baking if he took up a job. There were plenty of shops. It would be great!

He bit into a chocolate and vanilla that Kelly-Lee had put out for him. He hadn't protested, even though after the lunch he'd just had, he'd have put money on not eating again for about a week. It wasn't bad – a little sweet for his taste, and it didn't have the warm, fresh out-of-the-oven taste that Issy's cakes had. But that was fine; good in fact. Maybe she could come over here and make them even better! She would like that.

'Send a dozen,' he said boldly, thinking he was behaving like a New Yorker already. Kelly-Lee took down the address and promised to call it through.

'Well, I'm so glad you like us!' she said, smiling at him appealingly. But it was wasted on Austin. Sitting back after his second bite of the cupcake, in the cosy, familiar-seeming fug, he had fallen straight into a deep sleep.

Chapter Six

Recipe for a Bad Cupcake

2 cups bleached flour

2 cups corn syrup

1 cup partially hydrogenated soybean and
   cottonseed oil

1 cup sugar

1 tspn dextrose

water

½ cup high fructose corn syrup

½ cup whey powder

1 egg

1 tbsp soy lecithin (emulsifier)

1 tbsp corn starch

pinch salt

1 tsp sodium aluminium phosphate baking soda

3 drops white colouring

1 tsp citric acid

½ tsp sorbic acid

Send through machine. Bake for 20 minutes until partially cooked. Freeze until needed fully cooked, then zap for 10 minutes at high temperature.

Back in London, Issy unwrapped the box in disbelief.

'What the heck?'

Under the ribbon on the green box was emblazoned the large flower-embossed logo of a huge, internationally successful cupcake chain. And sure enough, inside was a selection of a dozen cupcakes in different flavours. They did look, it was fair to say, absolutely exquisite, all perfectly piped, and decorated with glitter, tiny stars and iridescent raspberry dust.

'Wow,' said Caroline. 'They are so chic. Look at the attention to detail.'

'That's because they're made in a factory,' said Issy darkly. 'You need a few wonky ones here and there to know they're home-made.'

'Why would he send you those?' said Helena. 'I don't understand. Are you sure they're from him?'

'Yes, look,' said Issy.

The card said, 'To Issy from Austin'. No kisses, nothing. It was very strange. It was less strange if you knew that Kelly-Lee had had only the barest of details to go on

when she called in the order over the head of a profoundly fast asleep Austin. And possibly an ulterior
motive when it came to not putting kisses on the card.

Issy shook her head. 'But why would he? I don't
understand.'

'Maybe he's trying to show you they have better cupcakes,' said Caroline, helpfully.

'Maybe he's the least imaginative gift-giver ever and
knows you like cupcakes,' said Helena. 'I mean, come
on, he works in a bank. He's hardly going to be a super-
romantic soul, is he?'

'He's perfectly romantic,' said Issy, going slightly
pink. 'When he wants to be, and when he isn't running
late or too busy or just generally a bit distracted because
Darny's playing up.'

They all stared at the open box.

'Ooh, are those your new range?' said a customer.
'They look amazing.'

Chadani cruised over from the sofa, stuck a podgy
little paw into the box and started smooshing the cakes
all up together. For once, Issy didn't think Helena
needed to say anything to her, which was just as well, as
Helena was watching her daughter admiringly, as if feeling sorry for anyone whose baby wasn't as good at
bashing up cakes as hers.

Pearl came past carrying a pile of empty dishes. She
sniffed.

'What are you three all hanging around for?' she said.

'Austin has gone completely insane,' said Caroline. 'He's obviously trying to put Issy off him for some reason. Don't worry,' she said, touching Issy on the arm. 'I know break-ups can be messy. My divorce was just horrible. Awful. So I can help you through this.'

Normally Issy could laugh Caroline off, but this really was a bit odd. She bit her bottom lip. Pearl noticed immediately.

'Oh for goodness' sake stop being a big bunch of divs,' she said. 'He's thinking about you. Obviously.'

'But why send something so insulting?' said Issy.

'Because he's a man,' said Pearl. 'I said he was being thoughtful. I didn't say he wasn't being a total and utter idiot.'

'Hmm,' said Issy. 'I think I am going to go and knead some panettone.'

Pearl and Caroline exchanged glances.

'You do that,' said Pearl.

Issy turned to go downstairs. Then she turned back. She sighed crossly.

'Well, I'd better try them, I suppose.'

She broke a bit off one of the big sparkly ones in the middle. It did look immaculate, there was no doubt about that; all the cupcakes perfectly even and exactly the same height. She took a bite and her nose wrinkled up.

'Oh, yuck,' she said.

'I think they say "gross" in America,' reproved Caroline.

'Too sugary,' Issy pronounced. 'And they're not using all butter. You can tell. There's a horrible oily aftertaste. That means industrial quantities, not hand-milled. This is raspberry extract, not real raspberry. And the crumb is too dense. Bleurgh.'

'There you go,' said Pearl. 'He obviously sent them to you to point out your clear superiority over them.'

'Or else he can't tell the difference,' said Issy, worried.

'Or perhaps he thinks these are better,' said Caroline, who always managed to go one worse than everybody else.

'Thanks, Caroline,' said Pearl pointedly. Issy turned away and stomped down the steps to the cellar bakery.

Doti the postman was finishing off his Christmas round outside the Cupcake Café. He liked to come to them last, especially on cold days. Partly because he had a sweet tooth, and partly because he had a soft spot for Pearl and liked to flirt with her. Pearl had Benjamin to contend with, but liked Doti very much.

Today, however, Doti was with someone else, a definite first. She was, Pearl noticed, rather pretty, in her thirties, long dark hair tied back in a ponytail, large hooped gold earrings and very white teeth. It was hard to tell what her figure was like in the unflattering postal uniform and fluorescent vest, but Pearl was putting money on pleasantly curvaceous. She sniffed. They were laughing together as they jangled through the door.

'Hello,' said Pearl, stiffly. Doti smiled.

'Ah, beautiful Pearl. This is beautiful Pearl,' he said to the woman.

'Hello, beautiful Pearl,' said the woman, nicely. That annoyed Pearl even more. Nice pretty people made her feel uneasy.

'This is Maya,' said Doti. 'She's my temporary Christmas postie.'

'Oh, hello,' said Pearl, trying not to sound narked. She shouldn't sound narked. It was just that Doti was the first person who'd shown the slightest bit of interest in her since Louis was born. Still, they couldn't be together, so she couldn't expect to be surprised if he liked somebody else. He was probably too old for Maya anyway. And they were only working together.

'Doti has been *soo* helpful,' said Maya, looking at him in a way that almost immediately put paid to their relationship being merely professional. Doti was pretty handsome, Pearl supposed. His hair was shaved, and he had a very finely shaped skull with small ears and a long neck and . . .

'What can I get you?' she said.

'I promised Maya I'd let her try the finest coffee and cake emporium this side of N16,' said Doti. 'So here we are.'

'Oh, it's lovely,' said Maya. She glanced at the blackboard and her face fell a little. 'It looks expensive, though.' She lowered her voice and spoke directly to

Pearl. 'I really needed this job,' she whispered. Pearl understood.

'Well, we're glad you got it,' said Doti heartily. 'Very glad. And coffee is on me.'

Louis ran in with his best friend Big Louis, scattering rucksacks, hats, scarves and gloves all over the place before the bell had stopped ringing.

'MUM!' he yelled, and Pearl put down the milk she was steaming and stepped over to give him a big kiss and cuddle.

'My special guy,' she said. 'My number one boy.'

Louis beamed. 'I was SOOO good today,' he said. 'Here is who was not good. Evan. Gianni. Carlo. Mohammed A and Felix ... '

'OK, OK,' said Pearl. 'That's enough.'

Louis looked grave. 'They have to sit on a rug. You would not like to sit on a rug.'

'Why not?' said Pearl. 'What happens?'

'You have to sit on a rug! And EVERYBODY knows you have done some naughty behaviour.'

'Hey, Louis,' said Doti.

Louis' face lit up. 'DOTI!' he yelled. They were great friends.

Doti crouched down. 'Hello, young man,' he said.

Louis looked suspiciously at Maya. 'WHO'S THAT?' he whispered very loudly.

'That's my friend who is also delivering post.'

'A lady postman?' said Louis dubiously.

'Of course! There are lots of lady postmen.'

'We're called post*women*,' said Maya. 'Hello. What's your name?'

Louis still looked at her suspiciously, and, unusually for him, didn't immediately start chatting.

'Doti has a friend already,' he announced loftily. 'He has me and also he has Mummy. Thank you very much.' Then he turned away.

'Louis!' said Pearl, genuinely surprised and secretly a bit pleased. 'Where are your manners! Say hello!'

Louis stared at the floor. 'H'lo,' he muttered.

'It's very nice to meet you,' said Maya. 'Oh, Doti, you weren't wrong about these mince pies.'

Pearl gave her a look.

'It's December,' said Doti. 'We can celebrate Christmas now.'

'Oh yes,' said Maya. 'Definitely. Yum.'

Louis tugged at Doti's trouser leg. 'Have you any letters for me?'

He asked this every day. Issy often reflected that it did slightly ameliorate the effect of getting endless and ever-higher electricity bills when they were delivered by a cheerful four-year-old wearing a hat shaped like a dinosaur.

'Well, as a matter of fact, I do,' said Doti. 'You know how normally you have to do a special delivery to Auntie Issy?'

Louis nodded.

'Well, today it isn't for Issy. Today it's just for you.'

Louis' eyes went wide.

'And you won't BELIEVE who it's from.'

Pearl was as surprised as Louis when Doti handed him an envelope covered in snowflakes and addressed Louis Kmbota McGregor, c/o the Cupcake Café.

Doti winked at her. 'The post office does it every year,' he whispered. 'I thought he might like one.'

Louis, who could recognise his own name printed in gold, was turning the envelope over and over like it was the most precious object he'd ever seen.

'Mummy!' he breathed.

'Are you going to open it?' said Pearl.

Louis shook his head. 'NO.'

'Who do you think it's from?' said Doti.

Louis held it away from him, still with a wondering look in his eye.

'Is it . . . is it from Santa?'

Doti took the envelope. 'See this,' he said, pointing. 'This is a postmark. Remember I showed you before? It tells you where the letter was posted and what date.'

Louis nodded.

'Well, this postmark says . . . the North Pole.'

'THE NORTH POLE?'

'Yup!'

'MUMMY! I've got a letter from Santa! At the NORTH POLE!'

'That's lovely,' said Pearl, mouthing a thank-you to Doti. 'Come on, darling, let's open it.'

Louis shook his head again and put the card behind his back.

'I can't,' he said. 'Too preshis.'

'Why is it too precious?' asked Maya.

Louis shrugged and kicked his foot against the counter, even though Pearl was always telling him not to.

'Monster garage,' he whispered. 'Santa might say I can't have a monster garage. Even though I did not do naughty behaviour and I did not have to sit on the rug. Like Evan and Gianni and Felix and Mohammed A but not me.'

Pearl bit her lip. That damn monster garage. Ever since he'd seen the advert, he'd been on about it. It was a garage that fixed monster trucks; big trucks, with big monsters inside. But every single monster cost a lot of money, and every single truck was sold separately and they cost money too, and the basic garage itself even before you bought a single monster or truck was well over a hundred pounds, and anyway they didn't have room to store it even if they got the damn thing, which she couldn't afford in a million years because she was going to have to buy Louis new trainers, as he'd grown out of the old ones and they were horribly shabby, and he needed a proper winter coat, and new pyjamas and loads and loads of basic stuff that probably other kids just got when they needed it and not at a special time of year, but that was just how it was.

And it hadn't helped that Benjamin had seen him looking longingly at the advert and said, without even thinking, of course you're going to have a monster garage; no son of mine is going without. They'd had a furious argument outside about it when he'd gone for a cigarette – which by the way also cost a fortune they couldn't afford – especially when he'd said, stubbornly, that he would get the fucking garage for his son and she could see by the glint in his eye not to argue, which just made her worry and panic even more because she hated to think what lengths he might go to to get it.

And every time Louis had mentioned hopefully about the monster garage and asked leading questions about whether Santa would bring him one on his sleigh or whether it would be too heavy and perhaps he would send some real monsters to carry it, or maybe a special dinosaur, she had hummed non-committally, and prayed for his little four-year-old head to latch on to something else.

So far, it hadn't. She hated Christmas.

'Well,' said Doti, 'when I went to empty Santa's letter box, he did say that he had heard that there was a par-ticularly well-behaved boy in N17, so I think he'll probably try his hardest. And now we must be heading back to the depot.'

Doti and Maya departed together, chatting head to head like a couple of teenagers.

Pearl let Louis have a mince pie. Then she ate two more herself, crossly.

Kelly-Lee had let Austin sleep until closing time – he was sweet, it wasn't like he was a tramp or anything, although he did appear to be wearing odd socks, but perhaps that was some of that fabled charming English eccentricity she'd heard so much about. But finally it was seven o'clock, pitch dark outside, Hussein and Flavia had already gone and it was time to shut up shop.

'C'mon, Hugh Grant,' she said gently. He looked nice asleep; he didn't snore or dribble or fart, like that fat little TV producer she'd dated in the fall, who'd come round, eat all her food and then try and get in her pants – she wasn't that dumb, plus she'd felt his little dick prodding up against her thigh when they'd been making out, and frankly she'd lost interest pretty sharply after that. It didn't stop him talking almost constantly about how many beautiful actresses hit on him every time he stepped out of his condo, and dangling hints about her maybe working in the studio one day. She sighed. She bet this guy wouldn't do that. Kelly-Lee put on her perkiest smile.

'Hello, hello?'

Austin blinked. He felt awful. All he wanted to do was crawl under his duvet and sleep for a day and a half. For a second he couldn't figure out where he was. He pulled out his phone; the little red BlackBerry light was blinking at him ferociously. He had nine new emails and six new voicemails. The first was from the bank head in London.

'I don't know what you've done to the Yanks,' it started. 'Maybe they like staff with hair like an unmade bed. Anyway, they want to make you an offer. Get in touch.'

The next two were from his PA, Janet, insisting he call her as soon as possible. And there was one from Merv, saying how much they were looking forward to having him aboard ...

Austin clutched the side of the sofa. This was going very fast. Much too fast. Half of him was excited by the rush of being in demand; half of him was petrified.

'Good news?' said Kelly-Lee, watching him stare at the BlackBerry screen in consternation and run his fingers through his lovely thick hair, all tufted up like a small boy's. Austin blinked several times.

'I ... I've just been offered a job. I think.'

Kelly-Lee's eyebrows went even higher.

'Boy, that's great! Congratulations! That means we'll be seeing you again!'

'Yes, well ... wow. I suppose.'

'That's brilliant.'

Kelly-Lee selected the largest of the day's leftover cupcakes – an enormous red velvet – and swiftly put it in a little box, which she tied up expertly with bright bows.

'Here you are,' she said. 'Congratulations. And welcome to New York.'

'I thought New Yorkers were supposed to be unfriendly,' said Austin.

'Well, you're about to discover that just ain't so,' said Kelly-Lee.

Austin shrugged on his heavy greatcoat and long scarf.

'Well, goodbye,' he said.

'See you again soon,' said Kelly-Lee, and flashed him her enormous smile.

Outside, the snow was horizontal and blowing into his face. He hurried along looking for a cab. New York in the snow was a lot more picturesque in the photos. In reality it was utterly bloody freezing, far colder than he'd ever felt in London. He found a yellow taxi and ordered it to take him to his hotel, then fumbled in his pocket for his phone again and made a resolution to buy a pair of gloves. That was odd, nothing from Darny and Iss. He checked his watch; what was the time difference again? Anyway, it didn't matter. This was news! Big news! A big job. Oh my goodness, a big job.

Austin had never meant to be a banker. He'd never really thought of doing anything much. When his parents had died in a car crash, he had been ambling gently through a degree in marine biology, after enjoying many diving holidays with his mum and dad before the extremely late and surprising new baby had come along after a silver wedding anniversary party went a bit crazy.

In the hideous blur that followed the accident, his little brother was bombarded on all sides by well-meaning aunties, social services, distant cousins, friends of his parents he'd never met. Austin had had to grow up extremely quickly, cut his surfer hair (for the best, he thought now when he saw old photos), leave university and find a job that would allow him to take over his parents' unexpired mortgage on their little terraced house in Stoke Newington.

It hadn't been easy convincing everyone that they were fine the way they were, with or without the fifteen shepherd's pies that arrived every morning on their doorstep unsolicited. As long as Austin kept the front room and the hallway reasonably tidy, he'd found, and the upstairs windows open to circulate any boy smell, they got by all right. But it had been a struggle. A long road.

By the time he'd discovered he had an aptitude for his job, he was already caught up in getting Darny to school and running the house (badly) and getting to work on time, and before he knew it, he had become one of those working mothers at school who were always dashing in late with the wrong PE kit and never contributed to the Christmas fete. Except those mothers weren't particularly friendly towards him because all the stay-at-home mothers would cover for Austin and bake him Christmas cakes and have Darny round to sleepovers to give him some time to himself, whilst simultaneously sneering at or pitying the working mothers, which made the working mothers furious.

But Darny was older now, grown up enough to at least remember to brush his own hair once in a while, even though he'd rather not, and turn on the washing machine (turning it on was rarely the problem; removing the clothes when they were finished instead of leaving them there to stew was the main stumbling block at the moment), and now Issy was there too, and maybe it was, kind of, time for Austin to do something with his life, or rather something with his life that he himself had chosen.

He wouldn't have changed one thing about his life with Darny, not one thing, he told himself fiercely. That was the hand he had been dealt, and he'd played it. He loved his brother so much. But this was beyond his wildest dreams ... a big job in New York ... a cool apartment, maybe? Darny could go to school here. And Issy ...

He needed to talk to Issy.

'Hello?'

The voice was trying to be friendly, but struggling. By the time Issy had risen at six to start baking, worked a full day in the shop, cashed up and done the accounts, helped Darny with his homework and cooked supper, there wasn't much left of her. She went to bed very early.

'Iss?' said Austin. 'Iss, you won't believe this. It's amazing. This huge bank. They want me! They want me to work for them! They're offering … well I don't know what they're offering but it seems like they really want me, and, I mean, well, obviously I haven't said anything, but, I mean, they have been talking about sending me overseas for a while, and well. Anyway.'

He was conscious Issy wasn't saying anything.

'Anyway. I just thought I should let you know what is going on. Kind of thing.'

Issy had been half asleep when she'd answered the phone. She was wide awake now. And she realised that on some level she had always expected something like this to happen. Who wouldn't want Austin? She did. Things were always too good to be true.

She suddenly wished Helena was here. Helena would tell her, ferociously, to buck up, that she was more than good enough for Austin, thank you, and that her stupid mind would talk her out of anything, which was how she had ended up with a loser like Graeme, and she didn't want that again, did she?

She did not.

But Helena wasn't here. She would be walking Chadani up and down the flat (Chadani was too sensitive to sleep well; it was a sign of hyper-intelligence), and there was only Darny, snoring loudly next door, a dark house with new, unhung curtains and, on the other end of the line, four thousand miles away, sounding happy and carefree and light, the only man she'd ever truly loved, telling her he was never coming home.

'Congratulations,' Issy had finally managed to stammer out. She had tried to cover up her consternation by yawning ostentatiously for as long as she could; then it had turned into a real yawn that she couldn't stop until she could feel his impatience on the other end of the phone. 'I mean, well done. It's really happening. New York, New York! I mean. Wow. I'm so happy for you ...'

Austin winced. She didn't sound in the least bit happy. That fake yawn hadn't fooled him in the slightest.

'It's such a step up,' he said, feeling a note of pleading creeping into his voice. 'I mean, it just changes everything really. I don't even know how I could come back to London and say no to it.'

'No,' said Issy. 'Of course you can't. You've worked so hard. And you're good at what you do.'

'Thanks,' said Austin.

There was a windy, wobbling pause across the ocean. Then Issy remembered with a pang of annoyance the cupcakes he'd sent.

'I got your present.'

Austin couldn't remember at first, he'd been so sleepy and fuddled when he'd ordered them. Then he did.

'Oh, the cakes! Ha, yes, I thought you'd like those. So you see, they do cupcakes over here too.'

'Well of course they do,' said Issy. 'They invented them. Until the Americans, they were just known as fairy cakes.'

'Oh,' said Austin. 'I thought you'd think it was funny.'

'They weren't very good.' Issy hated sounding sulky. She had to stop this.

'Want to come out and make them better?' said Austin.

There was another pause.

'Austin,' said Issy. 'I miss you so much.'

'I miss you too,' said Austin. 'I really do. I only got the cakes because I was thinking of you. Was it a stupid thing to send?'

'No,' said Issy.

'Yes,' said Austin.

'Yes,' agreed Issy.

'Oh, bugger,' said Austin. 'It's hard, this long-distance stuff, isn't it?'

Issy felt an icy grip of fear in her stomach. What did that mean? Did it mean they were going to have to get used to it? Did he mean it was so hard, maybe they shouldn't bother carrying on? Did he mean they were just going to have a lot of trouble from now on?

'Hmm,' she said.

'I wish you could come out,' said Austin. 'Why don't you just come out? You'll LOVE it.'

'Well,' said Issy, 'I'll just kill Darny and leave his body in the garden for the foxes, set fire to the shop, then I'll be right there.'

Austin smiled. 'Look,' he said, 'I think I'm going to have to be here for a while longer. Whilst everything gets sorted out, you know. Contracts and stuff. And I have to meet a few people.'

'You are coming back?' said Issy, suddenly panicked. 'You're not asking me to parcel up your stuff and send it on, are you? Put Darny on a plane with a little ticket around his neck like Paddington Bear?'

'Of course,' said Austin. 'Of course I'm coming back.'

'But you don't know how long for,' said Issy. 'Or when.'

Austin didn't answer. He couldn't.

Chapter Seven

Mince Pies

If you don't make your own mincemeat, you might as well just buy mince pies from a shop. Using pre-packed mincemeat, you're basically just putting stuff in an envelope. It isn't difficult to make, and it is less expensive, and if you get some of those nice-looking fancy jars, you can give it away as Christmas presents, although make sure you give it to people who like stewed fruit and know what to do with it, otherwise they tend to look at you as if you've just given them a jar of fresh rabbit droppings, which is rarely a welcome gift unless you have a friend with a very very tiny garden to compost.

The nice thing about mince pies is that they can officially be made to taste utterly delicious by the official worst baker in the world. They are as hard to mess up as peppermint creams. This is not one of those recipes where if you don't use precisely the exact measure of butter you might as well throw the entire thing in the bin. These are going to turn out absolutely perfect and fine. Trust me. Also, make them on a Sunday, as you can hang around and read the papers whilst the kitchen starts to smell absolutely and utterly delicious. The only weird ingredient is suet. Yeah. It's weird. Don't enquire as to what it actually is too closely.

Mincemeat

200g small cubes of apple

200g raisins

200g sultanas

1 tbsp nutmeg

1 tbsp mixed spice

Juice and zest of one lemon

Juice and zest of one orange

250g suet, cut into small pieces

The night before you need the mincemeat, put all the ingredients in a big bowl and mix well. Leave overnight covered in a clean dishcloth. In the morning add brandy (I'll leave it to your discretion how much) and then stick in the oven at 120°C/gas mark ½ for three hours.

Let the mincemeat cool and then pop into sterilised jars (to sterilise, dampen jar for one minute in the microwave). Cover with brown paper, then seal. It should keep for up to a year. If it keeps for up to a year, you're probably giving it to the wrong friends.

For the pastry, rub 200g flour and 200g cold, chopped-up butter together. Add 100g of golden sugar, a pinch of salt and a little water until it is ready to roll out and cut. Pop in baking tins, spoon in mincemeat and put pastry lids on pies. Brush top with beaten egg and sprinkle a little more golden sugar, then 20 minutes at 180°C/gas mark 4, and . . . ta-dah!

Caroline stomped into the shop the next morning in high dudgeon. Issy looked at her with bleary eyes. She'd hardly slept a wink after speaking to Austin the night before and was on her third coffee. She felt so daft, but it was the unfairness of the whole thing that was getting to her. She'd finally got her life together; she finally felt like she was doing what she had always longed to do and had met a man she loved, and now it was all going horribly wrong.

On a deeper level too, she knew why she was so upset; why she was so bad at talking about all this to Austin. It being this time of year didn't help . . . and now . . . No, she was catastrophising. Taking the worst possible view of the situation. Surely London would give him another job and it would all be fine; he couldn't possibly want to uproot what they had, how could he? Then she remembered something she hadn't thought about for a long time: she was at church on Christmas morning, wearing a too-tight red dress, with Startrite shoes that gave her blisters at the back, holding hands with Gramps, who knew everyone, of course, and would have been liked by them even without a bag in his pocket full of gingerbread. A woman she recognised from the shop, posh and loud. She didn't like her, although she didn't know why. The woman was wearing a blue hat with a large peacock feather in it, and she leant forward to Gramps and said, 'She couldn't POSSIBLY want to leave at this time of year,' and Grampa Joe hushed her, crossly, more cross than she'd ever seen him.

'So Richard is turning out to be even more of an UTTER ARSEHOLE than usual,' declared Caroline, banging the door and whisking her tiny arse – in white jeans, in December – into the shop. She was wearing a huge furry stole thing that made her legs look even more sticklike, and that Issy fervently hoped was fake. Issy blinked herself out of her reverie and tried to wake up as Caroline shook off the cold. It was freezing outside; everything was iced over, and the clouds in the sky were heavy and dense with snow.

'What's he done now?' she said. Caroline's divorce seemed to be taking rather longer than the marriage had lasted.

'He said no hampers. No hampers. Can you believe it? He stopped our hamper account.'

Issy looked puzzled. 'What do you mean? Those boxes with tins in?'

'They are not just boxes with tins in!' said Caroline in shock. 'They are traditional luxury items sent at Christmas as a token of esteem, and are therefore part of my totally normal family expenditure.'

'But don't they cost a total fortune for like a can of jam and some fancy nuts?' wondered Issy. 'And they're probably full of stuff you don't even like, like olives stuffed with beetroot. I always wondered who sent those.'

Caroline sniffed. 'Everyone does,' she said.

'So are the children looking forward to Christmas?' Issy tried to change the subject.

Caroline sighed dramatically. 'Oh well, you know what they're like.'

'Delightful,' responded Issy, promptly.

'Hermia is just looking forward to the opportunity to eat for the entire holiday. I will have to keep an eye on that girl. Can you believe it, she prefers eating a sandwich to practising her flute. A sandwich! I don't even keep bread in the house!'

Issy made Caroline her small decaf espresso, black, and handed it over. Caroline downed it quickly.

'Hit me again,' she said. 'And can I have it caffed?'

Issy raised her eyebrows. 'That bad?'

Caroline shrugged. 'Well,' she said. 'Well ... ' She blinked heavily several times. 'It's just ... Richard said ... Richard said ... ' And she dissolved into tears.

'What is it?' said Issy, rushing round the other side of the counter.

'He said ... '

Issy suddenly felt terrified for her. He wouldn't fight for the children, would he? OK, Caroline left them with nannies and ignored them and denigrated them, but ... no, surely not.

'He said that if he's going to keep paying for them, he wants them sent to BOARDING SCHOOL ... '

Caroline collapsed into sobs. Issy put her arm round her.

'Oh no,' she said. 'But I thought you always said that boarding school was the answer to everything and would do all those rioters a lot of good?'

Caroline sniffed loudly and took out a cloth handkerchief. Issy was stunned that she carried a cloth handkerchief, but didn't say anything.

'Yes, but not for mmmyyyyyyy ... ' She couldn't finish the sentence.

It was odd, thought Issy. If you heard Caroline talk about them – although sometimes she seemed to forget she had children at all – you would think she wasn't really that interested; that having children was something she'd done simply because it was expected. She seemed to find them more of an annoyance than anything else.

'They would miss me,' said Caroline. 'I think they would miss their mother, wouldn't they? Achilles is only five.'

'They would,' said Issy, from bitter experience. 'Of course they would. It's ridiculous. He's being completely unreasonable.'

'I know!' said Caroline, bawling. 'What am I going to do?'

'Hang on,' said Issy, straightening up. 'I've got an idea.'

Caroline glanced up at her, her tear-stained face almost unrecognisable.

'What?'

'Why don't you just tell Richard to go screw himself? Say, sod off, Richard, they're not going to boarding school. You can send them to the local school! Louis goes there, it's great.'

Caroline paused for a second. Then she fell once more into massive gobbing sobs.

Pearl and Louis came in, tinging the bell.

'What's up with Princess Twinkle?' asked Pearl.

'Don't ask,' said Issy. 'I mean it. Really. Don't ask.'

'Don't be sad, Caroline,' said Louis, reaching up to stroke her fur wrap. 'I like your wolf.'

'Please don't touch, Louis,' Caroline managed between sobs. 'It was very expensive.'

Louis turned round to Issy. 'ISSY!' he yelled. 'I MOST FORGOT! IT'S SNOWING!'

Issy glanced up at the windows. Sure enough, in the early-morning gloom, the little lamppost next to the tree showed up the flakes that had silently begun to drift down into the little alleyway.

'Oh, so it is!' said Issy, almost forgetting her tiredness in her delight. 'Isn't that gorgeous!'

'Can you come out to play in it with me?' said Louis, grabbing her hand.

'I can't, my love,' said Issy. 'But I can make you a hot chocolate.'

Louis smiled. 'YAY!' He turned to Pearl.

'CHRISTMAS! It's snowing! It's snowing! It's Christmas! It's Christmas! YAY!'

Pearl half smiled. 'All right, all right,' she said. 'It's going to take us four hours to get home tonight, that's all I can say. Let's get that hot chocolate warmed up.'

As they bustled around, cleaning, scrubbing, baking and generally getting the shop ready for the first of their chilled, hungry customers, Louis stayed with his face pressed against the glass. It was barely light at all, with the blizzard and the clouds so close to the ground. People passing by on the main road had their scarves over their mouths and their hats pulled down over their eyes, and were leaning in to the wind at an angle, grimly set on their destinations. It was an extraordinarily cold storm out there.

'I might take some samples out to the bus stop,' said

Issy, bringing up a huge tray of sticky gingerbread. 'More of a mission of mercy than anything else.'

'MAMMA!' shouted Louis suddenly, his chubby little finger pressed up against the glass, his breath forming a cloud of condensation on the window. ' MAMMA!'

Pearl rushed over and followed his finger.

'Jesus Lord Almighty,' she said, and without stopping to grab her coat, ran out of the shop.

Issy and Caroline were right behind her.

'What on earth ...?'

When you opened the door, you realised how freezing and horrible it was outside; a true maelstrom, with flakes swirling every way, blinding you. The cold grabbed you with a metal grip; the wind bit at your throat.

Pearl's heavy figure was lumbering over to the other side of the alleyway. Issy was just behind her, and gasped when she realised what it was Louis had spotted.

Standing just behind the now bare tree was a small boy, younger than Louis. He was in his bare feet, wearing nothing but slightly grubby cream pyjamas with fire engines on them. His hair was blond and standing straight upright, and he was crying his eyes out.

Pearl scooped the little thing up in her arms like he was nothing, and they all rushed back inside. Louis was excited at his discovery.

'I found the boy, Issy,' he said importantly.

Issy was horrified. She had dashed out on to the main road, expecting to see a terrified mother running up and down searching frantically for her little boy, but there was just the usual queue of frozen-looking early commuters. She said hello to her friend Linda and asked if she'd seen anyone looking for a child. Everyone had looked confused, but shaken their heads. Issy told them that if anyone did come looking for him, he was safe with them, then dashed back to the shop.

Old Mrs Hanowitz, one of their regular customers, was at the door already. She gasped when she saw the little boy, in his cream-coloured pyjamas, cradled in Pearl's arms.

'The Christkind,' she said, shaking her head. 'Look at him.'

She came closer and put her fingers through his golden curls.

'A child at Christmas,' she whispered.

'Don't be daft,' said Pearl. 'This child is lost. What's your name, sweetheart?'

By the time Issy got back, the child was wrapped up warmly in a tartan blanket that normally sat on the back of one of the old leather sofas. The child, who looked to be barely eighteen months, seemed too shocked even to cry. He grabbed the label on the blanket and started to rub it gently between his thumb and forefinger, then stuck his other thumb in his mouth. He looked rather comfortable.

'He needs a cake,' said Louis. 'And an Advent chocolate. OH NO, THERE AREN'T ANY, AUNT ISSY.'

'Louis, hush about that stupid Advent calendar,' said Issy. 'It's not going to get chocolate in it.'

'It is a very sad Advent calendar,' observed Louis.

Pearl sat down on the sofa with the boy still wrapped up in the blanket. Issy tried to tempt him with a piece of gingerbread, but he wasn't terribly interested in it, preferring to stare around the room with wide eyes. His little feet were blue; he was wearing no socks or slippers.

'I'll call the police,' said Issy. 'Someone must be going frantic.' She glanced out of the window again into the blizzard. 'Where are they, though?' she said. 'Unless he's come from miles away.'

'What's your name?' Pearl asked again, but it elicited no response. Then Louis came forward.

'What is your name, baby boy?' he asked kindly. 'Can you talk, baby?'

The boy took his thumb out of his mouth.

'Dada,' he said.

'Well, that's a start,' said Pearl. 'What's your name, sweetie? We'll get you back to your daddy soon.'

'DADA,' said the little boy, louder.

'He's the Christkind,' said Mrs Hanowitz, who had followed them back into the shop even though they weren't officially open and was looking openly at the boy's untouched gingerbread.

'I really don't think he is the Christkind,' said Issy. She took the phone from its cradle. 'Do you think this is a 999 situation? It's not, is it? Or is it? What's the one for things that aren't quite as important as 999? 888?'

'One oh one' reeled off Pearl at once. 'What?' she said, seeing Issy's surprised face. 'Oh, well done for you. You live somewhere where you're unlikely to be a frequent victim of crime.'

Just as Issy started to dial, she saw someone tentatively enter the alleyway and look around. It was a young, confused-looking woman, not dressed warmly enough for the weather. Issy put down the phone and went to the door and stuck her head out.

'Excuse me,' she said. 'Are you looking for a child?'

The young girl turned, looking relatively unconcerned.

'Oh, do you have him?'

Issy looked at her for a moment. She couldn't just have heard that.

'Are. You. Looking. For. A. Child?' she repeated in case the girl couldn't hear her.

The girl sauntered over. 'Have you got him?' She was chewing gum and her eyes looked tired and a little blank.

'Um, yes,' said Issy. She wondered for a tiny second if she was being a bit of a nosy old busybody – was it perfectly normal for small children to go wandering about in their pyjamas in snowstorms? Was it none of

119

their business? Then she turned and saw the tiny thing sitting on Pearl's lap and realised it wasn't.

The girl walked into the shop.

'Oh, there you are,' she said resignedly. 'Come on then.'

The boy made no move to go. Pearl looked at the girl.

'What are you talking about?' she said. 'Did you let this little boy walk out in the snow on his own?'

'Durr, nooo,' said the girl. 'He wandered off. Come on, Donald.'

'Dada no,' said the boy.

'Well, that explains that,' said Pearl. 'Is your name Donald?'

'Dada,' confirmed the boy, then stuck his thumb back in his mouth.

Pearl looked at the girl again. She didn't look old enough to be his mother. Plus, one would imagine his mother would probably be a bit more pleased to see him. Especially a mother who bought fire engine pyjamas.

'Right, I take him,' said the girl, looking bored.

'Have you got socks for him? A coat?'

The girl shrugged. 'It not far.'

'Hang on,' said Caroline suddenly. 'Is this Donald? Donald Gough-Williams?'

The boy's eyes lit up at the mention of his name.

'Yeah,' said the girl unwillingly.

'You *know* this child?' said Pearl. 'Why didn't you say?'

'Oh, they all look the same to me,' said Caroline.

'This is Kate's baby. Are you the new Gough-Williams nanny?'

The girl shrugged reluctantly.

'There are the twins too,' said Caroline. 'Where are Seraphina and Jane?'

The girl turned on her with exhausted eyes.

'Yes,' she said. 'The twins.'

'Who's looking after the twins now?' said Issy suddenly.

'CBeebies,' said the girl. 'Come on, Donald, let's go.'

Pearl stood up and handed over Donald, complete with the blanket.

'Bring this back later,' she said. 'Don't let him catch his death.'

'Yes, I say OK,' said the girl. Slinging Donald over her shoulder like a sack of potatoes, she turned and left the Cupcake Café.

Caroline stared after them. 'I wonder what's up with Kate?' she said.

'She hasn't been in here for ages,' said Issy. 'I think it was just after the baby.'

'No, she's gone completely off radar,' said Caroline. 'I just assumed she was in rehab.'

Caroline, Pearl and Issy looked at one another.

'Would you mind terribly ...' said Mrs Hanowitz.

'Take it,' said Issy, without a glance. Mrs Hanowitz started to eat Donald's unwanted gingerbread. Issy knew it was difficult for the old lady to heat and eat on her state pension.

'Now, I don't have children . . .' started Issy.

'I'll have to have a word,' said Caroline, shaking her head. 'That nanny is just awful. There's obviously some very juicy gossip going on.'

'That girl looked about sixteen,' observed Pearl. 'What's she doing looking after three children? How old are the twins?'

'Six,' said Caroline. 'Little girls. One thinks she's a boy. Adorable, mostly.'

'They are,' said Issy, remembering. Kate was always trying to separate them, but they insisted on doing everything together. 'I wonder what's happened?'

Caroline had already taken out her phone.

'Ooh, I wonder if it will ring in the Priory. Hello? Hello, Kate darling . . . Where? Oh, Switzerland?'

Caroline's voice dropped noticeably, but she pulled it back.

'How GORGEOUS! Got lots of the fluffy stuff? Oh DELIGHTS, darling. Say hello to Tonks for me . . . and Roofs . . . Oh, are Bert and Glan there too? Oh really, all of you . . . Sounds very jolly . . . No no, you know me, working girl these days, no room for that kind of stuff, just busy busy busy . . . Oh yes, Richard's coming down, is he?'

Her voice turned to steel.

'Well, that's great news. You and Richard and all our

friends. I'm so glad to hear it. I do hope you all have a wonderful time. Oh, they're both ... No, no, of course I don't mind. Why would I? He's nothing to me. He'd just better not be spending the children's fucking school fees, that's all I can say ... '

There was a pause.

'Now, listen. We just had your Donald in the shop. He'd got out of the house. I think you need a new nanny ... Yes, again. Well, you know, they don't know how to work, these girls. I agree, totally lazy. New Labour. Issy was on the point of calling the police.'

Issy was now very relieved she hadn't got to the point of dialling.

'Yes, well, no, he was totally fine. Yes, he was still sucking his thumb ... seems like a bit of delayed development to me ... '

They exchanged a few more words before Caroline hung up. Her face sagged, and Issy caught the hurt and pain there. Then she pulled herself together.

'That lazy girl. I think Kate's going to change agencies. She said they've sent her six totally useless characters now.'

'Maybe she should have all six at the same time,' said Pearl.

'Do you know, that's not a bad idea,' mused Caroline.

Issy rolled her eyes. 'The longer I spend in Stoke Newington, the less I understand it,' she said. 'Is everyone really rich now?'

'Hmmph,' said Mrs Hanowitz, across the counter. 'Although I am pleased the Christkind brought me this good luck. That was truly bitte good.'

🧁

Carmen Espito clicked her heels up the passageway in front of Austin. None of this, he reflected, felt quite real. But here he was, on the forty-ninth floor – forty-ninth! It even had a special express lift – of the Palatine Building at Forty-fourth and Fifth, right in the very heart of Manhattan. The office was on a corner, and consisted mostly of huge glass windows, one of which faced north and included the Empire State and all the way to Central Park; while to the east he could see the Hudson river with the Brooklyn Bridge spanning across into the ware-houses and riverside cranes of Brooklyn.

All around the great tower snow whirled, soundlessly turning the whole of Manhattan into an enormous snow dome. It was heartstoppingly beautiful, one of the loveli-est things Austin had ever seen.

'Wow,' he said, standing so close to the floor-to-ceiling windows he felt as if he could step right out into the sky. 'My little brother would LOVE it in here. How does anyone get any work done?'

Carmen smiled. She was used to the bank staff being very sophisticated, and if they were impressed by any-thing, absolutely refusing to show it. Before she had lost sixty pounds, got her nose fixed and tattooed on her eyebrows, she had been just a normal girl from Oregon, and Manhattan had transfixed her too.

'It is nice, isn't it?' she said. Then her bright red lips closed again, and she sat down at the empty desk.

'Now,' she said. 'I'm a lawyer, specialising in immigration and employment rights. Mr Ferani wanted to get all of this red tape sorted out as soon as possible, and I'm sure you do too.'

Austin told himself this was just a bunch of paperwork; not at all irreversible, just some stuff to look at and think about later. Then he realised, looking at the obviously sexy but also obviously very serious Carmen Espito, that these were legal documents she had in front of her. This wasn't just a little American chit-chat. Obviously they liked things done and they liked them done quickly. And they doubtlessly expected him to jump at the chance.

As any sane person would, of course. The chance to grab a fabulous job, a whole new life, at his age, well. It was a dream come true. Anyone else, he was sure, would be biting her hand off.

'Can I ... ' he asked. 'Can I take the contracts and stuff back to take a look at, just before we're all done?'

Carmen raised an eyebrow.

'Of course, they're pretty much standard boilerplate,' she said. 'If you want to get your lawyer to call me ... '

Austin's lawyer had been a seventy-five-year-old grandmother who'd advised him to ignore social services when they wanted to come and poke about and ask Darny if he was getting his five a day, to which Austin would always answer yes, having come to the conclusion some time ago that he was just going to have to include potato.

'Uhm, yes, maybe I will,' he said hastily, trying to sound businesslike. 'Great. These are great.'

Carmen handed him several heavy sheaves of documents.

'Just bring them back with your passport.'

'My passport?' said Austin, feeling slightly panicky. It felt a bit like they were trying to hold him against his will.

Behind him the door opened with a boom, and Merv Ferani marched in. Today his bow tie was covered in small leaping reindeer, and his waistcoat was red. He looked like a small Jewish Santa Claus.

'How are we going here, Carmen?' he said. 'Finishing up?'

'Mr Tyler wants to get his lawyer to look it over,' she said, swiftly. Merv's face registered surprise.

'There's something you're not happy with?' he said.

'Oh, no, I'm sure ... It's just, you know, I'd ... I mean. I kind of do have to talk it over with my little brother.'

'He's your business analyst, is he?'

'No ... no, he lives with me. And my girlfriend,' he added hastily. 'I just ... I mean, it's a huge uprooting ...'

'To the greatest place on earth!' said Merv. He was genuinely confused – and he had a right to be, Austin conceded, given that Austin had agreed to come to New York in the first place.

'Well, yes,' said Austin. 'I realise that.'

Merv looked out of the ceiling-height windows.

'Hey,' he said. 'I've got a great idea. We'll fly 'em out for the weekend. What do you think about that, huh? Let them have a look, realise how great your life here is going to be. Take the kid to some museums and shit, catch a show, eat some real food. I'll get my PA to sort it out.'

Austin looked at him, stupefied. Then he remembered he was meant to be this super-cool hip banker from the UK who was completely blasé about this kind of thing happening all the time. He didn't think he could pull that off.

'Well . . . ' he said.

'That's my boy,' said Merv. 'I'll pass you on to Stephanie, you'll love her.'

Why did everything have to move so fast? thought Austin, feeling his throat tighten nervously. But then, Issy was going to love it. She *was* going to love it, wasn't she?

Chapter Eight

Peacekeeper Christmas Spice Cookies

225g butter, softened

200g sugar

235ml treacle

1 egg

2 tbsp sour cream

750g all-purpose flour

2 tbsp baking powder

5g baking soda

1 tsp ground cinnamon

1 tsp ground ginger

pinch salt

14g chopped walnuts

145g golden raisins

145g chopped dates

In a large mixing bowl, cream the butter and sugar together. Add the treacle, egg and sour cream; mix well. Combine the flour, baking powder, baking soda, cinnamon, ginger and salt; gradually add to creamed mixture. Stir in walnuts, raisins and dates. Chill for 2 hours or until easy to handle.

On a floured surface, roll out dough finely. Cut with a 21½ inch round cookie cutter. Place on greased baking sheets. Bake at 160°C/gas mark 3 for 12–15 minutes. Cool completely. Allow to be inhaled by hungry cross people.

Issy was at Darny's school, and, currently, feeling a complete and utter fraud. Actually, it was awful. She was surrounded by people who all knew each other and were chatting furiously amidst peals of laughter, under fluorescent lighting, the smell of cheap mulled wine failing completely to cover up the undercurrent that was still after all these years so familiar to Issy: sweat, horrific aftershave rendered by the bucketload, trainers, illicit cigarettes and a harder-to-place hormonal fug that made everyone a little louder and more excitable.

She shouldn't even be here; she had just been so horrified when Austin had remarked casually that he didn't normally go to Darny's end-of-term concerts any more because Darny hated him being there so much and played up and they both got embarrassed.

'I thought watching kids in nativity plays was the good bit about having them,' she'd said, outraged.

'After the year with the politically motivated capitalist innkeeper being portrayed as the leader of UKIP, and the dope-smoking shepherd? No. We all kept out of it after that,' Austin had said wearily. 'Anyway, now he's at secondary school they don't do a nativity any more, they do some contemporary stuff.'

'Shit,' said Darny helpfully. 'He means contemporary shit.'

'And have you got a part?'

Darny had shrugged his shoulders, which Issy took to mean yes, I do, and Issy had insisted they were going and both the boys had slumped in a way that made them look less like brothers and more like identical twins.

'You have to encourage young people,' said Issy, who felt strongly about this after a year of watching increasingly dejected teenagers turn up looking for work with barely literate CVs. None of these kids had a job or any experience and she wished she could do more for them; but the CVs were all full of grandiose claims about empowerment and being an envelope-pushing people person and horrible sub-*Apprentice* claims that, when she looked at the slouching, embarrassed adolescent in front of her, didn't seem to be helping anyone. Austin called her Jamie Oliver, but he agreed. Just not when it came to Darny.

'It'll make things worse,' he said. 'Darny doesn't need an excuse to open his mouth.'

'No, he needs to know when it's appropriate,' said Issy. 'That's why we need to be there for him.'

But then, of course, Austin had got called away to the land of women with pin-thin legs and spiky heels and amazing luxury and being cosseted all day long, and it was she who had to pull on as many layers of clothing as she could manage after a long day at the café and try to catch out Darny as he insisted that they'd been instructed to be all in black as Miss Fleur had convinced them that that would make it more dramatically powerful. Issy had sighed and finally agreed.

It had been bracingly cold outside, and they'd passed other families rushing towards the main school building on Carnforth Road. Words of merry excitement filled the air, and Issy couldn't help but feel a momentary pang; everyone was excited about being with their families at Christmas time, and she hadn't even heard from her bloody mother, while Austin was miles away and Darny was already, before they'd even got to the school gates, disappearing into a vast sea of adolescents, most of whom were impossible to tell apart. Issy supposed it was a true sign of growing older when you couldn't really tell what young people looked like; individually they just looked young.

Oh, she missed her Gramps so much. He was good at young people. He liked them, encouraged them. He'd hired lots of apprentices in the bakery, some of them from awful backgrounds, and the vast majority had thrived and done well and gone on to other jobs and lives elsewhere, and for so long they'd received hundreds of Christmas cards every year from happy customers and family friends and ... Issy didn't even open email Christmas cards. She just couldn't see the point these days.

Of course everyone else knew where to go, so she played with her phone to make it look like she was very busy and engaged, and followed the general stream towards the gym auditorium. Someone had obviously tried to make it look festive – there were paper streamers hanging from the ceilings – but it couldn't disguise the fact that this was an inner-city school trying its best, not a posh luxury private school with theatrical societies and fully equipped sound-mixing desks.

Issy paid a pound for a plastic cup of scorching, slightly bitter mulled wine to give herself something to do, and reminded herself to stay out of the line of sight of any of Darny's teachers; that was strictly Austin's department. One of the reasons, she figured, that she and Darny stayed on reasonably friendly terms was that she hadn't once interfered in his schooling or how he was getting on, even when her fingers itched to do so, and she knew it was the right thing. He had frequent letters home and detentions, and Austin would sigh and beg him to behave, and Darny would put forward very rational arguments as to why he shouldn't have to, and it would go back and forth until everyone was exhausted and frayed and Issy would retire to the kitchen and whip up some Peacekeeper cookies and hope that one or other of them would grow out of it.

She didn't know a soul at the school. She texted Austin quickly. He was just leaving another meeting and texted back, 'I told you not to go', which was of course not helpful and made Issy wonder what the emoticon was for mild frustration. She sipped her mulled wine – the second sip was slightly better than the first, on balance – and wondered who to text next. This was danger hour for Helena, who would be trying to settle Chadani into bed, a process that could take several hours. Then her other friends ... but it had been so long, and they all (she tried not to count, but they mostly did) had children now, and had moved away, or were travelling all the time, or didn't really know what to talk to her about once they'd got past cakes. She really needed someone to whom she could say, 'Isn't this just total hell?'

'OH MY LORD, isn't this just TOTAL hell?' came a strident voice. She glanced up. To her utter surprise, Caroline, in a bright red fitted dress that was almost totally inappropriate for a school concert, but which also still looked slightly amazing, was marching through the serried ranks of other parents, who parted to let her through.

'Darling, thank GOD there's someone I know here. Everyone else looks COMPLETELY feral.'

Issy winced and tried to make a 'she doesn't really mean it' face to the rest of the world.

'Sssh,' she said. 'What on earth are you doing here?'

'Oh GOD, well, if that bastard goes through with what he's threatening, I'm going to have to send Hermia to this hellhole one day and have her mugged for her watch and shoes before she's even made it through the metal detector.'

'Caroline, can you keep your voice down?'

Caroline looked mutinous. 'I was hoping they'd ban me, then the Bastard would have to keep them at their private school like any rational human being. I don't understand how he can be so evil.'

'I think it's rather a good school,' said Issy. 'It's integrated, progressive—'

'I don't want progressive,' hissed Caroline. 'I want them hit on the hand with a ruler three times a day and doing cold runs in their underpants. Build a bit of bloody backbone, that's what this country needs.'

'But doesn't that turn out bastards like your ex?' said Issy. The mulled wine must be stronger than she'd thought.

'Well, quite,' said Caroline. 'He shafted me before I had the chance to shaft him. If it wasn't happening to me, I'd probably be quite impressed.'

A slightly fusty-looking older man was standing on the

platform, speaking into a microphone that bent feedback in and out. 'Can everyone sit down, please?' he was saying, his tone of voice indicating that he fully expected to repeat that exact sentence several times before anyone actually listened to him. The sole spotlight reflected off his bald head as he bent over to look at his notes.

'Christ,' said Caroline. 'Is there anywhere we can get a drink round here?'

'I think he's asking us to sit down,' said Issy.

'Well, I can see what you were like at school,' said Caroline.

'Yeah, likewise,' said Issy, steering her gently up the aisle and passing over her mulled wine. Caroline tasted it and made a face. Everyone had started shuffling in and Issy couldn't see a seat anywhere. All eyes were on Caroline in her bright tight dress. Issy was burning up.

Finally they landed right at the front.

'Oh God,' said Caroline loudly. 'I think I've seen enough, actually.' She stared meaningfully at the teacher on stage.

'I will take you out,' said Issy warningly.

'What?' said Caroline. 'We're paying for this school, I think we deserve to see how it stacks up.'

'Actually it's a publicly funded school so everyone's paying for it,' said Issy. 'It can kind of do what it likes.'

Caroline snorted again. 'Ha, as if Richard pays tax. Right, if he says "Winterval", I'm out of here.'

'I think Winterval is an urban myth,' said Issy.

'Like Kwanzaa?'

'No, I think Kwanzaa is a real holiday.'

'Welcome, ladies and gentlemen, to the Carnforth Road School Christmas celebration – happy Christmas, Hanukkah, Winterval or Kwanzaa, whichever you would like.'

Issy cringed as Caroline gave her a pointed look.

'We have, this year, with the help of our wonderful drama mistress Miss Fleur, put together something of an alternative event for you ... *The Tale of the Spaceman*.'

There was a flourish of excited applause, as the overhead speakers came on and started with an enormous burst of synth chords. The curtain went up to reveal a perfectly black stage with nothing visible on it except, hanging from the top of it, a torch.

'Hang on,' said Issy. 'Is that "A Spaceman Came Travelling"?' She glanced at Caroline. 'OK, it is. You win. Let's go.'

'I LOVE this song,' said Caroline, suddenly looking fascinated.

In fact, despite the inevitable silliness – some very painfully sincerely delivered homilies on being an alien sent to earth to discover the terrible fate that it had been left to; a long piece on polar bears dancing that was obviously meant to be very moving but in fact left most of the audience in uncontrollable fits of mirth; a line of girls dressed as sexy penguins which was obviously meant to be funny but was in fact profoundly uncomfortable as row after row of fathers pretended they weren't secretly figuring out how old they were; and a truly horrible orchestral interlude that wasn't improved by being right next to the tuba player – on the whole there was a definite effort being made, which made Issy feel proud and Caroline fiddle with her telephone.

Then it was Darny's turn. One of the smallest in the lowest year in the school, he stepped forward boldly. Issy was used to thinking of him as a large presence in their lives, as denoted by his enormous smelly trainers and pots of cheap hair gel strewn across their only bathroom, but now he seemed tiny, a small boy amidst the hulking teens and young adults.

Issy, however, had finally relaxed. Something with a strong environmental message was surely well within Darny's remit for being on message. She quickly pulled out her phone and took an illegal photo for Austin. They were all supposed to buy the official, non-paedophile photo album afterwards, but she wasn't sure she could wait that long. And he would have been proud, despite himself, that Darny had such a large speaking role.

Darny walked confidently towards the podium with the microphone. Issy realised she was nervous for him. She couldn't bear speaking in public; even welcoming people into the café was hard enough some days. It didn't seem to bother Darny at all, though. Come on, she found herself thinking. A nice little speech about saving the planet for tomorrow and they'd be home free and ready for another glass of terrible mulled wine. Caroline might even take her for a real drink.

Darny lifted up his speech as he got to the podium.

'Written on recycled paper,' he quipped, which got an appreciative laugh from the audience. He paused, then began.

'I wrote a bunch of crap in this essay – which my teacher really liked by the way, so thanks, Miss Hamm – about how to save the rainforest and protect biodiversity for future generations . . .'

Issy felt herself sit bolt upright all of a sudden.

'Well, you know it's crap and I know it's crap. Everyone in China wants a fridge, and everyone in India wants an air-conditioning unit, and to deny people that kind of thing when they're working incredibly hard under conditions we can't even imagine is frankly totally smashed up. So why do we waste our time sorting out our sodding milk cartons and tea leaves? It's not going to make one tiny blind bit of difference to the polar bears, you know that already. I guess we're just filling in time here at school and talking about stuff like this for OFSTED, but really we all know it's crap.'

Issy let out a low groan and her chin sank on to her chest.

'So instead of fannying about with recycling water bottles – which is a joke anyway; if they were serious about this, you wouldn't even be able to buy water in bottles because it's arse – we might as well—'

Darny's great ideas for a solution to all the problems of the world were cut off suddenly in their prime by a howling wail of feedback as Miss Hamm launched herself up on stage and grabbed the microphone out of his hands with a look on her face that indicated she regretted the passing of corporal punishment in schools to the very depths of her being.

'DARNELL TYLER, REMOVE YOURSELF FROM THE STAGE THIS INSTANT.'

She turned to face the crowd. Darny still stood there, looking totally unbowed.

'Ladies and gentlemen, I must apologise for the unprompted showing-off of one of our younger pupils ... Is the guardian of Darnell Tyler in tonight?'

With hindsight, there couldn't have been a better time for Austin to reply to the photo Issy had sent him with the words 'Want to leave the country?'

'Oh God, it was awful,' said Issy the next day. 'Awful awful awful. I was so embarrassed.'

'I don't see why,' Caroline was saying. They were making eggnog coffee in the shop. Issy had expected this to be disgusting – it certainly sounded disgusting – but had inadvertently become completely addicted to it and was mainlining it that morning. The night before had been tricky; she was in no position to tell Darny off, but neither could she let him think that he was the hero of the hour, as his classmates apparently had (it was unlikely they had listened to what he was saying, but they had adored the bravura and the disruption).

But every time she brought it up on the way home (it didn't help that Caroline had sighed and said, yes, she might have expected this kind of thing in a sink school, which as she'd just sat through over an hour of carefully put-together entertainment made Issy want to kick her), Darny had just shrugged and said well if she'd only let him explain, and she'd had to say that wasn't the point, and Darny had said well that was hardly an argument was it, she must know he was right and everything was cyclical.

Issy tried to ignore Caroline's nihilistic take on the whole thing, but she was surprised when Pearl weighed in on Darny's side.

'I'm not taking his side,' Pearl explained patiently. 'I'm just saying, it was quite a brave thing to do.'

Issy tutted. 'Don't be daft. My mum was always trying to get me to do stuff like this. Talk about CND or refuse to wear a skirt or something. She wanted me to be some kind of school mouthpiece.'

'So what's wrong with Darny doing it?'

'I never did it!' said Issy, horrified. 'Cause everyone a bunch of trouble for nothing!'

Pearl and Caroline exchanged a rare smile.

'What were you like at school, then?' said Issy, stung.

'Mine was a great school and I loved it,' said Caroline, with a blank expression on her face. 'I made friends for life and I loved boarding.'

Now it was time for Issy and Pearl to glance at each other.

'What did you learn there, Caroline?'

Caroline ticked it off on her fingers. 'How to eat tissue paper if you get really really hungry. How to pretend to be ordering chips in a restaurant then change your mind at the last minute. How to never ever tell a girl you like her boyfriend or she'll call you a slut in front of the entire year. How to withstand prolonged and intense psychological warfare. And Latin.'

'Happiest days of your life?' said Issy.

Caroline shivered. 'Please. Please let that not be true.'

'What about you, Pearl?' said Issy in a gently mocking tone.

'I didn't see the point of school,' said Pearl. 'And my mum never made me go, not really. I liked sitting up at the back of the class and teasing the teachers and hanging out with my homegirls and just having a laugh really. We didn't care. We'd have eaten you two for breakfast.'

Issy agreed fervently with this.

'Yours sounds the most fun,' she said.

Pearl shook her head. 'I can't believe I wasted what I had,' she said, with only a trace of bitterness in her voice. 'They offered me a decent education and I chewed gum and smoked on buses. I envy Darny so much – he wants to learn, he wants to communicate and tell people stuff and engage. I couldn't be bothered doing anything like that.'

She shook her head. 'I tell you what, Issy, I hope Louis turns out like him.'

Issy sighed. And she hadn't even told them about Austin's job yet. She watched Louis patting the Advent calendar. 'I wish your chocolate comes back one day,' he was whispering to it. You were never supposed to want to swap worries with anyone, but for once she felt she could make an exception.

Chapter Nine

In fact, although she'd tried to make light of it, Issy had been close to tears by the time they'd got home the previous evening. She knew it was ridiculous – Darny's outburst had nothing to do with her, and he was completely unfazed anyway – but it hurt that he didn't even mind that she was upset with him. Everything she had ever told herself about not interfering in Darny's life, not caring about him … well, she did care about him. Of course she did. So it was galling to see that he didn't feel the same way about her – why would he, some girlfriend of his stupid big brother?

Deep down, too, she knew that if she had pulled a stunt like that, no matter what the nuns at St Clement's would have said, her mother would have been delighted. Thrilled with her, so proud. Her mother wasn't often very proud of her. It occurred to her she ought to get Marian and Darny together.

'So you mean it?' Austin had said excitedly when she picked up the phone, exhausted.

'What?' she said, dispiritedly. She'd thought he was only sending her the message 'Want to leave the country?' as a joke, and had texted back, 'YES PLEASE.'

'Look, Darny did something . . .'

'Did he bite anyone?'

'No.'

'Oh lord,' said Austin, thinking back to what Mrs Baedeker had said. She couldn't mean it, could she? She wouldn't seriously exclude Darny. No. He convinced himself she wouldn't. Darny hadn't hit anyone or stolen anything. It was freedom of speech. There'd be a row, but in that case it was an even better idea to get him out of the way for a few days. Yes. That would do it. And he'd make him apologise and everything would be fine.

'Listen, I've got good news: the bank has invited you guys out for a few days!'

'What do you mean, "out"?'

'To New York!'

'Why does the bank want me to go to New York?'

'To see if you like it, of course. And Darny.'

'Well, after Darny's little stunt, he'll probably be excluded,' said Issy.

'What did he do now?'

'He deviated from the script in his school play. A bit. A lot.'

'Oh yes,' said Austin. 'Yeah, I knew how he felt about that.'

'And you didn't tell him to stop it?'

'I think he's got a point.'

'But how is that the right way to make it?'

'I am imagining you as the goodiest goody two-shoes at school,' said Austin.

'Just because I behaved myself!'

'Well, as long as Darny didn't bite anyone, I'm sure he'll be all right to come. Don't you think it's amazing? Haven't you always longed to see New York, Issy?'

This was a low blow. Of course she had. She paused.

'But ... I mean, is this it? Are you staying there for ever?'

'Of course not!' said Austin. 'I can leave whenever I like,' he added, skirting round the truth. 'I mean, it's really just a taster, then I can take it or leave it.'

'If they're flying us out, it doesn't sound like they particularly want you to leave it,' said Issy.

'Well, tough luck for them, then.'

Austin didn't have, Issy reflected, that same desire to please everyone that she had. She admired that. Normally.

'But won't you owe them something?'

'Nope,' said Austin. 'I'm in demand, baby!'

Issy smiled. 'Anyway. I can't, it's a crazy, busy time of year for us.'

'That's why you've employed two excellent staff members,' said Austin. 'To cover for you. Cut down on the cake styles to the ones Pearl can do, or leave mix or whatever it is you do ... It should be like leaving a dog in kennels, shouldn't it? Hey, you could take on a temp cook and—'

'A temporary cook three weeks before Christmas?' said Issy. 'Right.'

There was a silence.

'Well, I thought you would like it,' said Austin finally. 'It's only a few days.'

'I know, I know. It's just impossible,' said Issy. 'Come home.'

'I will. Soon,' said Austin, deflated. 'Can I speak to Darny?'

'Are you going to tell him off?'

'Um ... I'll do my best.'

Issy had sunk down on the bed, utterly deflated. Why was she doing this? Why was she lying? Of course she wanted to be in New York. Of course she wanted to get on a plane, leave everything behind her, fly to Austin, jump on his hotel bed ... of course she did.

But Austin, she had to be honest, wasn't the only thing she loved. She loved the Cupcake Café too. More than loved it; she had built it, nourished it, grown it. It supported her and her friends, and was the single best thing she had ever done in her life. And she knew Austin was pretending this didn't mean anything, that it was only a holiday, a bit of fun, that he could say no whenever he wanted to, but it didn't feel like that to her. It felt like soon, down the line, he was going to make her choose between the loves of her life. The thought was unbearable.

From the other room, she could hear Darny shouting. So Austin obviously had tried to give him a telling-off. She didn't know what he was going to do about Darny either. Moving him right now seemed to her a very bad idea. But she was only the girlfriend. What did she know?

'So you're going?' said Caroline and Pearl simultaneously when she told them about it.

'I can't,' said Issy. 'We're so busy, look at us, we're overrun. I need the cash this time of year.'

'A free trip to New York,' said Pearl. She shook her head. 'A free trip to New York. At Christmas. Can you even imagine how many people would dream of something like that?'

'Oh, I used to go with an empty suitcase,' said Caroline.

'Whatever for?' said Issy.

'To fill it up with stuff, of course! We'd just shop all weekend and then I'd take off all the tags to avoid paying tax at customs. Brilliant days.'

'Shopping and tax avoidance?' said Issy. 'Well, it does sound wonderful.'

'You're the one turning down the free trip to New York,' said Caroline. 'So I will decide not to listen to you.'

But she couldn't turn her head away for long.

'Where's he staying?' she said. 'Because 72 E45th is fine these days but the Royale is really going downhill and you won't believe what they've done to the Plaza . . . all those awful condominiums.'

'What's a condominium?' asked Issy.

Caroline sniffed. 'You know. A condo.'

'I don't know,' said Issy. 'It's just something Americans say, like bangs, that I've never really understood.'

'Well,' said Caroline, bustling off to tidy up, 'I don't have time to explain it to you now. In fact, why don't you go to the States and find out?'

'And cilantro,' Pearl called to her retreating back. 'What's cilantro, Caroline?'

Pearl and Issy shared a smile, but it didn't help Issy's problem. The bell tinged as Doti came in, without Maya today.

'Where's your glamorous assistant?' said Pearl, far too quickly, in Issy's opinion, for someone who was meant to be making a go of it with someone else and wasn't at all interested in the postman. Even Doti looked surprised.

'Oh, she's doing so well I've let her take some of

148

the run on her own,' he said, unleashing a block of cards wrapped up in a small red elastic band, and a large box.

'Hurrah,' said Issy. She had been completely surprised when people had started sending Christmas cards to the shop – it would never have occurred to her to do so. But they'd had one from Tom and Carly; Tobes and Trinida; from the students, Lauren and Joaquim, who had looked longingly at each other across the smallest, cheapest cappuccinos for months on end before finally plucking up the courage to talk to one another and were now madly in love, which was fantastic for them, but a bit of a loss of income; from Mrs Hanowitz, even though she didn't celebrate Christmas, who thought Louis might like a picture of a polar bear wearing a hat (he did); and even from Des, the estate agent who'd rented them the property in the first place. And as Issy had strung the cards up around the shop (Pearl grumbling about dust), more and more people had joined in, and now they had a lot. So Issy had thought about it and decided as a marketing cost (she said this to placate Pearl and Austin) to get some printed up. She'd enlisted her printer friend Zac, and Louis' artistic talents, and now they'd come back and they looked lovely.

Caroline had sniffed and said why didn't they go for minimalist, and Issy had pointed out that when you sold cakes with three inches of pink glitter icing sitting on the

LOUIXS

top, nobody was going to mistake you for a Scandinavian furniture shop, and didn't Caroline think Louis' drawing was nice, and Caroline had said you had to be careful not to over-praise children – it was bad for them and meant they'd never achieve – and Louis had overheard and asked Issy what ovah-pwaze meant, and Issy had come closer to sacking someone than she'd ever thought possible.

'Well, aren't they lovely?' said Doti.

Issy nodded, then sighed. 'Better add getting these out to my to-do list.'

Pearl rolled her eyes. 'She won't go to America to see her boyfriend on a free flight,' she said. 'Boo hoo hoo.'

'Why not?' said Doti kindly.

'Because there's too much to do and I don't want to leave the shop,' said Issy, expertly making up three hot chocolates and handing them over to some backpackers while spraying whipped cream on a nut latte for a fourth.

Pearl slipped four cranberry and fig cupcakes decorated with holly on to a plate whilst pouring two orange juices, wiping the surface, taking money, giving change and rearranging the front of the glass cabinet.

'Why can't you leave the shop?' persisted Doti.

'Because we're too busy,' said Issy. 'Which is nice, but it means I can't really go.'

Doti looked confused, as Maya clanged open the door behind him.

'Oh, I love this place,' she said, beaming her lovely smile.

Pearl gave her a surly look. 'Hello, Maya,' she said. 'I like your outfit.'

Maya looked down at the standard-issue postman anorak she was wearing, which looked at least four sizes too big for her.

'Really?' she said, then anxiously, 'You're joking, right?'

'She *is* joking,' said Doti sternly. 'Pearl is actually very nice, aren't you, Pearl?'

'Do you want coffee?' said Pearl.

'I've finished my round!' said Maya. 'We're a good team.'

Doti looked at Issy. 'What's that, Maya? You've finished for the day? Wouldn't it be lovely to have an extra job at Christmas time?'

Maya glanced at Doti and then at Issy.

'You're not hiring, are you?' she said, a flare of excitement in her eyes.

Issy shot Doti a cross look.

'No, no.'

'It's quite hard,' said Pearl. 'You'd need training.'

'Ha,' said Caroline from down in the kitchen.

'I don't understand,' said Doti slowly. 'If Maya could work for a few days so you could go and see your beloved, wouldn't that be a good idea?'

'It's not that simple,' said Issy. She was very reluctant to say that she would worry about not being in charge.

'Can't Pearl be in charge?'

'Well . . . ' said Issy.

'Don't you think I could do it?' said Pearl.

'Of course you could,' said Issy. 'Of course. I mean, yes, we could narrow our menu . . . I'll leave my book.'

'I'd be completely fine,' said Pearl. 'And also, when I cash up, mine comes out even.'

'Don't rub it in,' said Issy.

'I . . . ' Maya's face looked excited, then fell a little. She looked extremely young. 'Sorry,' she said. 'It's just . . . I've been job-hunting for six months. The idea of getting two . . . well. It would be amazing.'

'It would only be for a few days,' warned Issy.

'It would be such a help,' said Maya.

'She's a fast learner,' said Doti.

'Issy, did you break the new bowl?' shouted up Caroline from the cellar.

Issy's phone buzzed with a text. It was from Austin and said simply, '17.35 Heathrow Terminal 5. YES!!!!!'

This should, she knew, fill her with joy and excitement. Instead, irrationally, it made her a bit cross. It seemed presumptuous and bossy, as if she was being railroaded into a decision that wasn't hers at all.

She noticed on her smartphone (a birthday present from Austin that Darny kept trying to show her how to use and she kept forgetting) that she also had an email. Most of her emails came direct to cafe@thecupcakecafe.com, so this was unusual. Trying to keep her cool as Pearl started firing questions at Maya as to whether she knew how to work a till and do more than one thing at once and Maya revealed that she had grown up working in her local Chinese at weekends which made her pretty undoubtedly qualified if the busy craziness of most Chinese takeaways Issy had ever been in had anything to do with it, she clicked it.

Darling Isabel, it began.

Only two people in her life had ever called her Isabel. Her beloved Grampa Joe, and . . .

Well, here I am! Just to tell you I
won't be celebrating Christmas this
year as I have met my soulmate. I now
live with a collective of Orthodox
Jews so we'll be passing it just as
any other normal day. However
Hanukkah is upon us as I'm sure you
know . . .

Issy internally rolled her eyes. She did know it was Hanukkah actually: Louis had shown her the menorah he'd made at school, and everyone had finally understood after a week of trying to work out what he meant by 'men over' with Caroline talking pointedly about speech therapy to Pearl and Issy having to stand between them at all times.

so I will be lighting a candle for you
in the window here in Queens . . .

'Caroline?' said Issy in a strangled voice. 'Where's Queens?'

'Oh, no one ever goes to Queens, darling,' came the voice from downstairs. 'Does that new girl know how to make royal icing?'

'Yes,' said Maya. Pearl shot her a look. 'I learn fast,' qualified Maya quickly.

Issy held up her hand to quieten everyone.

'Caroline,' she said, more slowly. 'Is Queens near New York?'

Caroline climbed up the narrow steps with a supercilious look on her face. She loved being in the know.

'Actually, it's part of New York,' she said. 'There's five boroughs ... Manhattan, Brooklyn—'

'Yeah, OK, all right,' said Issy. 'So it's close by?'

'It's part of it. You go through Queens on the way to the airport.'

Everyone stopped what they were doing to look at Issy, who threw up her hands.

'OK!' she said. 'OK, I give up. The universe is conspiring against me. Maya, get down there and learn to make royal icing. I'm ... I guess I'm going to New York!'

'Yay!' cheered some of the customers.

Doti smiled. 'This is all going to work out great.'

'Thank you! Thank you!' said Maya.

Pearl didn't say anything as she handed over a box of a dozen red velvet and mint icing cakes for an office party.

'Don't smoosh them in the photocopier when you're taking pictures of each other's bums,' she warned the giggly girls with reindeer antlers waiting to pick them up.

'No fear,' said one. 'We're going to hand-feed them to the best-looking men in the office.'

'Well, there's no way that can possibly backfire,' said Pearl as they disappeared, giggling their heads off.

Issy's mind meanwhile was in a whirl; half-excited,

half-terrified, and trying to work out the practicalities. Pack ... tell Darny's teachers ... get organized ...

'I'll pick up Darny en route, he's at his friend's,' she mused. 'He'll be delighted ... No,' she corrected herself. 'He'll be the exact opposite to whatever emotion I expect him to have. Pearl, you're in charge.'

'It's a Christmas miracle!' said Caroline. 'This is wonderful.'

'Hmm,' said Issy, nervous and excited all at once.

'Hang on!' said Caroline and disappeared back down the stairs. 'I have something for you.'

Pearl looked up. Spontaneous acts of generosity weren't exactly Caroline's thing. Two seconds later she reappeared.

'It will be freezing in New York,' she said. 'Proper real American freezing, not a bit blowy and damp like it is here.'

She held out, at arm's length, her white fox-fur coat. It was cut very short, like a biker jacket, with great screeds of fur down the front and metal stud detail at the top, and a leather collar and cuffs, and was, beyond a shadow of doubt, the most hideous coat Issy had ever seen in her entire life.

'That's sooo kind of you,' said Issy in agony. 'But I couldn't possibly. How will you get home?'

Caroline shrugged. 'Can't I do something nice?'

'Yes, but you know, I don't really believe in fur ...'

'It's fake,' said Caroline. 'I know, it doesn't look it, it

looks like the real thing. And it was practically as expensive as the real thing. But as I said to the Bastard, can't you share a little kindness in the world? I mean, he can't, obviously, he's a total bastard. So that's me rebalancing our chakras. My therapist says it's good karma.'

'Your therapist believes in karma?' said Pearl wonderingly, but Issy was just standing there, floored by the generous gesture.

'Send me lots of pictures of you wearing it,' said Caroline. 'I love New York so much and never get to go there any more. You can take the coat instead. It'll be almost as good as going myself.' Her eyes had gone a little misty.

'Uhm. Thank you,' said Issy. 'Thank you. That's very kind.'

'Try it on!'

'Yes!' said Pearl. 'Try it on!'

Caroline's narrow shoulders and thin frame meant that at least the ludicrous cut of the jacket made it look like it was done on purpose. On Issy's soft white shoulders and large, gentle bosom, it didn't have a hope in hell. Her arms stuck out at the sides like Buzz Lightyear's wings.

'I don't think it fits,' said Issy.

'Nonsense,' said Caroline, pulling and fussing with the creaking leather till it came to an approximation round her middle. The fur tickled Issy's nose and she could feel the studs through the shoulders. 'It's perfect.'

Issy risked a look at Pearl. Her face was utterly blank

and she couldn't meet Issy's eyes, which told Issy all she needed to know. Even more when two seconds later she turned round to greet Louis coming in early from school.

'Issy!' he said, looking concerned. 'Is your coat sore, Issy?'

'Thank you, Louis,' said Issy. She glanced at her watch. 'Oh Lord, I'm going to have to go.'

She searched for the words that involved taking off the jacket without insulting anyone. They would not come. Pearl, still completely straight-faced, hung her handbag off her outstretched arm. Doti and Maya clapped and waved her a cheery goodbye, and she struggled her way out of the door, heart pounding, arms wide.

Just outside, in the chill of the courtyard, she turned back. Everyone except Caroline was, as she'd suspected, bent double with laughter at her new outfit. But that wasn't what she was looking at.

The little café was full to bursting with happy cheery people sharing their nut lattes and mince pies, showing each other their big bags of gifts, some with long rolls of red and green paper sticking out. Children were running around pointing at the Advent calendar, which Louis was guarding fiercely, doling out one window a day without fear or favour. The queue was almost out the door and steam was rising from the tea urn, and Issy felt, already, only a few metres away, a deep and abiding nostalgia for the place. She was on a journey now, heading somewhere else, far away, and she did not know if things would be the same when she returned.

Chapter Ten

Express Airlines Altitude Cookies

If you live up very high (or are flying) you have to bake differently, because things don't rise the same way or taste the same. In fact, hardly anything tastes of anything in the air, which is why you like to drink tomato juice even though at ground level it's a bit nasty. Here are some airline cookies you may want to bake in advance if you have to go on a plane. They make a lot, so you can hand them out on the plane and make a lot of new friends.

Altitude Cookies
125g salted butter
125g white sugar
125g brown sugar
1 large egg

1 tsp vanilla essence

350g sifted flour

75g hot chocolate powder

1 tsp salt

1 tsp baking powder

350g chocolate chips (whichever colour you like)

pinch cinnamon

Cream butter and sugar together, then add egg
    and vanilla essence.

In a separate bowl combine the dry ingredients.
Fold in the wet mix, then mix the chocolate chips
in (yes, you can eat some; you don't have to pretend
they fell on the surfaces or anything). Chill the
whole mix in the fridge for at least an hour, then
preheat oven to 180 degrees.

Cut out with a glass to about ½ cm thickness
and place on baking tray covered in baking paper.
Bake for around 10 minutes, or until brown (9
minutes if you prefer a softer cookie).

Attempt to avoid eating them till you get on the
plane – warning, they are VERY rich for ground
level!

☕

Issy was dashing about the house in a panic. Helena had
agreed with frankly surprising alacrity to take her to the
airport, muttering something about getting out of the

house, but time was running short. Issy had no idea what to take – cocktail dress? Ballgown? Five hats? – and Darny was point-blank refusing to pack anything apart from his usual hoodie and fifteen DS games. He scoffed at every hat she held up as if it were for a five-year-old and couldn't seem to get his head around the fact that they were going to a different climate, which, since the only place he'd ever been to was Spain on a package trip, where it had rained every day, was possibly not that surprising but was infuriating Issy.

'Why are we even going?' he had grumbled. 'Doesn't Austin want to come back here? Why can't he come and see us?'

Issy had tried to come up with a good explanation. She wasn't doing very well.

'Hello!'

Kelly-Lee was delighted to see the rumpled-looking Englishman again. Now that he wasn't half asleep, she noticed how handsome he was, with a distracted look about him which implied his mind was on higher things. Austin was in fact wondering what exactly to say to Merv if Issy and Darny simply didn't arrive. He knew on one level that it was his fault for making everything so tricky; on another level, there was a bit of him, more childish, that said it was unfair that he didn't have anyone – truly anyone – around to say, wow, Austin, that's just so amazing!

162

Even his PA, Janet, who was normally his biggest cheer-leader, had got very sniffy about the whole thing and was making pointed remarks about how wonderful it was for people who got to go and work in America and how there wasn't much call these days for old washed-up PAs who got put out of work, and Austin had tried to laugh it off and explain that he wasn't going, and she sniffed loudly and he remembered how many more things Janet seemed to know than he did and felt guilty.

So no, nobody was happy for him, not really. He did like to think that his mother would have been pleased. But would she? She hated bankers; both his parents had been totally unreconstructed old socialists. She had absolutely adored him going off to study marine biology, had loved the concept of him travelling the world and diving. And if she hadn't only gone and been hit by a bloody nineteen-year-old driver – well, then he might have been doing just that. At least he was doing the travelling the world bit.

He had a few photos of his parents, but not many; developing pictures was expensive in those days, and they were mostly of him and Darny, which as far as Austin was concerned was pointless and completely unnecessary. Sometimes they were with his dad – tall and with the same mop of unruly red-brown hair as Austin – but there were very few of his mother. He guessed it was always her behind the camera. He tried to conjure up her image, but he still found it hard to believe how young she had been. It became worse the older he got. Sometimes he would imagine her in the kitchen cooking up something nice, but this was a complete fallacy; his mother hated to cook and would dole up sad-looking vegetable stews or lentil hotpots under sufferance. The fact that Issy actively enjoyed being in the kitchen was something he could never quite understand; his mother used to mutter a lot about Germaine Greer and slavery. He saw so much of her in Darny. He missed her such a lot.

'You look like you've lost a dollar and found a nickel,' said Kelly-Lee. Austin smiled weakly.

'Hello,' he said. 'Sorry, lost in thought.'

'Ooh, a thinker!'

'Well, I don't know about that,' said Austin, as she made him a cup of burnt-tasting coffee large enough to sail the QE2 in.

'So,' she said in a conspiratorial tone of voice. 'Did your girlfriend love the cupcakes?'

Austin frowned. 'Hmm,' he said. 'Not exactly.'

Better and better, thought Kelly-Lee.

'Oh no! That's too bad. Is she on a diet?'

'Issy? On a diet?' Austin grinned at the thought. 'Uhm, no.'

Kelly-Lee had been on a diet since she was thirteen years old, though she always claimed she wasn't and was just lucky she could eat what she liked.

'So what was the problem?'

'Well, she's a baker, so ... '

'They're all made to the highest of standards.'

Kelly-Lee picked up a coconut cookie wrapped in cellophane. 'Here, try this.'

'Actually,' said Austin, 'I'm not that crazy about sweet things.'

He didn't even care for sweets. This was perfect, thought Kelly-Lee. They might as well have broken up already. He was moving here, she wasn't here, she didn't like his present, he didn't like her cakes ... No court would convict her.

She quickly glanced at herself in the reflecting side of the cake cabinet. She looked pretty good, her wide mouth painted a nice delicate pink and her teeth very straight and sparkly white. She blinked whilst looking at the floor – an old trick, but a good one, she'd found – then glanced up at Austin through her lashes.

'Well, if you don't want anything sweet ... ' she said tentatively, pretending to be nervous, 'maybe a drink later?'

'Uhm.' Austin furrowed his brow in confusion. 'I don't ... '

'I just thought a friendly thing when I finish my shift ... nothing more. Sorry. I'm just ... I'm new in town too. I'm sorry, I just ... I mean, I just get lonely sometimes.'

'You?' said Austin, genuinely surprised. 'But you're so pretty! How can you be lonely?'

'Do you really think so?'

Austin was starting to feel this conversation was getting out of his control.

'Anyway, I have to go to the airport tonight. My girl-friend is ... well, at least I *think* my girlfriend is arriving.'

'Oh, great,' said Kelly-Lee. 'You must come on by, show her the place!'

'I will,' said Austin, relieved.

'But you don't know if she's coming for sure?'

Austin winced a bit. 'Well, it's hard for her to get away, you know; she runs a business and everything ... ' He checked his phone, instinctively, then put it away when it showed nothing.

Too busy to look after her man, thought Kelly-Lee without a qualm.

'Well,' she said. 'If she decides not to come, you come here and get me and I'll take you to this little Manhattan watering hole I know where they serve Jack Daniel's and play jazz. You'll like it.'

'I'm sure I will,' said Austin, gulping down as much coffee as he could handle – about an eighth of the gigan-tic cup – and heading for the door.

'Hang on,' said Kelly-Lee. She grabbed a notepad and pen and jotted down her number. 'Just in case,' she said, popping it in his top pocket.

There was a letter on the hall table that looked official. Even though Helena was honking furiously outside in the car and a pair of tights were trailing out of Issy's gigantic bag like they were attempting to escape, she stopped to pick it up. Darny was wearing shorts, mismatched socks, a hoodie and nothing else. Issy threw one of Austin's coats at him – very briefly she caught Austin's comforting smell of cologne and printer ink – and banged open the door with a clang. Helena was gesticulating wildly, Chadani Imelda howling her head off in the back seat. Behind them, a large white van was also honking, trying to get past on the narrow road that was lined both sides with parked cars.

'DARNY!' called Issy in frustration. Darny slouched out as slowly as he dared, pretending to read *The God Delusion* in one hand as he went.

Helena stopped honking when she saw what Issy was wearing.

'What . . .' Her mouth dropped open.

'Shut up. It's a favour to a friend,' said Issy. 'An acquaintance. Someone I don't like. Whatever.'

She tried to throw her bag in the boot of the car, but Chadani's gigantically oversized turbo buggy was already in there taking up all the room, so eventually, crosser and crosser, she laid it on the back seat and made Darny sit on it.

'We're going to miss this flight,' she grumbled.

'We won't,' said Helena, cheerily flicking a V at the irate van caught behind her. 'And if you do, you can catch the next one, and if you don't want to, you can come home and have some wine with me and I'll show you all of Chadani's new photographs and finger paintings.'

Issy sighed. 'Hello, Chadani,' she said to the back seat. To her horror, Chadani was wearing a white fake fur coat not unlike Issy's own, except Chadani's was huge and had big pompom buttons. She looked red-faced, hot and cross.

'WAORGH!' she cried, then opened her mouth and started screaming again, and Issy began to think that paying a fortune to take the Heathrow express might not have been so bad after all.

'Hello, baby,' said Darny in a conversational tone.

Immediately Chadani stopped hollering and looked at Darny with huge chocolate-brown eyes.

'Stop crying,' he said, fastening his seat belt beside her. 'It's annoying and I have to sit next to you.'

Chadani held out her little finger. Darny took it, and she coiled her hand around his second finger, then held it tight. Issy and Helena looked at each other.

'How do you *do* that?' said Issy.

Darny shrugged. 'Because I don't judge everyone the second I meet them like you do.'

'Well, one, I do not do that,' said Issy. 'And two, Chadani is a baby.'

'She's a person,' said Darny.

Helena pulled out.

'I can't believe,' whispered Issy to Helena when Darny had put his earphones in, 'that I get all the annoyingness of a child and none of the cute and cuddly bits.'

'Oh, you can keep your cute and cuddly bits,' said

Helena. 'Chadani Imelda pooed on her own head this morning.'

'Maybe you could send that to *Britain's Got Talent*,' said Issy.

Helena snorted. 'She has many, many talents,' she said, her voice softening. 'But delicate, feminine pooing is not one of them. Although the other day—'

'It's all right!' said Issy quickly. Helena's ability to talk freely and enthusiastically about poo might, she supposed, be considered absolutely cool and normal in her parenting group, but Issy still found it a bit alarming.

Helena swerved round the corner and shook her head.

'I can't understand why you aren't excited,' she said. 'I can't imagine waking up one day normally then suddenly getting whisked off for free to New York. I mean, I have to look after Chadani every day ... FOR EVER.'

'But you love doing that,' said Issy.

'You love eating cupcakes, but you don't eat them every day ... Hmm, bad example,' said Helena.

Issy sighed. 'Actually,' she said, 'I hoped you'd understand. Everyone else thinks I should be over the moon to be going away, and I feel like the most ungrateful, selfish person on earth.'

Helena grinned, before fiercely flicking a V at a lorry driver. Issy didn't think he'd done anything wrong; it was just habit.

'What's the matter, it's not a posh enough hotel?'

Issy grinned back. 'No, it's not that. It's just ... you know, the Cupcake Café is my baby.'

'Smells better than mine,' said Helena.

Issy looked at her curiously. It was very unlike Helena to talk in anything other than glowing terms about motherhood.

'What's up?' she said.

Helena let out a big sigh. 'Do you know how many hours junior doctors work?'

'Lots?' asked Issy.

'*All* of them!' said Helena. 'So it's just me and Chadani cooped up in that crappy little flat all day ...'

Issy bit her tongue.

'Then he comes home and he's knackered and has to study and we have to be quiet and all he wants to do is sleep and he thinks my life is very easy but all I get to do is change the baby and take her out for walks which is oh my God so boring, I just push a pram about all the time and no one will talk to me because apparently a pram makes you invisible and all the other mothers go on about their kids all the time and it's *so* boring and I miss my life.'

Helena stopped suddenly and took a deep breath as if she'd surprised herself by what she'd said.

'I love Ashok and I love Chadani Imelda,' she said fiercely. 'Don't get me wrong. I love them more than anything.'

Issy felt horribly guilty. She should have listened

more, been around more for Helena. She hadn't thought motherhood made you lonely – how could it when there was someone new in your life? – but maybe it did.

'Why didn't you say?' she said. 'You always seemed so happy.'

'I *am* happy!' said Helena in anguish. 'I've got everything I've ever wanted. My stupid brain is just taking a bit of time to realise it. And whenever I try and see you, you're so busy and professional and successful and doing nine things at once and it's taken me three hours to leave the house and wipe banana off the walls, so I just think what could I possibly have to talk to you about, when you're jetting off on the spur of the moment to New York like a model or something.'

'You can talk to me about anything!' said Issy. 'Except Chadani's poo, I don't like that.'

There was a pause, then Helena burst out laughing.

'I've missed you,' she said. 'I really have. I just didn't know how to talk to you any more.'

'Well I've missed you too, so much,' said Issy. 'I have plenty of people I work with, and I have Austin, when he's not on the other side of the world, but I really really need my friend.'

'Me too,' said Helena.

'So aren't you going back to work?' ventured Issy. 'You love your job so much.'

Helena sighed. 'Well, Ashok and I felt it was so important for Chadani Imelda's first years . . .'

Issy shot her a look.

'Am I going on about "what's best for baby" again?'

Issy nodded vigorously.

'Sorry. I got into the habit at my mothers' group. So much for the sisterhood. It's like *The Apprentice* in there, but with breast pumps.'

She reflected.

'I mean, obviously I'm winning, but it takes a lot of effort. There's masses of puréeing and stuff.'

'So?'

'Oh fuck, yes, as soon as I possibly can. I am totally bored off my fucking tits. Also I need gin.'

Issy nodded. 'We do. We need to go out and get some gin.'

'We should,' said Helena. 'But you're leaving the country.'

'Yes,' said Issy. 'I shall return with duty-free gin.'

'Well, I am envious,' said Helena. 'But I do understand. And I would say, enjoy it as much as you can. December in New York – amazing! Forget all the other stuff. You and Austin will sort it. You're both reasonable people. Love will find a way.'

'Hmm,' said Issy. 'I will just have to try and remember the difference between compromise and giving up everything for a chap. My mother would be horrified.'

Helena smiled. 'And she spent a year in a nudist colony.'

172

'Please don't remind me about that again. Please please please please.'

'The photo Christmas card was my favourite.'

'Stop it! Stop it!'

When they arrived at Heathrow, Helena got out and even ignored – for five seconds – Chadani's cross mewling noises to give Issy a huge hug, which Issy returned with gusto.

'Now don't start buying too many presents for Chadani,' she said sternly.

'Sssh!' said Helena. 'She still believes in Santa Claus.'

Darny slouched out of the car.

'Have you got a hug goodbye for your auntie Helena?'

Darny regarded her. 'I wouldn't feel comfortable embracing you at this point,' he said.

Helena shot Issy a look. 'Good luck,' she said.

'Thank you!' trilled Issy. 'Come on, Darny, shall we go see Austin?'

Darny shrugged his shoulders. 'I'd have been all right in the house by myself.'

'Of course you would,' said Issy. 'Right up to the catastrophic fire at five past four. Come on!'

Helena held Chadani Imelda's arm up to wave as they disappeared into the futuristic glossiness of Terminal Five, lit up like a spaceship in shades of purple and blue. Then she cuddled her little girl close to her in her smart red coat.

'I love you so much,' she said. 'But Mummy has stuff to do too.'

'MUMMY!' said Chadani cheerfully, and bit her affectionately on the ear.

There was a queue of hundreds of people at check-in. It made Issy tired just looking at it; she'd been up since 5.30. Lots of screaming children, obviously travelling for Christmas, and loads of complicated-looking baggage being checked in. The queue wound round and round the metal poles with strips to pull out and fasten to mark the line; several children were pulling them back, hurting their hands and causing disagreements in the queue. One harassed woman at the check-in desk had a grim set to her jaw that said she was getting through her day by sheer willpower alone, so not to try and cheek her.

Down in the main lobby of the terminal a brass band was playing 'Once in Royal David's City' so loudly Issy couldn't hear herself think. She felt a headache coming on. This was a stupid idea. They shouldn't have come. She had a very ominous-looking letter from Darny's form teacher in her pocket that she was taking to Austin that she recoiled from touching whenever her hand strayed in that direction and Darny was making the kind of loud sighs and eye rolls that generally precipitated an outburst against the world, and Issy felt ridiculously hot and stupid in her white coat; she knew her cheeks were red and her black curly hair had tangled itself in the humidity.

They heaved their stuff forward towards the front of the queue, where a man was checking boarding passes. Theirs had been lying on the hall floor when Issy had arrived home – she'd assumed Janet had dropped them in, but now she saw that they'd actually been couriered. She handed them over, feeling as she did so a mild panic that they were the wrong ones and the realisation in the pit of her stomach that she hated flying; it scared her stiff even though she'd never admit it in a million years.

The man studied the documents and glanced at her briefly. Issy felt herself go even redder. It would be entirely like Austin to get the date or the plane or the time wrong; once they'd been to Barcelona for a mini-break whilst Darny stayed with the dreaded aunties, and he'd booked the hotel for the wrong weekend. Typical. Issy chose to forget for the moment that instead they'd hired a scooter and gone off and explored the country-side, ending up in this completely amazing finca with a waterfall in the grounds and the most amazing paella, and had had the best trip ever.

The man finally looked up, smiled brightly at them and said, 'This isn't the queue for you.'

Issy thought she might burst into tears. They were going to have to turn round and head all the way back into town with all their stuff, and Darny would be a nightmare and she'd have to explain to everyone what she was doing back in London and Austin would probably extend his trip and she'd have to spend Christmas by herself because her mum was Jewish now and . . .

The man was pointing to the side. 'You go over there.'

She followed his hand. It was indicating a red carpet, leading off behind a purple-tinted wall with a sign overhead saying, 'Business and First-Class Passengers'.

Issy did an enormous double-take. She couldn't believe it. She looked at the tickets but still didn't really understand them, then smiled an enormous wobbly grin.

'Really?'

'Really,' said the man. 'Have a good flight.'

Suddenly, everything changed. It was, Issy told Helena later, like being whisked through the wardrobe to Narnia. There was an entire section for check-in just for them; no queues, no waiting to get through security. Even Darny was quietly impressed. They went up to the lounge, which had every magazine and newspaper and snack and drink imaginable, then, on the plane itself, they went upstairs, which was beyond exciting.

If Austin thinks this will change my mind about everything . . . thought Issy, sinking into the heavy pillows and pushing out the footrests as the plane banked over the twinkling lights of the city. For the first time ever (and with Darny in the window seat), she'd completely forgotten to be nervous on take-off, quickly texting Austin to say they were on their way (which he'd received with some relief). If Austin thinks …

But the weeks of late nights and constant early starts at the café, the worry and the work, coupled with the slow steady burr of the engines below, was too much for Issy, and she fell fast asleep, waking up six hours later to find, to her utter and total disgust, that they were commencing their descent.

'I missed dinner,' she said crossly.

'Yes,' said Darny. 'It was amazing. Delicious. You could have anything you wanted. Well, I wanted wine but they said no.'

'And I missed …' Issy flicked quickly through the inflight magazine. 'Oh no! They had *all* the good movies I wanted to watch! I haven't been to the cinema in a million years. I can't believe I missed them all!'

She looked around. Businessmen were removing their slippers and putting their shoes back on; pushing back TVs and footrests.

'Nooo!' howled Issy. 'The only time in my life I will ever ever ever get to go business class on an aeroplane and I've wasted it all.'

'Your face looks crumpled,' observed Darny.

'Nooo!' Issy jumped up. The airline mirror reflected the fact that she looked absolutely gruesome. She did her best with the make-up she'd managed to grab on the way out. Then she added a bit more. Then she put some lipstick on her cheeks to try and stop herself looking like the walking dead. Instead she looked like a clown. She told herself, sternly, that she had woken up to Austin every single day for over a year and he hadn't recoiled in horror yet, but deep down she realised how nervous she was. Not about him, but about what was going to happen. And maybe a little bit about him.

Austin was nervous too, standing in the airport arrivals. He was excited to see them, of course he was. It was just … he hoped … well, he just wanted everything to be good and happy and nice. But he also wanted – indeed, had pretty much promised – to come and live here now. To try things out. To travel, to experience life in the big city. He bit his lip. A brass band was playing 'Once in Royal David's City' in the terminal forecourt. It was dreadfully loud.

Issy and Darny came through passport control first. Darny looked excited and nervous; he burst into a huge grin when he saw his brother, then instantly tried to look cool and nonchalant, although his eyes were darting everywhere: at the security marshals with their guns and dogs; accents so familiar from the television but so strange at the same time; different signs and instructions coming over the tannoy.

Issy looked tired, and sweet, and had for some mad reason put red clown spots of make-up on her cheeks, but he decided to ignore that for now. And she was wearing … what was she wearing?

'What are you wearing?'

Issy looked up at him. Had he changed? She couldn't tell. He looked the same – his thick browny-red hair flopping over his eyes as usual; his horn-rimmed glasses; his tall, slim figure with the surprisingly broad shoulders.

But he also looked – kind of at home here. Like he fitted in. He had a briefcase and a long overcoat and a rather nice red scarf and a suit, and suddenly Issy saw him as one of the men on her flight; casually bored of being in business class instead of finding it a big adventure; working every free moment they had. She had never thought of Austin as one of those people. But maybe he was.

'Hey,' she said. Then she let herself be enfolded in his strong arms; drinking in his scent and the familiar warmth of him.

'Hello,' he said. He kissed her firmly on the mouth. 'You haven't answered my question.'

'I liked the plane tickets,' she said.

Suddenly Austin stopped looking like a smooth, rich businessman and looked like himself again.

'I know, coool, huh? Did you play the games? Did you visit the bar? Did you get a massage?'

'No,' said Issy crossly. 'I fell asleep and missed all of it.'

'No way! Did you not even try the barbecue? What about the swimming pool?'

Issy giggled. 'OK, now you can shut up.'

Austin caught Darny in his other arm. 'Don't think you're getting away without a hug, you.'

Darny grimaced. 'Yuck, that's disgusting. Brothers aren't meant to hug anyway.'

'You'd do well in communist Russia,' said Austin. 'C'mere.'

Darny continued to grimace, but did not, Issy noticed, pull away.

'Shall we get going?' she said, eventually.

'No,' said Austin. 'Not until you tell me what you're wearing.'

'Ahaha,' said Issy. 'It's for the cold.'

'But it comes up past your bum. Is that real fur?'

'No.'

'Have you joined . . . a band?'

'Shut up.'

'Are you retitling it the Cupcake Café and Pole Dancing Club?'

'I'm warning you . . .'

'Am I being insensitive? Are you actually being eaten by a polar bear? Do I need to call an ambulance?'

'I'll just take a taxi by myself.'

'No, no, we'll accompany you. Pingu.'

The taxi queue was surprisingly short, which was a relief, as the cold hit them with the force of a wall when they left the heated building.

'Only a taxi?' said Issy. 'I was expecting a limo.'

'They did offer me a town car,' confessed Austin. 'But I didn't know what that was, so I said no.'

He didn't mention that they had offered to send a car

to get Issy and Darny without him, so he could start picking up on things that were going on around the office, attending some meetings and getting up to speed. He didn't mention that at all.

Darny promptly fell asleep in the car, but Issy was glad. At first she was a little odd with Austin – she didn't know why, she just felt slightly sad, which was ridiculous, as it was hardly his fault that he hadn't been around; it wasn't like he'd taken off on the holiday of a lifetime. But she couldn't resist his childish enthusiasm as they came over the crest of a hill in Queens and Austin nudged her going, 'Now! Now! Look! Look!' and grabbed her and pulled her on to his lap as she saw for the first time in real life the lights of Manhattan.

It was so strange and so familiar all at once that it took her breath away.

'Oh,' was all she could say. As if choreographed, the cab driver let out a string of expletives, and a light snow started to fall, wreathing the huge buildings in a cloud of smoky whiteness; softening the lights so that the entire island of Manhattan appeared to glow. 'Oh,' she said again.

'I know,' said Austin, their heads together out the right-hand window.

'What's that old song?' said Issy. 'The buildings of New York ...'

'... look just like mountains in the snow,' finished

Austin. 'Oh, except I don't know that song. I don't listen to girl singers. Mostly I like heavy metal and rap and boy songs.'

'You don't know any rap.'

'All Saints are rap,' said Austin.

'Yes, all right,' said Issy, squeezing his hand with hers. It was breathtaking. Whatever was going to happen, this was still them together, coming into New York.

'Put up that goddam window,' barked a voice from the front of the cab. They complied immediately.

'Well, it's not exactly the Plaza ...' said Austin, leading them into the lovely little old-fashioned boutique hotel on the west side of Central Park. It had stable doors beneath, and gabled windows, like an English country cottage thrown into the middle of the iron and steel of the city. A log fire burned in the corner of the lobby and the receptionist welcomed them like old friends, calling in a waitress, who brought them three foaming cups of hot chocolate with marshmallows in whilst she processed their check-in. It wasn't grand like big hotels she had seen before, Issy thought, looking at the cashmere throws over the sofas, but it was the most gorgeous, homey luxurious thing she could imagine.

Austin led them up a small creaking staircase into their bedroom, then he added, 'But look what it has ... ta-dah!' And he threw open the connecting door to reveal an extra bedroom for Darny, complete with flat-screen TV and its own bathroom and games console.

'Wow,' said Darny, whom they'd had to haul bodily out of the cab, suddenly wide awake. 'WOW!'

'I reckon these old beams are nice and soundproof,' said Austin, winking at Issy.

'It's beautiful,' she said, awestruck at their own room, which also had a fire burning in the grate. The room was small, but the bed was huge and gigantically soft and pouffy-looking, made up with soft white linen; there was a huge flat-screen television, a fridge and a bottle of wine. Outside the window, the snow was piling up on the sill; yellow cabs cruised the quiet back street, but further behind she could hear honking traffic and feel a buzz in the air with the looming skyscrapers above. She popped her head into the bathroom and noted the great claw-footed bath, lined up with luxurious full-sized products and towels that would need their own postcode.

'Oh yes,' she said. 'Oh yes oh yes oh yes. I want one of these very much. And room service, seeing as I didn't manage to eat a single thing on the plane as I am a total idiot. But even if I missed that, there is no *way* I am not enjoying every second of this.'

Her clothes felt stale and hot, and she sniffed the bubble bath with a smile, then winked at Austin.

'I am *so* glad I came,' she said suddenly, filling up with happiness. She went to embrace Austin, who was, however, frowning at his watch.

'Ahh,' he said. 'Well. Um, we're due at dinner in about twenty minutes. Sorry.'

'Dinner?' said Issy, who despite her nap was still feeling tired and distinctly grotty after the flight, and whose body clock thought it was about one o'clock in the morning. 'Can't we just stay in and have a lovely time?'

'I would love that,' said Austin firmly. 'But I'm afraid having dinner with you and . . . ' He nearly said 'my boss' but checked himself just in time, ' . . . Merv is just part of the deal.' He grinned at her. 'Come on, we're going somewhere posh. It'll be fun.'

'I want to have fun here, in a bubble bath, with you, followed by my very first American cheeseburger, which I was hoping would be larger than my head,' said Issy a trifle sadly. 'Then falling asleep in about an hour.'

'I've booked the babysitter,' said Austin relentlessly.

'I don't need a babysitter,' came an adamant voice from next door. The rooms obviously weren't as sound-proof as they looked.

'She's just going to pop up every half-hour,' said Austin. 'Make sure you aren't playing eighteen-rated games or touching your private area.'

'Shut up.'

Issy jumped in and out of the strong American shower, but it wasn't quite the same as a long soak fol-lowed by a long lie in bed with Austin.

'Smart?' she asked, remembering that she'd packed in

about four seconds flat and couldn't actually remember what she'd brought.

'Oh yes, well, hmm, I don't know,' said Austin, who had enormous trouble noticing what women wore.

Issy suddenly remembered with horror that her best green dress that she'd bought for her birthday party was at the dry-cleaner's and she hadn't had time to pick it up. That was her only really lovely thing; everything else she wore was really to be comfortable to work and get around in, which meant lots of slightly faded floral dresses with elbow-length sleeves teamed with opaque tights and boots and a cardigan if it was cold; in other words, she dressed like the student she hadn't been for ten years.

She wasn't sure this was going to cut it.

She hauled through her suitcase – turning the perfect little hotel room into a midden in the process, she noted sadly – and came up with three near-identical grey floral dresses, two of which were far too light for the winter chill; two pairs of jeans (who needed two pairs of jeans on holiday? she wondered to herself); four formal shirts for Darny (what was she thinking?), and her old college ball gown, which was covered in netting and pinched under the arms and would be far too formal.

'Bugger,' she said. 'I think I will have to shop tomorrow.'

Austin, who never normally noticed time at all, was looking anxiously at his watch. 'Um, darling ... ' he was saying.

'OK, OK.'

With horror, Issy realised that the only thing she had that was mildly suitable was the black jumper and trousers she had travelled in – travelled in, and slept in for six hours. At least black could look a bit dressy, and she could stick a necklace on, and her boots could go under the trousers . . .

She sighed. Then, tentatively, pulled on her slightly stale clothes.

'I feel like Haggis McBaggis,' she said gloomily, gazing at herself in the tastefully soft-lit mirror. Austin glanced at her and just saw that the steam from the shower had made her cheeks go warm and pink, which he liked, and she was biting her lip like a nervous child, which was also cute.

'You look great,' he said. 'Let's go.'

Chapter Eleven

Bananas Foster

1 banana, peeled and cut in half

2 eggs, beaten

1 cup breadcrumbs

1 cup vegetable oil for frying

For the sauce

¼ cup butter

1 cup brown sugar

½ tsp cinnamon

¼ cup banana liqueur

¼ cup dark rum

2 scoops vanilla ice cream

Heat the oil in a thick-bottomed pot. Roll the bananas in the egg then the crumbs to coat and set aside.

When the oil begins to smoke, gently place the banana halves in pot and cook until golden brown. Less than 1 minute.

Combine the butter, sugar and cinnamon in a flambé pan or skillet. Place the pan over low heat on top of the stove, and cook, stirring, until the sugar dissolves. Stir in the banana liqueur. Remove from heat and add rum. Then continue to cook the sauce over high heat until the rum burns off – the sauce will foam.

Slice cooked banana into quarters and place in dish. Scoop vanilla ice cream on top. Generously spoon warm sauce over the top of the bananas and ice cream and serve immediately.

Pearl got home late and was bone tired. Louis had uncharacteristically whined the whole way. It had taken a lot longer to cash up and clear up without Issy there, and that was before they batched up for the next day. Because Pearl did so much of the cleaning, she often felt she worked very hard. Which she did, but as she filed the payroll reports, she realised she didn't quite appreciate how much Issy did to keep everything ticking over. No wonder she couldn't think about going to New York without falling into a panic. There were a million different things to remember.

Too tired to think about supper, she'd given in to

Louis' proddings and as a special treat picked up some fried chicken on the way home. She knew she shouldn't; she knew eating it would only make her feel more tired in the long run. But right at that moment, resistance was low and the weather was freezing and wet and windy, and she wanted nothing more than to sit down in front of *In the Night Garden* and cuddle her (slightly greasy) son.

The doorbell rang. Pearl and her mother looked at each other and frowned. They didn't have many visitors. There wasn't the room, for starters. And Pearl usually met her friends after church, not at seven o'clock at night in the middle of a storm, unannounced.

She got up from the futon, her knees creaking as she did so. She cursed inwardly to herself; she was young, still. She shouldn't be creaking and huffing like an old lady. She shouldn't have eaten all that chicken.

Standing in the shadow of the alleyway, in the space that was meant to be lit by security lighting but that the council never got round to fixing, with his finger to his lips, possibly a little tipsy, was her ex, and Louis' father, Benjamin.

'Sssh,' he said.

In the cab, Issy suddenly sagged. The cold had cut through her like a knife as she'd stepped out of the cosy lobby of the hotel; her watch said 2 a.m. British time; and she envied Darny, who had gone straight to bed, very much. Never the less, she wanted to be as supportive as she could.

'So who's going to be there?' she said, trying to stifle a yawn.

'Well, Merv,' said Austin. 'He's the guy in charge. And his wife. I haven't met her. And some other director of the bank. I haven't met him. And *his* wife, I suppose.'

'We're walking into a massive group of people we haven't met?' said Issy, feeling suddenly terribly anxious. 'Who are basically interviewing you for a job?' She took out her make-up case nervously.

'Don't ... I mean, you've probably got enough stuff on your cheeks,' said Austin.

Issy's eyes were hugely round and fearful. 'What do you mean?' she said.

'Nothing,' said Austin quickly. 'Nothing. I mean, you look fine.'

'They're all going to be trendy New Yorkers, though,' said Issy. 'And I'll just be scuzz. Mind you,' she added, 'maybe that'll make them change their minds about the job and you'll have to come home on the next flight with me.'

She'd tried to sound light, but she was aware she'd touched on a sensitive issue. Austin looked at her, but in the passing street lights it was very difficult to see his face. As the cab bounced downtown on one of the large, open avenues, he pointed out the Chrysler Building, all lit up in Christmas colours. It was so familiar and so wonderful all at once that she couldn't help being impressed. Then she sniffed.

'They've done the BT Tower up in red and green,' she said casually. 'Oh, and the whole of the South Bank is a festival of light. And a Christmas market.'

The snow flurries were becoming thicker and thicker. The driver turned down a little old-fashioned-looking street lined with houses with brown steps up to their front doors, which reminded Issy of *Sex and the City* and the days when she and Helena used to watch it and wish they got their Chinese food delivered in little boxes, or that they too were asked out by suave gentlemen every five minutes (Helena did get asked out every five minutes, but only by drunks on a Saturday night when she was bandaging them up in Accident and Emergency).

The restaurant had large plate-glass windows that reminded her of the café, but this place was painted grey, not green. Inside, it seemed to glow; the lights were soft and warm and yellow and gave the place the most inviting, exciting atmosphere imaginable. Happy, stunningly beautiful men and women – all dressed, Issy noticed glumly, up to the nines – were chatting, laughing and generally having a wonderful time.

'Hello,' said Austin cheerily to the doorman. He never felt intimidated anywhere. Probably because he wasn't really noticing it, thought Issy. And that made him comfortable and that in its turn made him likeable and that made him confident and so things always went well. It must be nice. She smiled in an ingratiating way at the doorman and wondered whether to tip him as he opened the door.

Inside, a stunningly beautiful blonde woman gave Austin a smile that made her look as if she'd been waiting to see him all day.

'Good evening, sir!' she said, displaying gorgeous teeth. 'Do you have a reservation?'

But 'Austin! Hey, Austin!' was already booming across the room, and at the back of the restaurant – it was much larger than it appeared from the outside – a short, wide man was rising up from a comfortable-looking banquette.

The blonde whisked away their coats, then threaded them through the tables. Issy decided it must be jet lag that had made her think she had just passed Michael Stipe having dinner with Brooke Shields. All she could say for sure was that every person in the room looked gorgeous, had obviously just had their hair done, was talking animatedly about interesting things and looked a hundred per cent absolutely like they were supposed to be there. Unless someone asked her about flour grading, Issy reflected sadly, she wasn't going to have anything to say. And, after all, she was only the girlfriend. If *Sex and the City* was accurate, there were millions of beautiful girls in New York just desperate to snap up some gorgeous hunk.

Issy tried to snap herself out of it and smile politely and the men stood up as they approached the table.

'Hello,' she said, as the women revealed themselves to be almost terrifyingly skinny. Merv's wife, Candy, was at least three inches taller and twenty years younger than him. The other couple's names she didn't even catch, and she muttered 'hi' whilst feeling nine years old, hopelessly intimidated, furious with herself and furious with Austin for some reason she couldn't quite articulate.

'Hi,' said the women, blankly and without interest. Presumably if you didn't have poison injected in your face every ten minutes and starve yourself to death 24/7, you didn't deserve even the faintest glimmer of attention round here.

Austin, on the other hand, was, she noticed, the object of ritual scrutiny. In her cornered state she couldn't help but be slightly mollified; yeah, she thought, you guys are all a lot thinner and richer than me, but at least I don't have to pretend I like having sex with Merv just because he's rich.

Mind you, that said, compared with everyone else there, Merv was a lot of fun.

'D'ya just get off the plane?' he said. 'There's only one answer to that. A martini! Fabio!' A stunningly handsome young barman appeared at Merv's elbow. 'Get this young lady a martini straight up. She needs a wake-up. Gin – she's a Brit. With a twist. Quick as you can, OK?'

Austin looked at Issy in a slight 'he's always like this' way, but Issy didn't actually mind. Anything that would make her feel more at home.

'Bottoms up,' she said when her drink arrived, and took a large gulp.

The only martini Issy had had before had been one her mother had made for her when she was fifteen and had come back miserable from a party because none of the boys had wanted to dance with her, which almost certainly had something to do with the fact that whilst all the other girls were in Lycra and legwarmers, she was in a macramé dress her mother had made for her in Peru and insisted on her wearing, and as it was one of her mother's periodic homecomings, she had given in. It had had martini bianco and lemonade and had been delicious, and she'd sat up late while Marian had told her that no man was to be trusted. As Marian herself was not to be trusted, and the closest man in Issy's life was Grampa Joe, who clearly was, Issy had gone slightly too far the other way and endeavoured to trust most of the men she ever met, far too much for far too long. Which had often turned out to be a mistake. Until Austin. She looked at him and took another gulp.

This martini, on the other hand, was pure alcohol and, frankly, rocket fuel. She put it down spluttering, her eyes watering.

'Ooh, got ourselves a party girl,' said Merv approvingly, as the rest of the table looked on superciliously. Issy thought she heard the director's wife mutter something about 'British drinkers'.

'Actually, Isabel runs her own business,' said Austin.

'Oh, really? Doing what?' asked the other man.

'I make cupcakes,' said Issy.

'Oh, that's so *cute*,' said Candy. 'I wanna do that, Merv.'

'Course you can, darling,' said Merv.

'Oh, wow, it must be so much fun, you must just have such an awesome time!' said Candy.

'Every second,' said Issy. She glanced at Austin, glanced at the table, and determined to finish the entire drink, even if it did taste like very expensive petrol.

'What is it?' hissed Pearl. 'Ben, you've got to give me some warning when you come round! It's not right. I'm just about to put Louis to bed. He's got school tomorrow.'

'I know,' said Ben. 'Ssh. Come see this.'

He dragged her closer for a kiss, and she could smell hash on his breath. Her heart sank.

'You been eating chicken?' he said. 'Got any more? I'm hungry.'

'No,' she said. 'What is it, Ben? You haven't been by in weeks.'

'Yeah, but look.'

He beckoned her out in the freezing wind – she wished she'd grabbed her coat – to a beat-up old van that wasn't his, as far as she knew, and flung open the back door.

'Ta-dah!'

Pearl peered inside, lit only by the street light. At first

she couldn't quite figure out what it was. Then she realised. It was a huge box. The writing on it became clear.

'A monster garage,' she breathed.

'I told the little man I wouldn't let him down,' said Ben.

'But ... but ... I mean, have you been working?'

She knew what she meant by this. If he was working, he was meant to give her some money. That was the deal.

'Oh, just a bit, here and there ...' said Ben. He couldn't quite meet her eyes.

'Do you mean working properly, a proper job? Where? Was it cash in hand? With Bobby or who?' demanded Pearl.

'Oh, well, I thought you'd be pleased,' said Ben, cross now. 'I thought you'd be happy that we got the little man the one thing he wants more than anything ... thought we could wrap it up too, you know, with a big bow, the whole works. Maybe I'll just throw it away, huh? Just set it on fire because I haven't got my P60 and a receipt and everything else ...'

'Ben,' said Pearl, desperate not to start a fight. 'Ben, please. It's just it's so expensive ...'

'I know how much it is,' said Ben, his handsome face set like stone. Pearl swallowed. She wanted to believe he had a job, she did, but why couldn't she get a straight answer out of him?

She didn't say anything more. Ben cursed quickly under his breath then turned to go.

'Don't you want to come in and see Louis?' Pearl said, a little reluctantly.

Ben shrugged, then slouched past her in through the door of the little ground-floor flat.

'DADDY!' Louis' shout of joy, Pearl reflected, could be heard halfway down the street.

Pearl never swore. She thought it showed an uncontrolled mind. But she got extremely close to it right then. She looked around. Someone had built a snowman from the dirty leftover snow of a few days ago. Someone else had taken the carrot off its nose and put it where a penis would be. Pearl sighed, and went back indoors, out of the freezing cold, feeling very far away from wishing goodwill upon all men.

'So, Austin,' Merv was saying, sitting back in his banquette and grumbling, presumably not for the first time, about the fact that he couldn't smoke his cigar indoors. 'What would you say our prospects are vis-à-vis ...'

Issy had realised that frankly there wasn't a single thing she could contribute to the conversation – Candy was playing with her phone, like Darny would have been doing, and the director's wife, who was called something like Vanya or Vania or something that sounded like it might be a name but wasn't really, was making a massive point of differentiating herself from Issy and Candy by insisting on joining in with the men's conversations in a highly technical and competitive way.

Candy yawned every so often quietly behind her hand, but then would lean in and stroke Merv's thigh in an affectionate manner. Issy realised that a charming waiter was refilling her glass every time she took so much as a sip of the ambrosial white wine, so she kept at it. Since neither Vanya nor Candy ate at all, Issy went at the bread basket in an almost passive-aggressive manner. Meanwhile Austin was talking about Europe and money and futures and micro-trading and other things Issy hadn't even heard of in a way that was completely beyond her and very impressive.

She wondered what Austin thought about her job – he saw her at work, she supposed, making coffee and baking cakes and handling the customers, but she didn't think he found it very impressive (she was quite wrong to think this; Austin thought what she did was amazing). Meanwhile, here he was, eating a very rare steak and explaining why the future of Europe was as luxury-goods merchants to roaring emerging economies, whilst everyone nodded sagely and listened to everything he said. Suddenly Issy wished Darny were there to wind Austin up and say something cheeky.

Cosy in the warm restaurant, drinking quite a lot of wine and eating her food without saying very much, Issy had felt herself start to slightly drift off when she heard her name.

'It's like Issy's business model,' Austin was saying. 'High-end products, immaculately made and presented, not mass-market. That's the future, because everywhere else we can't compete.'

The table turned towards Issy, who felt very fuzzy in the head.

'What?' she said.

'Is that true, Issybel?' asked Merv. 'Are you the future of commerce? When you're awake?'

Everyone laughed as if he'd said something funny, and Issy blushed bright red and couldn't think of a single word to say.

'Well?' said Merv.

'Do you think your model is going to drive European-zone regeneration?' snapped Vanya, as if they were in court or something.

'Ha, well, hem,' said Issy. She was bursting with embarrassment and bright red. Austin hadn't told her this was a bloody job interview for her too. Even worse, because she hadn't been following the conversation, she didn't have a clue what to say. And even if she had, she didn't know what the right answer was anyway.

'Well, gee, it's nice to have a hobby,' said Vanya with a large fake smile, turning back to her salad and mineral water.

Austin took Issy's hand under the table and gave it a

sympathetic squeeze. This made things worse as far as Issy was concerned; she didn't need his sympathy: she needed not to be put on the spot. The conversation moved on to real-estate prices, but Issy still sat there, burning up with crossness and feeling stupid and inferior.

Finally, when the pudding menu was coming round and Vanya and Candy were holding their hands up against it as if it were a list of poisons (which, Issy reflected, taking it, was probably exactly what they did think), Issy was ready. She launched in.

'The thing is,' she said, 'if you make stuff that's really good, people realise it's a superior product. Well, most of the time. They still sell lots of squirty cream in cans. Anyway, that's not important. The important thing is that even if people have less money, they'll still buy themselves small lovely things as a treat. Sometimes even more because they're staying in a lot, trying not to buy too much, so they'll have a little reward ... '

'Yeah, yeah,' said Vanya, sounding bored. 'But what does that mean on a macroeconomic level to you?'

Issy spluttered. 'It means ... I'll tell you what it means,' she said, drunker than she'd realised, and suddenly sick of being patronised and talked down to and ignored and treated as the uninteresting dumpy girl-friend of the brilliant and fascinating man by these stupid, annoying glamorous Americans. 'It means I wake up every day and I do a real thing. I get my hands dirty. I create something from scratch, with my bare hands, that

I hope people will love, and they do, they really do; and I turn out something perfect and beautiful, that is meant to be enjoyed, and people realise that, and they do enjoy it and they pay me money for it and that is the best job in the bloody world and we should all be lucky enough to do something like that and that's where we should be focusing our efforts. What did you create today, Vanya? Did anyone pick up one of your reports and smell it and give you a big smile and tell you it was absolutely bloody amazing?'

She paused to savour the open mouths round the table.

'No, I didn't think so.'

She turned to the waiter.

'Does the gateau de fôret noire come with fresh cherries or marinated? Tell the chef fresh if he can, it's far better; the acidity balances out the sweetness instead of making it cloying and overbearing. Of course, I'm sure he already knows that. On a macro level. So I'll take it.' And she shut the menu with a triumphant snap.

The party headed out rather mutedly, except for Merv, who had suddenly found Issy a bit of a one and asked her lots of cake-based questions and whether she could make a decent kugel, which actually she'd never heard of, then described his grandmother making it in their little Long Island kitchen and complaining that she couldn't get kosher sugar and that the base wasn't right, and Issy tried to talk him through it to see if she could figure it out.

No one else spoke to her at all; even Austin seemed stiff, and Issy, through her slightly drunken haze, started to worry that in fact rather than putting her point in a cool and measured way, she had perhaps shouted at everybody else at the table completely unnecessarily. Oh well. She couldn't worry about that now.

As they got to the door, the beautiful waitress brought them their coats. Issy shrugged herself into Caroline's now even tighter ridiculous white jacket. Candy stopped short. Then she leaned closer.

'Oh. My. God,' she said, the first direct thing she'd said to Issy all night. 'Is that ... is that the new Farim Maikal?'

Issy didn't have the faintest clue who it was, but the name definitely rang a bell. And actually, now she thought about it, Caroline had gone on and on about the coat when it had arrived and been really smug about it and how she'd got one over on her friends and this would show them and all sorts of other stuff that Issy hadn't really understood. But Farim she thought she remembered.

'Hmm,' she said non-committally.

'It IS!' breathed Candy. 'Can I touch it?' She held out her hand, reverently stroking the ridiculous white fur and collar studs. 'Wow, the wait list at Barneys for this was like ... wow.'

Even Vanya was looking at it with a touch of jealousy.

'Shame they didn't have your size,' she said.

'Oh man, that doesn't matter, she looks amazing,' said Candy. 'Anybody would who got their hands on one. This is THE hot coat this winter.'

Issy bit her lip and suddenly felt a terrible wave of homesickness.

Chapter Twelve

Kugel

220g medium-wide egg noodles

65g butter

220g cream cheese

100g sugar

1 tsp vanilla

4 eggs

200ml milk

150g frosted flakes or corn flakes mixed with sugar

2 tbsp butter, melted

2 tsp sugar

2 tsp cinnamon

Cook noodles according to package directions.

In a large bowl, mix butter, cream cheese, sugar, vanilla, eggs and milk. Stir until smooth.

Drain noodles, and add to mixture, then pour into a large square pan, cover and refrigerate overnight.

The next day, about two hours before the meal, preheat the oven to 180°C/gas mark 4.

In a small bowl, crush the cereal and mix with melted butter, sugar and cinnamon. Sprinkle the cereal mix on top of the cold kugel, and then bake for 1¼ hours. Cool for 20 minutes before serving.

Issy fell asleep in the car, then sank into the beautiful bed, which made her feel like she was sleeping on a cloud, and even though she was woken incredibly early by both the jet lag and Darny banging hard on the connecting door, she already felt much better. She had been too tired even to give Austin a proper kiss, but as she turned over in the bed, she saw he was already up and in the shower.

'Hey,' she said as he came out with a towel wrapped round him and opened the door for his brother. Darny grunted at them, then headed into his own bathroom.

'Hey,' Austin said, without quite looking her in the eye.

Issy immediately panicked and sat up in the big soft bed. Last night was a bit of a blur.

'Was I ...' Her voice sounded weird, a bit husky. 'Sorry, was I really bad last night?'

'No, of course not,' said Austin, but his tone was a little distant.

'Well, you put me on the spot,' said Issy, looking round for something to drink. She picked up a bottle of Evian, then saw a sign next to it indicating that it was $7.50, which even she with her poor arithmetic skills could tell was outrageous, so she put it down again.

'Just drink it,' said Austin crossly, when he realised what she was doing.

'What's the matter with you?' said Issy. 'What did I do?'

'You were just ... you were just a bit aggressive, that was all.'

'*I* was aggressive? That Vanya girl wanted to bite me on the leg!'

Austin still looked unhappy.

'Austin,' said Issy, imploring him. 'Look, if you wanted me to behave in a certain way or dress like a tart and keep my mouth shut like that Candy girl ... you should have said so.'

'I didn't,' said Austin. 'I just wanted you to be your-self.'

There was a terrible silence.

'Maybe that *was* me,' said Issy quietly.

Austin looked as if he wanted to say something, then bit his tongue and didn't. Instead he glanced at his watch.

'Look ... '

'You have to go. I know. Me and Darny will go out and explore.'

'Good,' said Austin, looking relieved to be on safer ground. 'OK, cool. I'll text you. I should be able to get away this afternoon after five. I know this cool café we can meet at.'

'Well, we might need an afternoon nap,' said Issy. 'But definitely. OK.'

Austin came over and kissed her. 'We could do with some time, just the two of us,' he said. At exactly the same moment, Darny started up singing a loud and extremely tuneless version of a Bruno Mars song, whilst clattering loudly in the rainforest shower. Issy rolled her eyes.

'Mm,' she said. Then she smiled. 'Have a good day.'

Austin smiled back at her, but still, when he left the hotel room she felt a terrible anxiety in the pit of her stomach. Something wasn't right, and she didn't know if she could fix it. She didn't know the recipe for this.

'Well, *fix it*,' Pearl was saying, as patiently as she was able. Maya tried yet again, but her shaky hand meant that more of the latte slopped over the top of the glass.

It was Maya's first day, and Pearl had never had to be someone's boss before, especially not someone who was pretty, sweet, young, and appeared to have caught the eye of a person Pearl would never admit in a hundred years she had a bit of a soft spot for.

It was proving tricky for both of them. Maya was trying her best, but Pearl was so quick and efficient, she couldn't quite follow what she was doing; not only that, but she was nervous. Pearl seemed to have taken against her for some reason, and she couldn't work out why. And she'd been up since five on her post round and had been too anxious to eat any breakfast.

'Three lattes, a hot chocolate and four mince pies,' said Pearl, smiling nicely at the customer. 'Just ring it up like this.'

Her fingers flew deftly amongst the buttons and the till dinged open. Maya tried to remember what she'd done, but it didn't seem like it would be possible. She sighed, then went back to the coffee machine. Grind, pressurise – the big orange Rancilio terrified the life out of her. Even Pearl admitted it was temperamental, and likely to give you a steam burn at any moment. Steam the milk but not too much (skin) and not too little (freezing). Then combine, spoon the foam on the top, and powder a little cupcake shape with chocolate and a template Issy had had made up. Repeat a hundred times an hour, serve up with a smile ... Maya was getting panicked.

'Hurry up!' said Pearl, keeping a fixed grin on her face. Where the hell was Caroline? She'd been late the day before, too. When Pearl had called her on it, she'd shrugged and said, come on, the boss was away, and anyhow it was too cold to leave the house in the morning without her coat. Now she'd done it to her again. Pearl gritted her teeth. Sometimes it drove her beyond endurance to have to work with someone who only turned up as a sop to her ex-husband's divorce lawyer, and thought she was hard done by at that.

Maya turned round too fast and knocked the entire metal jug of milk on to the floor. Gasping apologies, she jumped to it, but Pearl was there before her.

'Please take these mince pies with our compliments,' she hissed, handing the customer back her money. 'I'll bring the coffees over when they're ready.'

Pearl got out the mop whilst Maya spluttered apologies that Pearl wasn't really in the mood to accept, particularly when they smelled burning and she realised she'd missed the oven beeper going off because she'd been crouched down cleaning up milk, and they'd lost an entire tray of Christmas cake cupcakes and the beautiful warm-scented ambience of the shop had gone, giving it instead a charred edge that was going to do nothing for business.

'This place smells awful,' said Caroline, wafting in twenty minutes late. 'Good lord, look at that disgusting pile of dirty dishes all over the tables. Yuck, who'd want to eat here?'

'Can you keep your voice down?' said Pearl, wiping sweat off her forehead. 'And get cleaning up.'

'Can't the newbie do that?' sulked Caroline. 'I just got my nails done.'

'The newbie is trying to learn how to make a cup of coffee without exploding anything,' said Pearl.

'Oops,' said Maya.

'Maybe try again when we're a bit quieter,' said Pearl through gritted teeth, getting her to start on the dishwasher, which she figured even Maya couldn't mess up. Wrongly, she discovered, half an hour later, when Maya tried to refill the soap dish with dishwasher cleaner and managed to somehow scoop the overflowing foam over an entire tray of fresh lemon slices.

'Oops,' said Maya, again.

There was a queue out the door, but not a good queue – it was a grumbling bunch of freezing people who'd waited far too long for watery coffee and nothing-like-as-good-as-usual cakes, being served up by three grumpy, stressed-out people instead of being soothed by the normal gentle smile and greeting from Issy. If one more person said 'Boss on holiday, then?' to Pearl, she was going to scream.

Just as one of their everyday regulars was looming up to the counter bearing a cake with teethmarks in it and an ominous expression, the phone rang. Pearl ducked down the stairs with the handset, leaving Maya to put on an apologetic look and try to explain why the strawberry tart tasted a bit soapy.

'Hello.'

'PEARL!'

'Oh, well, you don't have to shout.'

'Sorry,' said Issy. 'I'm not used to phoning from abroad. Wow, it's good to hear your voice. How are things?'

Pearl paused. As she did so, she heard the tinkle of falling crockery.

'Uhm, fine,' she said quickly.

'Really? You're all doing great without me?'

Issy's voice sounded slightly disappointed. She had rather hoped they would find it difficult to struggle on without her being there. Mind you, Pearl was so capable and had reassured her so many times that she could manage on her own. It was hardly rocket science. She thought back to that snooty woman at dinner last night. Maybe she was right after all.

'Well,' said Pearl. 'It's certainly not the same.'

'PEARL!' came Caroline's imperious voice. 'Did you remember to reorder the milk? Only we appear to be running out and it's only one thirty. And the sandwich boy hasn't been, so we've missed an entire lunchtime.'

'Bollocks,' muttered Pearl under her breath.

'What's that?' said Issy. 'This is a terrible line.'

'Oh, nothing,' said Pearl. 'Just congratulations from cheerful punters.'

'Well, good,' said Issy. 'I'm glad it's all carrying on fine.'

'Yup, don't worry about us,' said Pearl, catching with

her foot an orange that appeared to be bouncing down the stairs. They didn't even sell oranges. 'Don't worry about us at all.'

Issy wrapped Darny up against his strongest protestations and took out her guidebook. 'Don't complain,' she said.

'I am complaining,' said Darny. 'I'm considering a citizen's arrest, in fact. I don't want to go out. I want to stay in and play computer games. They have *Modern Warfare 2*.'

'Well I'm afraid you can't,' said Issy. 'We're in the greatest city in the world and I'm not letting you miss it. Any other kid would be desperate to get out there and explore.'

Darny's brow furrowed. 'Do you think so?' he said.

'Yes!' said Issy. 'It's a huge world out there, full of all sorts of things. Let's go explore!'

Darny stuck out his bottom lip. 'I think this is kidnap.'

Issy, hung-over, stressed, tired, worried about the café – she had thought she would be worried if it was wobbling, but no, nobody even seemed to have noticed she was gone, so a fat lot of use she was back there; and here she was nothing but a liability – had finally lost her patience.

'Oh for CHRIST'S sake, Darny, just do what you're asked one FRICKING time and stop behaving like a spoilt baby. It's pathetic. Nobody's impressed.'

There was a sudden silence in the room. Issy had never spoken to Darny harshly before. It was the tightest of drawn lines. He was not her boy. He was not her son. She had always promised herself that she wouldn't cross that line.

And she just had. She had been harsh and hurtful and it was hardly Darny's fault; he hadn't asked to come here. And neither had she. Oh, what a mess.

In total silence, Darny stood with her as they waited for the elevator. As they descended into the lovely lobby, the charming receptionist smiled nicely at them and asked if everything was all right, and Issy lied through gritted teeth and said it was, then they both steeled themselves to go out into the freezing New York morning. The sky was a burstingly bright blue and Issy resolved that the first thing they needed was sunglasses; the sun bouncing off the glass panes of the skyscrapers and the snow was almost blinding.

'Wow,' she said. For a moment she forgot everything that was going on, just how impressed she was with the fact that she was actually here. In New York!

'Come on,' she said. 'Let's go shop! We can have Darny at Barneys! There's a shop called Barneys, you know, very famous.'

Darny didn't respond.

'Look,' said Issy, putting up her hand to hail a taxi. It really was impossible to be outside for more than a couple of minutes. 'I'm sorry, OK. I really didn't mean what I said. I was … I was frustrated about something else and I took it out on you.'

Darny shrugged his shoulders. 'Doesn't matter,' he said. But obviously it did.

Barneys turned out to be horrifically expensive, so they left after Issy had swooned a little over the staggeringly beautiful clothes draped on the mannequins, and marvelled at the young, beautiful American women who were storming through and picking things up right, left and centre, commenting on them all the while. She spied a Gap across the road and they hurried across. Everything was much cheaper there, and she bought Darny a few things she thought he needed (most notably new underpants) that neither Austin nor Darny ever seemed to notice. Then she thought about it again and bought Austin a whole bunch of new underpants too. Couldn't hurt. And some shirts and a couple of jumpers. She liked buying for him. She couldn't ever have bought clothes for her last boyfriend, Graeme; he was very anal and particular. Austin probably wouldn't even notice, or care, but it made her feel like she was looking after him, and at the moment she didn't feel that she was looking after anyone particularly well – and worse, no one, from her customers to her boyfriend to his brother, felt particularly like they wanted looking after either.

She sighed, especially when she came across a beautiful, soft checked lumberjack shirt. It was lined inside, which would have made it comfortable and warm for her grandfather, who had, in his last days, always been cold but found hard fabrics scratchy and uncomfortable against his skin. She held it briefly in her hands, wishing she could buy it for him. But she couldn't.

Laden with bags, they jumped into another cab – Issy knew she should probably take the subway, but was terrified of getting lost or hopelessly confused. Anyway, she told herself, she hadn't had a holiday in over a year, she worked too hard ever to spend any money and the rest of the trip was free. She deserved a bit of time off and could afford to spend a little.

The Empire State Building didn't look like anything from the street; just another office block, except for the beautiful art nouveau signage outside. Issy hadn't considered that it was actually a working office block. Of course it was; what did she think, that it would just be empty, like the Eiffel Tower? She bought their tickets with excitement, glancing at the enormous, beautifully dressed Christmas trees in the lobby that seemed to stretch several storeys high, whilst Darny maintained his petulant silence. Issy tried to pretend he wasn't there. In the crush of the first lift, she watched the beautiful golden arrows on the floor indicator climb upwards and smiled to herself, feeling she was channelling Meg Ryan. But it wasn't the same, every time she caught Darny's tight-looking little face in the mirror.

Up on level 100, the cold and the wind and the sun were absolutely bracing. All Issy's jet lag and fuzziness was instantly blown away as she stepped out on to the smaller-than-she'd-expected platform. The jostling lift-load of tourists spread to all four sides of the building to gaze out over the far horizons: huge ships from China and the Middle East docking down in the Lower East Side; helicopters taking off south from Broad Street and circling round the island like giant wasps; Central Park, so ridiculously straight-edged and tidily cut, totally unlike the more organic outdoor spaces of London she was used to – then no other green at all anywhere, just building after building, their jagged tops and mirrored glass walls making them look like an infinite reflection of a child's Lego set. The sun glinted off the river and the island – a shape as recognisable to Issy as London; possibly even more so than her home city of Manchester, she realised, with a lurch of shame. Her breath was visible in front of her face and she instinctively took out her camera, before realising that the vista laid out before her was probably better bought on a postcard rather than taken through netting.

'On top of the world,' she called out to Darny, who was huddling in a corner against the cold, looking anything but. 'Come on,' she said. 'Shall we go up and look at the mast? Do you know, it was built to tether Zeppelins to? Can you imagine what it was like, bringing one of those down? Only it was too windy, so they had to stop.'

Darny grunted again.

'Darny,' said Issy timidly. 'I know you're cross with

me. But don't let it spoil your trip, OK. Or mine. I promise I won't think you're not cross with me if you have a tiny bit of a good time.'

Again, no reaction, and Issy bit her lip in frustration.

'Well, never mind about that,' she said, taking one last look around, lingering longest on the side with the little arrow that said it was 3,460 miles to London. 'Come on. It's time for lunch. There's someone we have to meet.'

Chapter Thirteen

Verity Deli Hot Chocolate Brownies

Calories: UK – a million, and can make you potentially nauseous all day; US – a light snack in between two gigantic meals, both of which have melted cheese on top. Can also be accompanied by caramel sauce, whipped cream, ginger ice cream, coronary surgery. Do make this, but please make very small brownies as a delicious melting snack. Death by chocolate is, truly, a horrible idea. The idea here is to feel delighted and pleased, not sticky and regretful.

185g unsalted butter
185g best dark chocolate
85g plain flour
40g cocoa powder

50g white chocolate
50g milk chocolate
3 large eggs
275g golden caster sugar

Melt butter and dark chocolate very slowly and carefully in the microwave. Allow to cool. Turn on oven to 160°C/gas mark 3 and line a baking tray with baking paper.

Sift flour and cocoa powder; chop the milk and white chocolate. Whisk together eggs and sugar till the mixture looks like a milkshake and doubles in size. Carefully and gently fold in melted chocolate mix until fudgy. Stir in chocolate chunks.

Bake for 25 minutes till shiny on top.

Issy followed the instructions she'd received in the email. Heartily frozen from exposure to the elements a hundred floors above ground, they were both relieved to escape back into the warmth of the building, then into a yellow cab. Issy was beginning to get the hang of cabs; Austin had explained that you didn't hail them and wait for them to come to you. You grabbed one and just opened the door and jumped in, otherwise someone else would take it. At first this had seemed rude and ill-mannered, till the first three times someone had managed to get there ahead of them and stolen their cab, which was of course even more ill-mannered, so now Issy was hopping in and out of them like a native, Darny at her heels.

They passed through the happy chaos of Times Square, full of pink-cheeked tourists looking around to see what all the fuss was. A Santa was ringing a bell at every cross-walk. People were buying tickets to Christmas shows and staring at the fabulously lit-up buildings, with their holidays wishes from Coca-Cola and Panasonic. Everything was a riot of lights and trees and every street corner had carollers or bell-ringers or men selling knock-off handbags which Issy looked at slightly regretfully before coming to her senses and moving on. She couldn't imagine the look on Caroline's face if she turned up with a fake Kate Spade, not to mention her horror of getting caught at customs.

The place they'd been instructed to show up at – early, it had been insisted – was a large corner block with old-fashioned fifties-style lettering advertising a soda fountain. It was called the Verity Deli, and its walls were lined with pictures of its illustrious clientele – Woody Allen was there, as was Liza Minnelli; Steven Spielberg and Sylvester Stallone. There was already a small queue forming. An elderly waitress with dyed orange hair and an alarming bosom crammed into a green uniform took them straight away to a much patched and darned banquette. Issy asked for a cup of tea and let Darny, eyeing her closely, order a root beer float, even though neither of them had the faintest idea what it might be. When it arrived, it turned out to be a gigantic confection of ice cream and fizzy flavoured lemonade, in a glass the size of Darny's head. He glanced at her again, but she didn't comment and he plunged in without checking twice.

They were waiting a long time. The waitress returned repeatedly – the menu was absolutely gigantic, with all manner of things to order: roast beef side; knishes; pastrami on rye and lots of other things that made no sense at all to Issy, who was already slightly shocked at the state of the banquettes and the slovenliness of the waitress. She wouldn't want to run her fingers across the top of the pictures.

After twenty minutes, as Issy fiddled with her phone and wished she'd brought a book, and Darny ate his way stoically through the root beer float until he looked like he was turning green, the door slammed open dramatically, bringing in with it a noisy gust of wind. A tall, imperious woman dressed in old-fashioned, very plain hand-made clothes and a large and rather elaborate hat swept in.

'Isabel!' she declaimed loudly, in an American accent.

'Mum,' said Issy.

Darny looked up for the first time that day.

Marian swanned across to their table. The elderly waitress was over in the blink of an eye, but Marian waved her away.

'Beverly!' she cried. 'Not until I've said hello to my precious daughter, whom I haven't seen in an age. Look at her, isn't she lovely?'

Marian wobbled Issy's cheeks up and down. Issy tried not to mind and hugged her mother back.

'And who's this? Have you had a child and not told me?'

'No,' said Issy and Darny simultaneously.

Marian sat down and waved away the laminated menu. 'We'll have pastrami on rye three times, no pickles. And three root beer floats.'

'No thank you,' said Darny, looking slightly queasy.

'Two root beer floats. You have to try these,' said Marian.

'OK,' said Issy.

Their drinks appeared in record time, while Marian was still looking her up and down.

'I haven't seen you since ... '

'Gramps' funeral,' said Issy. She'd put a notice in the *Manchester Evening News*, and had been stunned by the response. Over two hundred people who had remembered her grandfather – worked with him or eaten his wares over the years – had contacted her, and his funeral was full to the rafters. It had been rather daunting. Her mother had wafted around gathering compliments and looking artistic and brave whilst Issy had attempted to cater for an endless parade of well-wishers and mourners, many of whom were kind enough to say that she had inherited his talent.

There had been so many stories. Credit given when the man of the house was out of work; an apprentice taken on out of prison; a thief rapped sharply on the knuckles and sent off with a stiff lecture, never to offend again. There were stories of wedding cakes; christening cakes; warm doughnuts for cold hands off to school; growing up with the scent of fresh bread always in the nostrils. He had touched a lot of lives, and people wanted her to know that, and she was grateful to hear it.

She was glad to be busy too, all through the funeral and the sorting things out; there was always something to do and she had her hands full. It was when everything was tidied away and she'd returned to London that she'd spent her nights crying into Austin's shirts. He had been very good about it. He'd understood, perhaps better than anyone else could.

There had been a little money – not much. Issy was glad about that. Her grandfather had worked hard his entire life, and she had spent it all on the nicest home and the nicest people she could find to make sure he was as comfortable and happy as possible. She didn't grudge a penny of it. She had used her share to extend her lease and pay off some of her mortgage. Her mother had used hers to go to an ashram, whatever that was, and complain about all the inaccuracies in *Eat Pray Love*.

And here she was again, large as life, in a coffee shop in New York. It felt very strange.

'Hey,' said Issy.

'Well,' said her mother. 'Tell me everything.'

But before she could begin, Marian was looking over for the waitress.

'You know,' she confided, 'I shouldn't really be eating this. I went all raw food at the ashram. Apparently I have a very sensitive system and I can't process refined flour. But oy vey, as we say.'

'Mum,' said Issy. She looked at the sandwich in front of her. It was piled higher than her mouth could possibly open. She wasn't entirely sure what she was meant to do with it or how she should eat it. 'Are you Jewish now?'

Marian looked solemn. 'Well, I think on a very real level, every one of us is Jewish.'

Issy nodded. 'Except we're Church of England.'

'It's the Judaeo-Christian tradition, though,' said Marian. 'Anyway, I'm changing my name.'

'Not again!' groaned Issy. 'Come on. Remember the fuss you had with the bank when you tried to change back from "Feather"?'

'No,' said Marian. 'Anyway, it's not hard to remember. I'm going to be Miriam.'

'Why bother changing your name from Marian to Miriam? It's practically the same.'

'Except one honours the mother of Jesus, a great prophet to be sure, and one is the sister of Moses who led the Chosen People to the Promised Land.'

Issy had learned long ago not to take her mother up

logically on any of her latest crazes. Instead she smiled resignedly.

'It's good to see you,' she said. 'Are you enjoying living here?'

'It's the most wonderful place on earth,' said Marian. 'You must come visit the kibbutz.'

'You're in a kibbutz?'

'Of course! We're trying to live as authentically as possible. Saturdays are difficult, but apart from that . . . '

'Why are Saturdays difficult?' It was the first time Darny had spoken of his own accord all day.

Marian turned her attention towards him.

'And who are you?' she asked bluntly.

'I'm Darny Tyler,' he replied, his face heading back down towards his sandwich again.

'And how do you fit into all this? Is my daughter being nice to you?'

Darny shrugged.

'Yes, I am!' said Issy, cross. 'I'm nice to everyone.'

'You're too nice,' said Marian. 'Always trying to please people, that's your problem.'

Darny nodded his agreement. 'She always wants everyone to like her, all the teachers and stuff.'

'What's wrong with that?' said Issy. 'Of course I want people to like me. Everyone should like people to like them. The alternative is just wars and aggravation.'

'Or honesty,' said Darny.

'Quite right,' said Marian. They exchanged a glance.

'You two are ganging up on me,' said Issy, attempting at least the bottom half of her sandwich. It was absolutely delicious. As soon as she tasted it, all her doubts about the café and its standards completely disappeared. That was interesting, she realised, looking at the queue out of the door. People came here for one thing only: the amazing, fabulous food. The fact that the lino was a bit cracked or the windows smeary didn't matter in the slightest. She looked around at the other customers, rushing in, shouting out their orders, scattering salt sachets and coffee stirrers on the counter, jostling each other to get in. This was good. This was how people liked it. It might not suit her clientele, but it certainly suited its own.

'So tell me, how's school, Darny?' said Marian.

Darny shrugged. 'Awful.'

'It is not "awful",' said Issy. 'He gets top scores in maths and physics. And no scores in everything else, not because he's not bright but because he isn't interested.'

'I hated school,' said Marian. 'Got out as soon as I could.'

And got pregnant, Issy didn't say.

'Issy was such a little scholar, worked so hard, went to college, passed all her exams, proper little swot, and what does she do now? Makes cakes. Which is fine, I grant you, but it hardly needed her grandfather to pay for three years of higher education.'

'It's been very useful, actually,' said Issy, crossly.

'So you are who, exactly?' said Marian.

'I'm Austin's little brother. Austin's her boyfriend.' Darny made a face and Marian laughed.

'I didn't know you had a boyfriend,' she said.

'Austin,' said Issy patiently. 'The tall chap that was at the funeral? Whose house I live in? Whom I talk about on the phone?'

'Oh yes, ooh yes, of course I did,' said Marian. 'I must meet him one day.'

'You have met him,' said Issy. 'Four times.'

'Oh, of course I have. Good for you! Now, Darny, tell me some of the nonsense they've been teaching you in school.'

And to Issy's absolute surprise, Darny launched into a long story about their sex-education teacher who had got all wobbly and upset doing something unfortunate with a banana. It was a funny story and Marian listened carefully and asked pertinent questions, and then they both got stuck into a discussion of why they had to use rabbits for sex information and why couldn't they use those gay penguins, and Issy couldn't help but be struck by the fact that Marian was obviously enjoying the conversation – they both were – but also that she was talking to Darny as if they were both adults, or both teenagers, she couldn't quite tell which one. At any rate, in a way that they managed to understand one another. She watched them with some sadness. Darny was so sparky, so full of contrariness and argument. She found it wearing and problematic, but to her mother it was clearly a challenge. Yet she herself had spent so much time as a daughter trying to be good, and behave herself, and gain appreciation for that.

Well, Gramps had loved her for who she was. She knew that much. And Austin, too. No wonder he'd been so surprised by her outburst last night. She surreptitiously fingered her phone and wondered what he was up to. She glanced towards the restaurant kitchen, full of short-order cooks shouting, bantering, working the lunchtime rush. She wished she could bake something. It always calmed her down when she was agitated. But between the little hotel room and the big restaurant meals, that definitely wasn't possible. She was just going to have to grin and bear it. And be happy that Darny and her mother seemed to have made a connection. That was good, at least.

They added a hearty tip to the bill (Issy paid, and her mother let her), reluctant to leave the cosy banquette for the freezing street, but Marian mentioned that she had to go and pick up some knishes from Dean & Deluca, a sentence Issy didn't understand any of, so they headed out together into the cold.

'How long are you here for?' said Marian.

'A few days,' said Issy. 'Can we come and visit you?'

Marian frowned. 'Well, you know, it's very busy at the

commune ... Of course,' she said. 'Of course. I'll send you directions.'

She kissed them both freely.

'Mazel tov!' she yelled happily, as she marched off in her funny home-made clothes, walking across a stop light as if she'd been born in America.

'Your mum's cool,' said Darny, as they took a cab up to the Guggenheim Museum.

'People think that,' said Issy.

'Do you not see her very much?'

'No,' sighed Issy. 'But that's OK. I never did, really.'

A silence fell between them. But this time it felt a bit more companionable.

After an hour of trying to appreciate the art (and Darny running up and down the famous circular passageway), Issy was utterly exhausted. She was on the brink of suggesting they go back to the hotel and have a nap when her phone finally tinged. It was Austin, with one of the funny, short New York addresses made up of numbers. He was suggesting they meet up there, and Issy agreed.

Austin had sleepwalked through his meeting. He hadn't listened to a word anyone had said, just launched into an analysis of the business as he saw it. Amazingly, nobody seemed to have noticed that he hadn't listened. Maybe not listening was the way forward. Maybe it was how everything got done. But he couldn't help it. He was, he realised, unutterably miserable. Here they were, showering him with riches and offers and a whole new way of life; a way of life he'd never even dreamed of. Success, security for Darny and himself; a future.

But the person he wanted more than anyone to share it with didn't seem to want to share it with him.

Austin hadn't fallen in love with Issy straight away. He had found her quirky, then he had liked her, then it had gradually dawned on him that he never wanted to be without her. But it was more than that. He trusted her; he listened to what she had to say. They thought alike on so many things. And the fact that Issy clearly wasn't interested in being here with him … it shook his confidence, it really did. He'd grown to rely on her so fully, even, he realised, to the point of taking her for granted.

He kicked his way through the dirty snow. Everyone he met thought he was crazy in this weather, but he liked walking in Manhattan; there was so much to look at, and he fitted in with his regular long stride because everyone walked fast, and he liked the pulse of the city in his veins and the hum and buzz of electricity. He did like it. Issy would like it too.

That made him groan internally. He knew … he thought he knew … that if he begged her, if he made a big point out of it and insisted and strong-armed the situation – which was not his style at all – she would come. She would. Wouldn't she? But even if she did, Austin knew she wouldn't be happy. Couldn't be. She'd worked so hard, and it was her ... her purpose, he supposed. Issy, in the Cupcake Café, her hands covered in flour, her cheeks pink from the heat of the oven; with a pat on the head for every child and a friendly word for every cold and weary London passer-by. It defined her. To stick her in some glass box high-rise apartment in Manhattan whilst he worked ridiculous hours every day ...

He would turn them down in a heartbeat.

That much had been running round and round his head. That much he'd decided. Unfortunately, there was something else. Something that made all his good intentions towards Issy hardly count at all.

The letter Issy had grabbed from the hall table as she had left for New York. The letter, with its impersonally typed address and frank. It was slightly crumpled and stained from its trip on the plane and being stuffed in and out of bags. Issy had left it on his side of the bed. She didn't know, of course, how far things had gone.

Dear Mr Tyler,
We at Carnforth Road School are afraid that the behaviour of your son/ward has become, despite repeated warnings, too much for our school to take on. We are recommending a permanent exclusion. We do not feel Darny's particular needs are being met by this school ...

There was more, much more. Mostly of a legal nature. Austin had skipped that.

There was only one other school in the district, King's Mount, and it had been terrible and dangerous in Austin's time and it was still terrible and dangerous now. Parents avoided it like the plague; people moved so their children wouldn't have to attend it. Fights were regular; it was the dumping ground for children who had nowhere else to go, or a halfway house to borstal, or for those whose parents just didn't give a toss. It had been on special measures for ever, but they couldn't shut it as it was absolutely huge, and nobody else wanted the children who went there.

Darny would never survive there. Austin couldn't possibly afford to send him to another school. Not in London. Even if they'd take him, which with his record was probably a bit tricky. He gulped.

Merv had already handed him a brochure for the middle school his own children went to, assuring him he'd get a place for Darny. It had class sizes of twelve, its own pool, and weekly one-to-one seminars 'to develop social and creative potential' and encourage 'independence and clarity of thought'. Austin had had it half on his mind ever since. Part of Darny's intransigence was of course just down to his age; it was completely normal and would probably get thrashed out of him at King's Mount ... Austin couldn't bear it. Darny was small for his age. Small, not very brave, but with a big mouth. He remembered Issy saying in passing that she didn't like big gangs of schoolchildren in her shop (she let them in, but Pearl did bouncing if they got too rowdy), but felt like making an exception for the poor terrified mites she saw crawling out of King's Mount, with their pale, scared-looking faces.

Austin sighed. Would he drop everything, this job and everything else, for Issy? Of course. Yes, New York would be fun and an adventure, but he wouldn't jeopardise their relationship for that. Not if it was just him.

It wasn't just him. It was him and Darny; had been for a long time.

As soon as Issy saw the outside of the place where they were meeting, she knew, and couldn't help feeling a bit irritated. This was where Austin had got those other cupcakes. Those enemies ... She was curious, she couldn't help it. The New York City Cupcake Store, read the old-fashioned writing on the window. This was where so many of the great cupcake makers had started in this city ... perhaps she'd just had a bad batch. It would be a good thing to try some others out, have a look around and see if she could get any new ideas. She wished she'd thought of this before, actually, rather than following the guidebook and having to try and explain stuff to Darny in the art gallery that she didn't really understand, then answer his follow-up questions, which she definitely didn't.

The smell of coffee wafting out into the street – although it had that odd, slightly burned smell that she'd learnt to associate with American coffee shops – calmed her down a little. It felt more like home somehow. She sniffed. Something was odd. She could smell baking for sure, a warm smell that encompassed half the street. And she could see the cakes in the window. But the cakes in the window didn't chime with the smell, which was much breadier. Something was up.

She peered through the steamed-up window. Austin, to her amazement, was already there. It wasn't like him to be on time, never mind early. He was inside chatting to someone. They were head to head. Issy blinked. He hadn't mentioned bringing a friend.

'Come ON,' Darny was saying, hopping up and down. 'It's FREEZING out here.'

'OK, OK,' said Issy, and pushed open the door. The doorbell made an electronic noise. Issy preferred her real bell.

Austin looked up, almost guiltily. The girl he was talking to was, Issy noticed, almost ridiculously pretty, with her perfect teeth and rosy mouth and lovely scattering of freckles. Issy wondered if she was being paranoid, but the girl seemed to shoot an angry look in her direction. Issy was going too far in her harsh judgements of New York and its inhabitants. She needed to calm down

234

and lighten up a little. Everything was going to be better now.

'Hello,' she said as cheerily and generously as possible.

Austin smiled. He still felt a bit awkward about this morning, and had a sense that things weren't turning out quite as amazingly as he had thought they should be in his head.

'Hello,' he said.

'New York sucks,' announced Darny cheerfully, as if it confirmed all his long-held suspicions. 'It's freezing and really boring. But the food is good,' he added, looking at the cupcakes.

'Hello,' said Kelly-Lee. She was slightly discomfited. Girlfriends she could handle, but she didn't know they had a child. That was annoying. And Austin didn't look anywhere near old enough. 'Have you come to visit your dad?'

'My dad's dead,' said Darny rudely, as he always did under the circumstances. 'That's my brother.'

'Awww,' said Kelly-Lee. Darny knew that 'awww'. He and Austin exchanged glances.

'Come here, tyke,' said Austin.

'Here, little man. Let me get you a cupcake. I don't know if you have them in your country. It's a special American treat, and here's a Christmas one just for you!'

Darny rolled his eyes, but he wasn't about to turn down a free cake.

Issy smiled tightly. Kelly-Lee glanced up at her. 'Oh yes,' she said. 'I forgot, you bake, don't you?'

'Yes,' said Issy. She had realised what was weird about the smell; they were pumping it in. It was chemical. They hardly baked here at all.

'For a real job or just for fun?'

'It's a real job,' said Issy.

'Oh,' said Kelly-Lee. 'I wanted to be an actress for a real job.'

'Well, it's nice to meet you,' said Issy, slightly confused.

'Me and Austin here have been hanging out, haven't we?' said Kelly-Lee, playfully putting her hand on his lapel. Then she came out from behind the counter to pick up some cups littering the tables, making sure she bent over at each one so Austin and Issy could both check out how amazingly tight and rounded her bottom was, after several hours of Pilates a week.

Issy raised her eyebrows at Austin.

'Um, she's been very friendly,' said Austin.

'And don't forget to call me!' said Kelly-Lee. 'Don't worry, I'll look after him for you when you're not here!' And she smiled her enormous wide American smile right in Issy's face and gave her a cheery wave with her dishcloth before disappearing into the kitchen.

Issy was fuming. 'Who the hell is that?' she said.

'I don't know, some girl,' said Austin, confused.

'Some girl? Some girl? You just happened to walk into a cupcake shop and start chatting with some girl?'

'It was just chatting,' said Austin.

'So you didn't take her number?'

Austin thought back. 'Well, she did give me her number ... but I didn't ask for it. I don't even know where it is. She only gave it to me in case you didn't get on that plane.'

Issy blinked in disbelief. 'What, if one cupcake girl wasn't available, any one would do?'

'No! No!' said Austin. 'You're getting this all wrong. You're taking everything all wrong! You have done since the moment you got here.'

'I haven't seen you since the moment I got here,' said Issy, realising to her horror suddenly that she was on the brink of tears. They hardly ever fought. 'Which I suppose I'd better get used to, seeing as you're moving here with all the new people you know and all the cool New York stuff you do and I'll just go back home and get on with my dreary baking life, which, by the way, is REAL BAKING,' she shouted through the back so Kelly-Lee could hear. 'Not this plastic crap they're churning out here with fricking vegetable oils and sell-by dates. Do you know what the sell-by date of a cupcake is? It doesn't have one. About an hour. So this is crap and everything here is crap and you're coming here, for ever, and I realise I have to put up with that, but I don't see why you should bloody start flaunting your new girls and new interests in front of me before I've even left.'

Austin was stunned. He'd never heard an outburst like this from Issy before. He looked at her, upset. Also, he hadn't understood the bit in the middle about vegetable oil.

'Issy . . . Issy, please.'

'No!' said Issy. 'Don't turn this into me being all ungrateful and stupid. *You* make up your mind about what you want and don't tell yourself you don't know or that you're still weighing up options. I met the people you're going to be working with. They seem very confident that you're about to move away from everything we have. But don't worry about telling me, I'll just put it together all by myself.'

She turned round, grabbed her hat and stormed out of the shop.

'Is she all right?' said Kelly-Lee coming through from the back all wide-eyed and sympathetic. 'I'm sorry, I didn't realise she'd fly off the handle like that. Is she like that a lot? I hope I didn't say anything wrong. Some people are just very dramatic, aren't they?'

'Don't worry about it,' said Austin, not putting her straight, and leaving money for the coffee.

'This cupcake is awful,' said Darny. 'By any reasonable judgement, it's a terrible, terrible cake.'

'You're so cute,' said Kelly-Lee. 'I love your accent.'

Austin turned to Darny. 'Can you stay here for five minutes?' he said. 'I'd better go and get Issy.'

'With her? No chance,' said Darny. 'You can't leave me, it's illegal.'

'*Please*, Darny,' begged Austin.

Darny folded his arms and looked mutinous. By the time Austin had bundled him out on to the street, there was no sign whatsoever of where Issy had gone.

It was growing dark outside. It was icily, bitterly cold, as cold as Issy had ever known. People were dim outline shapes in enormous puffa jackets and huge hats and furs, like bouncy marshmallow men, hurrying and rushing to get inside. The sun was setting in bright pinks and reds and golds, cutting through the skyscrapers and casting endless shadows across the busy pavements. Issy hardly noticed; she ran, blindly, up the street, tears pricking at her eyes. It was time to face the truth, she knew. Austin was going to move here. He was going to make his home, and Darny's home, over here, and that would be that. And all the girls would be all over him like a shot, and ...

She could hardly think any more. She found herself back on Fifth Avenue, pushing blindly through the crush, the sheer weight of people slightly freaking her out when she was disorientated and just needed somewhere to have a really good cry, in private. There didn't seem to be a lot of privacy in this city.

Her phone rang. She fumbled for it in her pocket, her

heart thudding. Was this it? What was she going to say? Sorry, Austin, this is it for us? I'm leaving you because you're about to leave me anyway and I don't want to go through four months of torture whilst you faff around between London and New York unable to make up your mind? Or, Please please please come back to London with me and give up all hopes of an exciting future to be stuck behind a desk in Stoke Newington for the rest of your life?

She was tempted not to answer – nobody's name would come up on her screen because she was abroad – because she didn't know what to say, and a snot- and tear-filled gabbling wouldn't really help anyone. But to not answer would be worse, passive-aggressive and horrible and scary, and if Austin was putting things off, it wouldn't help if she did too.

'Hello?' she whispered into the phone, her hand where she'd taken off her glove to press the green button already feeling cold and stiff. Automatically she kept walking north to where it seemed quieter; up through Columbus Circle and skirting the bottom of Central Park.

'Oh thank GOD,' said Pearl. 'There you are. Issy, I may have been ... ahem ... slightly exaggerating before. About how things are.'

'What?' Issy snuffled, wrenched back to reality.

'Um,' said Pearl.

Pearl was standing in the basement kitchen of the shop. It looked like a bomb had hit it. Strawberry cake mix that Issy had carefully made up in advance was dripping off the walls. Receipts and pieces of paper were piling up on surfaces all over the place. It was the middle of the night and Pearl hadn't slept properly in two days.

'I think,' she said, finally, 'I think I've broken the mixer.'

'Frick,' said Issy. The industrial mixer was a central part of the operation. 'But it's Saturday tomorrow! It's a huge Christmas shopping day. The entire world is going to be out.'

'I know,' said Pearl. 'And some cake mix landed on the calculator and I'm having, um, some trouble cashing up. And possibly there's a health inspection due.'

Issy made up her mind. 'Listen,' she said, with a heavy heart. 'It's all right. I've got this totally posh plane ticket.'

She paused and took a deep breath.

'I'll fly straight back. I'll see you in the morning.'

Chapter Fourteen

It didn't take Issy long to pack. Apart from Caroline's ridiculous coat, she'd worn almost none of the unsuitable clothes she'd packed so quickly, with such excitement. Flicking pointlessly through the television channels, she saw *Sleepless in Seattle* playing on TCM and nearly burst into tears.

Austin arrived back at the hotel shortly after her, a grumpy Darny in his wake.

'This really isn't good for me,' Darny was saying. 'Having to deal with conflict in an already difficult childhood.'

'Shut up, Darny,' Austin said. His face fell when he saw Issy with her suitcase out.

'It's not because of you,' she said. 'Honestly. Pearl can't cope without me. Things have gone really wrong.' She looked at him straight on. 'Sorry. I can't leave the café.'

Austin looked straight back at her. His heart was pounding in his chest. Darny was sitting in the corner, his face drawn and tense. Austin didn't want to mention the letter in his pocket. It wouldn't make anything better. It would make everything worse; Issy might think he was blaming her, because it had happened in his absence. He never wanted her to think that she had done anything wrong; with Darny, with him. Not anything. He felt a terrible lurch. There was so much he wanted to say, but would any of it change that essential truth?

'I know,' he said, quietly.

There was a long silence after that.

Issy felt as if she'd been punched in the face. He was going to let her go, just like that. Without even vaguely trying to persuade her to stay. For some stupid job. For his career. Everything she had ever thought about her big, handsome, gentle Austin ... well, she hadn't imagined that this would happen. Not like this.

She put out her hand to steady herself. Austin saw her and wanted to burst into tears. She looked so vulnerable. But what could he do? If it wasn't now, it would be later. Should he just prolong the agony? He felt as if he were ripping apart inside; and yet here they were, words still coming out of their mouths, almost like normal human beings.

'I'm just going to phone the airline,' Issy said, feeling as if they were someone else's words, someone else's script. Surely she should be saying, let's take a ferry ride to see the Statue of Liberty; or go for a romantic evening in a cocktail bar where a pianist would be tinkling 'It Had To Be You' in the corner; or go and watch the adverts and the sailors down in Times Square and look at the great bows and Christmas lights that draped every corner of the city.

'I'll get someone to do that,' Austin was saying, like a robot.

'Someone at your office? In New York?' said Issy, then wished she hadn't. Everything was bad enough without being spiteful on top of it. 'Sorry. Sorry. I didn't mean that.'

'No,' said Austin. 'It's OK. *I'm* sorry. I mean …'

He looked so thoroughly miserable, all Issy wanted to do was take him in her arms and hold him till he felt better. But what good would that do? she thought. He seemed to have made up his mind. Prolong everything? Pretend to carry on a financially ruinous and technically impossible career between two totally different continents?

'Ssh,' she said. 'Don't worry about it.' She indicated Darny. 'We can talk about it back in the UK.'

'Mm,' said Austin. He couldn't figure out where exactly this had all gone so terribly wrong. Issy hadn't even taken a second to look around or tried to see the positive side of New York. She'd been against the entire thing right from the start, almost as if she'd decided that it was going to be a disaster, and therefore it had turned into one. It made him incredibly cross.

They stood a little while longer with neither of them saying anything.

'Well, this is boring,' said Darny. 'I can feel my ADHD kicking in.'

'I'll make the call,' said Austin.

'OK,' said Issy.

After a tense ten minutes, it was arranged that Issy could go back on a flight leaving very early the next morning. Just one more night to go.

'Do you want to go out?' said Austin.

'I think I'm finally going to have that nice bath,' said Issy, trying to paste a smile on her face and stop her voice from wobbling, though she didn't quite succeed. 'Then an early night; I'm going to be up to my eyeballs when I get back to the café.'

'Yeah,' said Austin. 'OK.'

But as they lay together in the huge, comfortable soft white bed, listening to the distant honks and whoops of the traffic, there was not the faintest possibility of sleep. Instead Issy cried; great silent tears, dripping down into her pillow. She tried not to make a sound or disturb Austin, until he turned over and realised her pillow was wet.

'Oh my darling,' he said, holding her tight and stroking her hair. 'My love. We'll work it out.'

'How?' said Issy, sobbing. 'How?'

But Austin didn't have an answer to that. Either way, it seemed, would leave one of them very unhappy. Which in the long run would leave them both unhappy; that much he understood. He sighed again. Why did life have to throw up speed bumps when they seemed to be running happily along? And this, he thought, stroking Issy's soft dark hair, this was a big one. Their tears mingled together on the expensive pillowcases.

Pearl had finally thrown up her hands and admitted defeat. She had phoned Caroline and asked her to come in early.

Caroline had turned up and tutted at the state of the place. Then she had made a call of her own.

'Perdita! Chop chop!' she had shouted at the pleasant-faced middle-aged woman who'd arrived, slightly frightened-looking, three quarters of an hour later. Perdita had instantly started scrubbing everything down from top to bottom, as Caroline briskly went through the figures.

'One thing divorce does is make it very easy to read a balance sheet, see where all the money's gone,' she growled.

Pearl was still gazing at Perdita. 'She's your cleaner? How can you have a cleaner and still come to work in a café?'

'Because Richard is an evil cunning bastard,' said Caroline. 'I've told you this before.'

Pearl eyed her shrewdly. 'But you must be getting close to a settlement now,' she observed. 'It's been dragging on for years.'

'Pearl, you're a terrific salesperson and a wonderful organiser in the café, but your paperwork is a dog's dinner and you bake like a wookie,' said Caroline tightly, ignoring her. 'Division of labour should have been sorted out properly before Issy flounced off.'

'She didn't exactly flounce off,' said Pearl. 'Caroline, I have a theory about you; do you want to hear it?'

'If it's about my astonishing self-control when it comes to food, I'll just tell you again, nothing tastes as good as skinny fee—'

'Nope,' said Pearl. 'That's bullshit. No, here is my theory: I think you work here because you like it.'

'*Like* it? Working? In a job a robot will probably be doing in two years' time? In a job that persistently refuses to recognise my creative interior design and organisational skills and insists on putting me in front of the general bloody public after I've already been a major player in the corporate world? Yeah, right. Perdita, you've missed a bit. And sort out the skirting while you're down there.'

'Yeah,' said Pearl. 'I reckon you really do like it.'

Caroline glanced at her out of the corner of her eye.

'Don't you ever dare tell a bloody soul. PERDITA! Did you bring those bags I asked you? Well, if it takes two runs at it, it takes two runs; just bring them in, would you?'

Perdita soon came in weighed down with two suitcases.

'What the hell is in there?' said Pearl.

'Aha!' said Caroline.

Maya arrived just afterwards, arm in arm with a girl with very short hair.

'Hi,' she said happily to everyone, beaming her lovely smile. 'This is Rachida. Rachida, this is Pearl and Caroline. They are being very patient with me.'

Pearl raised an eyebrow, feeling guilty because she had not been in the least bit patient.

'I've had her up all night practising,' said Rachida. 'Our friends have got a cappuccino machine. She's got it down to six seconds.'

'Thank you,' said Caroline. 'Do your friends do book-keeping too?'

'Shut up,' said Pearl, looking at Maya and Rachida.

Rachida left, kissing Maya full on the lips as she did so. Maya took off her coat and hung it up behind the door, unconcerned. 'See you tonight!' she yelled cheerfully. Then she turned round.

'OK,' she said. 'I reckon I'm ready.'

Pearl smiled a huge wide smile at her, ridiculously cross at how pleased she was.

'OK,' she said. 'Go bring up that new tray of mince pies. Surely I got them right sixth time out.' And Pearl started to slightly relax, leaning behind the counter and turning on the stereo. 'Deck the Hall with Boughs of Holly' came thundering out of the sound system, and she found herself joining in on the falalas. She must need sleep, she thought.

Issy cried all the way to the airport in the cab. She cried as she sat in the posh lounge, where she completely wasn't in the mood to sample any of the luxury treats. She cried all six hours across the Atlantic, pausing only to watch *Sleepless in Seattle* so at least it seemed like she had an excuse. She cried all the way back on the Heathrow Express and all the way back up the Victoria Line and all the way across town on the number 73.

Then she pulled herself together and walked into the café.

She stopped, and gasped. She couldn't help it. She hadn't really noticed from the outside; there were a lot of people with their faces pressed up against the glass, but she hadn't really taken it in. But here, inside, the entire place was transformed.

Snow lined the fireplace, which was thickly wreathed with ivy. Ivy also hung down in garlands from the ceiling, linking up so the café appeared to have trees growing out of it. Every table had a display of silver ferns and holly, and there was a huge wreath on the door, so the entire place felt like an enchanted forest. Most remarkable of all, however, was that some space had been cleared in the windows, taking out their display box. In its place was a snowy landscape, complete with white hills and a little wooden town, lit up with tiny lampposts. Figures were tobogganing down the hills; there was a school with children playing outside, a hotel with ladies in ballgowns descending the steps, and several cosily lit houses, and round it all ran a dinky steam train, with carriages with tiny people inside them. There was a station with a station master waving a flag and blowing a whistle, and vintage cars parked outside, and tucked behind the highest of the hills, against a backdrop painted with stars, was Santa Claus on his sleigh with all his reindeer. It was utterly enchanting.

'AUNTIE ISSY!' Louis hurtled out from behind the counter and leapt on Issy as if he hadn't seen her for months. 'AH DID MISS YOU!'

Issy let herself enjoy being bowled over and smothered in kisses.

'I missed you too, my love.'

Louis beamed. 'WE HAVE A TRAIN! DID YOU SEE OUR TRAIN? IT'S A REAL TRAIN! IT GOES ROUND AND ROUND AND THERE IS SANTA CLAUS BUT HE IS HIDING SO YOU DON'T SEE HIM!'

'I did see it,' said Issy. 'It's wonderful.'

'Well, my wretched children don't appreciate it,' sniffed Caroline. 'Why are you back so early? Did you get a stain on my jacket?'

Louis stroked Issy's hair. 'Did you bring me a present?' he whispered.

'I did,' whispered Issy, answering the easiest question first. She reached into her hand luggage and brought out a snow dome she'd bought at the Empire State Building. It had all the lovely buildings of New York – the Empire State, the Chrysler, the Plaza – with little taxis on the ground, and when you shook it, a snowstorm commenced. Louis held it in absolute awe, shaking it again and again in amazement.

'I like my pwesent, Issy,' he said, quietly.

Pearl came round from behind the counter, looking at Issy carefully. She wasn't her normal ebullient self at all. Pearl thought it could just be jet lag. But no, it was more than that. It was as if a light had gone out somewhere behind Issy's eyes. Her face was drawn and pinched-looking, with none of its usual rosy glow.

'That's a beautiful present, Iss,' she said, using the gift as an excuse to give Issy a big hug.

Issy nearly lost it again, but felt she was pretty much all cried out. She turned to Caroline.

'Did you do this?'

Caroline nodded. 'Well. My interior decorator did. I think it's dusty and clutters the house up, so I brought it here. Achilles did look a bit sad at our minimalist look,

251

but heyho. We should absolutely win that bloody *Super Secret London* prize for best shop.'

'It's beautiful,' said Issy. 'Thank you.'

She smiled at Maya, who was expertly balancing four coffee mugs on one arm whilst pouring off perfectly frothed milk with the other hand.

'Well, it didn't take you long to get the hang of things.'

'It did, actually,' said Maya. 'I've been up practising five hours a night.'

Pearl nodded to confirm the truth of this. Issy looked around. Everywhere were happy-looking people eating away. Many of her regulars waved. She wanted to cry again: it felt good to be home.

'I thought you were all having a total disaster,' she said.

'A temporary blip,' said Pearl. 'We're totally over it now.'

'I see that,' said Issy. 'Could I possibly get a cup of coffee?'

Austin cried all the way into the office, but hid it. Darny wasn't paying attention anyway. He washed his face in the men's room, installed Darny with his DS next to his secretary, marched into Carmen's office before he even had a chance to think, and signed the papers. Now he belonged to Kingall Lowestein.

'Hey!' said Merv, swinging by to shake his hand and

have his photograph taken with Austin for the bank's newsletter. 'You won't regret it.'

Austin already did. 'Can your PA send over those school forms?' he said.

'Sure thing,' said Merv.

Issy started the batches for the next day's cakes so they could get a bit ahead of themselves. Maya was looking at her with wide frightened eyes, imagining her instant dismissal, but Issy smiled and said they were so busy with the window display bringing shoppers in that would she like to stay for a while, and Maya grinned widely and gleefully acquiesced. Issy also thought privately that she wasn't sure she herself was up to being jolly in the shop all the time and might take some more time off. On the other hand, what else did she have?

'Can I come over?'

'Yes,' said Helena, with the fervour of someone who wasn't getting enough adult conversation. 'Whenever you like. Stay as long as you like. Bring wine. Chadani Imelda, stop putting that up your bottom.'

'Um,' said Issy. 'Um. Can I stay the night?'

There was a pause.

'Oh,' said Helena.

'Oh,' said Issy.

'Oh darling,' said Helena.

'Please don't start me off,' said Issy. 'At least wait till I get there.'

'Bring wine,' repeated Helena. 'I've suddenly decided to stop breastfeeding. Bring LOTS of wine.'

Helena had, Issy noticed blearily, actually tidied away some of the children's toys and clothes that normally littered the flat in anticipation of her arrival. This was almost more worrying really; that she would go to so much trouble.

'I also went out and got some gin,' said Helena. 'I think gin too. And tonic, obviously. Or perhaps martinis, what do you think?'

'When's the last time you had a drink?' asked Issy.

'Two years ago.'

'No martinis, please,' said Issy. 'Especially not for you; you'll fall out the window by five past seven.'

They sat down, whilst Chadani Imelda methodically emptied Issy's handbag of lipstick, change, tampons, and, heartbreakingly, a napkin from the New York City Cupcake Store. Issy picked it up and made to blow her nose on it.

'If I called this number,' she said, indicating the 212 dial code, 'he'd probably be there right now. It's only afternoon there.'

'Hush,' said Helena. 'Hush.'

She poured them both enormous glasses of Sauvignon Blanc.

'Now,' she said. 'You. Fantastic person. Him. Total delight. How the hell did you get yourselves into this mess, and how are you going to get out, you utter bloody blithering idiots?'

After Issy had explained – she could hardly bear to think about that last night, both of them lying there, totally alone in their hugely luxurious bed – Helena took a large slurp of her wine and let out a long sigh.

'Phew,' she said. Then, 'Well.'

'So I'm meant to give up my whole life and everything I've ever worked for for some guy?' said Issy, re-pouring.

'Well, it's not "some guy", is it?' said Helena. 'It's *Austin*.'

'AW-IN,' said Chadani Imelda, looking so like her mother even Issy couldn't help smiling.

'Why can't the two of you just talk it through?'

'We can't,' sighed Issy. 'This is a huge, huge deal they're offering him. Whereas the way things are in London, he might not even have a job for much longer. He doesn't feel he can turn it down for me. And I don't think I can destroy the Cupcake Café for him. Which makes me think ...' At this, Issy started to cry huge, racking, choking sobs, '... which means we can't love each other enough.'

Helena shook her head. 'You do. Of course you do. But you're human beings, and it's not a movie. You can't just dump everything and run off into the sunset. Life gets in the way. There's love and then there's things that are practical. You both have responsibilities. You have employees who rely on you, and he has Darny to look after.'

'Nobody ever looks after me,' said Issy.

'Well, that's just self-pitying bollocks,' said Helena. 'And completely unfair given how much time we all gave up to help you open that stupid café in the first place.'

'Oh yes,' said Issy. 'Sorry about that.'

She sighed and drank more wine.

'I was so happy, though, Leens. I thought I was tired and a bit stressed out and always super-busy and up at the crack of dawn and everything with the café, but ... actually, when I think about it, I had everything.'

'That's the ludicrous thing about happiness,' said Helena. 'You never know you're going through it at the time.'

Chadani Imelda hit her mother on the leg, rather hard.

'Apparently these are the happiest days of my life.'

'Oh yes, we're in our prime,' said Issy.

'I'll consider myself in my prime when I stop getting spots,' said Helena.

'And my heart broken,' said Issy.

'And eating fish fingers.'

'And learn self-control,' said Issy, pouring them both another glass.

'Bottoms up!' said Helena.

'You haven't even compared me to some kid that's getting its leg chopped off yet, like you used to when you worked in the hospital,' said Issy.

'Oh GOD, I am SO HAPPY WITHOUT A JOB AND NO SENSE OF PURPOSE OR DIRECTION IN MY LIFE!' shouted Helena, startling Chadani, who nonetheless burst out into giggles too.

'Ha, you girls sound happy,' said Ashok, opening the door to the sounds of hysterical laughter.

Issy and Helena looked at one another, then burst out laughing again. They only stopped when Issy accidentally burst into tears. Helena swallowed, then realised how drunk she was.

'Jet lag,' she tried to explain, but it didn't come out quite right.

Ashok came over and kissed her. He was slightly perturbed by all the empty bottles, but he hadn't heard Helena laugh like that in a long time, and Chadani seemed quiet for once, so perhaps on balance it was a pretty good thing.

'Hello, Issy,' he said. His face lit up. 'Did you ... '

'Bring you some cakes? I know, I know, that's all I'm good for ... '

'ASHOK!' Helena tried to whisper, but she wasn't used to the booze and couldn't keep her voice down. 'Be sensitive! Issy's just split up with Austin!'

'Not officially,' said Issy.

Ashok picked up Chadani, who had cruised her way towards him, and gave her a huge cuddle and a kiss.

'This is not possible,' he said sternly. 'You have not split up. You cannot. It is unacceptable to me.'

'I should have tried saying that,' said Issy, gulping.

'So. What was it? Something ridiculous? And small? Did he tell another woman she looked nice? Did he not buy you a thoughtful present for your birthday? Men are not always perfect, you know.'

'Are you diagnosing our relationship?' said Issy.

'Sometimes it is useful to take a dispassionate view,' said Ashok.

'Oh, it is definitely dispassionate,' said Issy. 'It definitely definitely is that. He has a job in America. I have a job here. He has to move to America to do his amazing job there, otherwise he'll probably lose the one he has here. I have a quasi-successful business running on a long lease that employs three people but can't manage without me. What's the outlook, Doctor?'

'Well, one of you will have to move,' said Ashok stubbornly, nuzzling Chadani's neck. 'Look at this. This is happiness. You deserve happiness.'

Helena snorted loudly. 'Happiness and lots and lots of stinky laundry.'

Chadani giggled and squirmed in her father's arms, and Issy wanted to cry again.

'Well, I can't and he can't,' she said. 'This isn't north and south London. This is real life, with real choices and real consequences, and we both figured the sooner we faced up to that the better.'

'There is always a way,' frowned Ashok.

'Well, yes,' said Issy. 'If I wait five billion years, the tectonic plates will eventually fuse together and I'll be able to cycle over to his apartment . . .'

She was off again. Ashok patted her on the shoulder and Helena rushed up with more wine and some tissues.

'I've got a great idea,' she said. 'Let's have a wonderful Christmas, all together. A big party, here.'

'Here?' sniffed Issy.

Helena looked innocent. 'I just thought it would be lovely to get everyone together at Christmas time. Chadani's aunties could all squeeze in, and you could see if Pearl and Louis want to come, and—'

'Not everyone would fit in here,' said Issy.

'But think how wonderful it would be, all together,' said Helena. 'So happy, such a great way to take your mind off everything.'

'But you don't have a big enough table!' said Issy.

'Oh, so we don't,' said Helena. 'If only we knew of somewhere nearby with great big ovens and loads of tables . . .'

'I'm not cooking Christmas lunch for six thousand people,' said Issy.

'Just think of how wonderful it would be to be surrounded by the people who care for you and love you,' said Helena relentlessly.

'Care for me enough to banish me to the kitchen for the whole of Christmas Day?' said Issy.

'OK,' said Helena. 'Was just an idea. What were you planning on doing?'

'At the moment,' said Issy. 'I couldn't feel less in a goodwill-to-all-men state of mind.'

Pearl was on a half-day the next day, and she felt like she desperately needed it. She left early, rather guiltily ignoring Issy's red-rimmed eyes, a combination of jet lag, crying and an ill advised nightcap. She needed the time off and could make it back before Louis got out of school.

Doti caught up with her at the bus stop.

'Well, hello there,' he said, with his customary twinkle. 'How are things with you?'

'Not bad,' said Pearl. She was pleased, but still a bit cross with him for slavering all over Maya. It had felt insensitive.

'Christmas shopping?'

'I might be.'

'I was just heading into town myself. Maybe I'll wait for the bus with you.'

'If you like,' said Pearl.

'So, Maya's worked out well for you? I thought she might.'

'She is a hard worker,' agreed Pearl.

'Have you met Rachida? They're a lovely couple.'

'You knew she lived with a woman?'

'Of course I did; they're on my round. Don't get much past the postman, you know.'

'Why were you all over her, then?'

Doti looked confused. 'What do you mean? I really wanted her to get that job, she needed it desperately.'

'I thought you ... I thought you fancied her,' mumbled Pearl, feeling her face grow hot. Where the hell was that bloody bus?

Doti burst out laughing. 'A skinny little thing like that? Not likely,' he said. He looked slyly up at Pearl under his thick black eyelashes. 'I like something a bit more ... womanly,' he said.

There was a silence.

'There,' he said, finally, kicking the heel of his black postman boot against the pavement. 'I said it.'

Pearl's heart was fluttering in her chest and she found it hard to get her breath. Her emotions fought with each other inside herself; she had an almost overwhelming desire – and it would be so, so terribly simple – to extend her right hand, just a few centimetres, to meet his left, just there, his large, strong, worker's hand, holding on fiercely to the uncomfortable bus shelter bench. She gazed at his hand, and then her own, and his eyes followed her gaze.

Then she remembered the sound of a little boy crying, triumphantly, 'DADDY!' Ben parading Louis round the sitting room on his shoulders like he was a football trophy or a crown; the two of them playing kung fu and breaking her mother's prized horse statuette; Louis laughing, laughing, laughing.

Her knuckles tightened involuntarily, and she froze.

'I can't,' she said, in a voice barely above a whisper. 'It's ... it's complicated.'

Doti nodded. 'Sure is,' he said.

Then he stood up, just as the 73 rounded the corner.

'I am actually going into town,' he said, in a much more conversational tone of voice. 'I wasn't just looking for an excuse. So can I still come ... just as a friend? As a normal person?'

Pearl smiled at him, touched. 'You will never be a normal person to me.'

It was fun, in the end. Pearl hadn't realised it would be; pottering around John Lewis, buying a cheap little horse statuette for her mother to replace the one the boys had broken; and walking up to Primark to buy some underpants with monsters on them so hopefully they would appear to Louis more of a gift and less of a basic necessity. All the way they looked at the beautifully dressed windows of the posh shops, filled with expensive goods, but Pearl, watching the sullen faces of the thin blondes passing in and out of them, wasn't sure they were having as good a time as she was, and she could barely afford anything. Doti asked her advice on buying make-up for his grown-up daughter – he and his wife had separated years before, when she had taken a job in a nightclub almost comically unsuited to his hours and ended up having an affair with a bouncer, for which Doti did his very best not to blame her, which Pearl appreciated, even if she thought his ex-wife patently mad. Then he insisted on treating her to coffee at Patisserie Valerie, down on Regent Street, having once overheard her say how much she liked it. Pearl was as touched by the fact that he had remembered as she was by the treat itself.

They walked down past Hamleys, the huge toy shop. As usual, there was an enormous crowd of people, children and adults alike, gathered to see the wonderful window display – this year it was a huge snowy fairground scene, with a real rotating wheel and carousel rides for the toys below. Outside a Santa Claus was ringing a bell, and several pirates and princesses were blowing bubbles to attract passers-by.

It was the first time Pearl had felt a pang all afternoon. Right by the main door, under a seasonal coating of white cotton wool, all lit up with fairy lights – there it was. The monster garage, with the monster mechanics and the monster trucks going up and down the special lift. She smiled at it and shook her head.

'Are you thinking about that for the little man?' asked Doti.

'Oh, no, no, he gets far too many treats,' said Pearl,

fiercely and quickly. She was never, ever going to admit to anyone what she could and couldn't afford.

Doti stayed in town, and Pearl just made it back in time to hide all the little parcels before the door of the café flew open and Louis ran in.

'MAMMA! Oh, no.' He stopped himself. 'MUM!'

'You don't call me Mum,' said Pearl indignantly. 'I'm your mamma.'

'Noooo,' said Louis, shaking his head crossly. 'That's what babies say. I'm not a baby. You're my mum.'

Behind him Big Louis stood nodding gravely at this sad fact of the world.

'I don't want to be Mum. I want to be Mamma. Or Mummy, at a pinch, if you want to sound like those namby-pamby kids you go to school with.'

'Whatever,' said Louis.

'Louis Kmbota McGregor, don't you ever say whatever to me ever again!' said Pearl, horrified. Issy looked up and laughed. It was the first thing that had made her smile all day.

Louis looked half terrified, half proud of himself for inducing such a reaction. He glanced at Issy, who beckoned him over.

'When you say "whatever",' she said, 'you have to make your fingers into a "W", like this ...'

'Issy, you stop that right now,' said Pearl in a warning voice. 'Louis, that is not allowed, do you understand me?'

Issy and Louis made the 'W' sign at each other, then both chortled heartily.

'Dear Santa Claus,' said Pearl, writing out an imaginary letter, 'I am terribly sorry, but Louis Kmbota McGregor has been very badly behaved this year, and—'

'NOOOOO!' shrieked Louis in sudden terror, charging over and hurling himself into his mother's arms, and showering her with kisses. 'I'm sorry, Mamma. I'm sorry. Sorry, Santa. I'm sorry.'

'I think I'm coming round to Christmas,' observed Pearl.

'I'm not,' said Issy. 'I'm closing up early today.'

There was a massive groan from the customers in the café.

'Shouldn't you all be out getting stocious drunk for Christmas anyway?' she asked.

'The cake is soaking up the stocious drunkness from last night,' shouted someone from the back, and a few people vehemently agreed.

'Oh, all right,' said Issy. 'I may leave you all to help yourselves.'

'Yay!' said the crowd.

'Don't worry,' said Maya, yawning but appearing efficiently at Issy's elbow with a cup of coffee. 'I can handle it.'

Caroline ostentatiously tidied away the white jacket in a dry-cleaning bag. 'Hardly a thank you,' she sniffed out loud. Issy turned to her. She knew why Caroline was in such a filthy mood.

'So, Caroline, what are your plans for Christmas?'

'I am going to go through Richard's old address book and fuck all his friends in alphabetical order,' said Caroline brightly. 'Why?'

Caroline had been blinking very tightly all day and Issy had caught sight of a solicitor's letter in her pocket. She guessed it wasn't good news, as Caroline was being even more of a pain in the arse than usual.

'Only I thought,' said Issy, ploughing on. 'Well, I'm going to be here ... '

'Alone?' said Caroline sharply. Issy didn't answer. She didn't see why she shouldn't pull rank once in a while, in the case of major insubordination.

'... and Helena and Ashok wanted to have some family around, so I was thinking I might hold a little Christmas dinner here, in the café.'

Caroline didn't say anything. Issy knew that if she hadn't wanted to be included, she would have said something very sarcastic.

'Would you like to join us?' Issy asked gently.

Caroline shrugged. 'Don't think I'll be doing the sodding clearing up,' she said, blinking rapidly.

'No clearing up, no coming,' said Issy. 'It'll have to be all hands on deck. But it'll be fun. Pearl?'

Pearl wrinkled her nose. Normally they just went to church and sat in front of the telly. But it might be more fun here for Louis, with Ashok's little cousins running about the place ...

'I'd have to bring my mum,' she said. 'I can't leave her on her own on Christmas Day.'

'Of course,' said Issy.

'And I don't know how we'd get here without buses or anything . . . '

'Oh, I'll pick you up in the Range Rover,' said Caroline. 'I won't be doing much else in the morning.' She remembered herself. 'Of course it's great to be alone on Christmas morning. I'm going to have a bit of a spa day, some real "me" time.' Suddenly she burst into tears.

As Issy comforted Caroline, Pearl thought about Ben. She hadn't decided whether to ask him for Christmas. Well, that was what she told herself. She still didn't like thinking about where he'd got that bloody monster garage for Louis. But if she wanted to keep things civil – and she did, she did – she'd have to pretend that it was from a job, and that she hadn't noticed her maintenance had dried up. She'd tackle him again in the new year. She thought that he thought she made more money than he did, or that she somehow didn't mind paying for everything. She sighed. Everything did feel bloody unfair sometimes.

'Um, and maybe . . . ' Issy looked at her, raising her eyebrows. 'Louis' dad?' she whispered. Louis, however, was totally hypnotised by the Christmas train and didn't notice.

Pearl shrugged. 'Well, you know. He's hardly Captain Reliable.'

'Hmm,' said Issy. She felt as if she had no idea who was reliable and who wasn't, not any more. Pointless trying to guess really.

'Fine,' she said. 'So we'll have a huge one. Right here. I'd better find the world's most gigantic turkey.'

'Can we come?' said a regular customer who'd been listening in.

'No,' said Issy. 'They don't do turkeys that big.'

There was a sigh from around the room.

'Be quiet and eat your cake,' said Issy, going over to phone her suppliers, see if anyone could recommend a really good last-minute gigantic turkey supplier.

'Merry merry merry merry Christmas!' Louis was singing to the train. It was a song they were doing at school. 'Merry merry merry merry Christmas. Ding dong! Ding dong! Ding dong!'

Chapter Fifteen

Chocolate Cola Cupcakes with Fizzy Cola Frosting

Makes approx. 12 large cupcakes

200g plain flour, sieved
250g golden caster sugar
½ tsp baking powder
pinch salt
1 large free-range egg
125ml buttermilk
1 tsp vanilla essence
125g unsalted butter
2 tbsp cocoa powder
175ml Coca-Cola

For the frosting
400g icing sugar

125g unsalted butter, softened
1½ tbsp cola syrup (I used Soda Stream)
40ml whole milk
popping candy, to taste
fizzy cola bottles, candied lemon slices, stripy
    straws or candy canes to decorate

Preheat the oven to 180°C/gas mark 4. Line two 6-hole muffin tins with papers.

In a large bowl, combine the flour, sugar, baking powder and salt. In a separate bowl, beat together the egg, buttermilk and vanilla.

Melt the butter, cocoa and Coca-Cola in a saucepan over a low heat. Pour this mixture into the dry ingredients, stir well with a wooden spoon, and then add the buttermilk mixture, beating until the batter is well blended.

Pour into your prepared liners and bake for 15 minutes, or until risen and a skewer comes out clean. Set aside to cool.

To make the frosting, beat together the butter and icing sugar until no lumps are left – I use a free-standing mixer with the paddle attachment, but you could use an electric whisk instead. Stir the cola syrup and milk together in a jug, then pour into the butter and sugar mixture while beating slowly. Once incorporated, increase the speed to high and whisk until light and fluffy. Carefully stir in your popping candy to taste. It does lose its pop after a while, so the icing is best done just a few hours before eating.

Spoon your icing into a piping bag and pipe over your cooled cupcakes. Decorate with fizzy cola bottles or a slice of candied lemon, a stripy straw or candy cane and an extra sprinkling of popping candy.

❦

Austin's newly assigned PA, MacKenzie, was incredibly beautiful. She was tiny, with a gym-honed body that could only be arrived at by a lot of lettuce and early rising. Her face was tight, her nose probably not original, her hair extraordinarily bouncy and shiny. She had two degrees and a string of letters after her name, and Merv had called her a paragon of efficiency. She was also, Austin suspected, the most colossal pain in the arse. He already missed Janet terribly.

'So I've just typed up your sked-u-al?' she said, talking in a rat-a-tat voice with an upward inflection that sounded like everything was a question. It was not, Austin was learning, a question. It was an order. 'And if you could, like, be on time for all your appointments so I don't need to make so many calls to keep people waiting? And if you could, like, check out my colour-coded filing system so you always have the right files to take with you? And if you could, like, have your lunch order ready by ten thirty every day so I can get it right for you?

And you need to look into contract apartment leases, like pronto? And we'll start work on the green card, like, before you go back to close down your London office?'

Austin bowed his head and did some quick nodding, hoping she'd leave him alone. She stood in front of him, arms folded. For such a tiny person, she made an awful lot of noise.

'And, you know, I realise you've just arrived,' she said, 'but I think it is, like, unprofessional to leave a child in my office? It's not really acceptable to me? You know I have a bachelor's from Vassar? And I'm not even sure that it's, like, legal?'

Austin sighed. He knew this was true. He couldn't keep dumping Darny around the place; it was driving both of them crazy. But he'd promised to stay a few more days and set everything up, then go home and work out a couple of weeks' notice – although Ed, his old boss, was so proud that his boy had gone to the big team, he wasn't really expected to do much more than go out for a few leaving pints. Ed had also confirmed what Austin had suspected: they wouldn't be filling his post. They did need to fillet; even though Austin had done well in the job, it was going to go to keep good on the bank's promise to shareholders. Which meant there hadn't really been a way back after all.

He didn't know what else to do with Darny. He wasn't enrolled in the school yet, and it wasn't like he could go to a nursery or a crèche, however much Austin wished he could.

'You would be prosecuted for doing this to a rabbit,' Darny had announced cheerfully as Austin had perched him on his sofa with a Spiderman comic and a packet of crisps the size of a pillow, which Darny crunched with a noise that drove Austin to distraction. 'I wouldn't mind seeing that old lady again. She was cool.'

'Which old lady?' said Austin, struggling to figure out who Darny was talking about. If she wasn't wearing a black pointed hat and living in a gingerbread house, he was willing to give it a shot at this point.

'Marian. No, Miriam. Something like that. Issy's mum.'

'Oh yes,' said Austin, warily. He'd forgotten she was here. They'd met a few times; he thought on the surface she seemed pleasant, a little batty, mostly harmless. Underneath, from stories Issy had told him late at night, he thought what she had done was much, much worse. But she could babysit, couldn't she? She owed Issy that much, at least.

Then he remembered, as he did afresh and anew dozens of times a day, the way things were with Issy, and wanted to howl with anguish.

He didn't. He couldn't. Darny shook out the gigantic packet of crisps so all the dust floated to the floor. Then he burped loudly.

'I'll call her,' said Austin.

Issy was up to her eyes in marzipan when the phone rang. Nonetheless, she knew, in the way that sometimes you just do. Some phone rings sound different to others. And it was just when she was thinking of Austin.

Although, if she was being honest, she had been thinking about Austin every waking moment and every sleepless-night moment and her few and far between early-morning dreaming moments too. So.

She wiped her hands down her striped pink apron and picked up her phone. Number unknown.

It wasn't unknown to her.

'Austin?'

'Issy?'

She swallowed hard. 'I mi ... '

Then she stopped herself. It had nearly all come tumbling out, all the heartache and the sadness and the terror she had that she was going to lose him. All her neediness and insecurities brought to the surface. But how would that help? What would it prove? That she could guilt him into giving up his amazing life? Did she think that would make them happy?

She tried again. 'I'm making marzipan. Acres of it.'

Austin bit his lip. He could just see her, pink with the exertion. Sometimes, when she was concentrating, she even let the very end of her tongue slip out of her mouth, like a character from *Peanuts*. There she was, doing what she loved best; happy and immersed in her kitchen. He couldn't take that away from her. He couldn't.

'I hate marzipan,' he said.

Issy gulped. 'Well, one, you are wrong. And two, you haven't tried mine.'

'But I don't like the flavour and I don't like the texture. I do think people should be allowed to have different tastes in food.'

'Not when they're wrong.'

'But you don't like beetroot.'

'That is because it is food for horses. Everyone knows that.'

'Well I think marzipan is food for ... rabbits. Or squirrels. Nut-loving squirrels.'

'I think it's illegal to give marzipan to a squirrel,' said Issy.

'I wouldn't know, I missed squirrel marzipan week at school,' said Austin.

There was a silence. Issy thought she would burst with longing. Why was he calling? Had something changed? Had he changed his mind?

'So?' she said.

'Um,' said Austin. He didn't know how to get the next bit out without sounding like the most terrible heel. 'The thing is,' he said. 'I have to stay on here a bit longer ...'

Issy's heart dropped out through her feet like a plummeting lift. She felt it crack and go, all the way down down down, and smash to bits, far, far below.

All she said was, 'Oh.'

'And, hem. Well. I wondered ...'

'I can't come out again,' she said, quickly, fiercely. 'I can't. Don't do that to me, Austin.'

Oh Christ, thought Austin. This was going even worse than he'd thought. Although he realised that as he'd made the call, there'd been a bit of him wondering if she might possibly say, 'Darling. Let's forget the last week. Let me fly back over. Let's give it another shot.'

Of course she couldn't. She was up to her elbows in marzipan. He was mad.

'Um, no. No. Of course not,' he muttered. He wondered what Merv would say if he were here. Something straight and to the point, he imagined.

'I wondered if I could have your mother's number.'

Issy almost burst out laughing, but she knew that if she did, the tears would be right behind.

'For what, a date?' she said.

'No, no . . . for Darny. To help with Darny.'

'What, because I flounced off?' she said.

'No,' said Austin. 'You did what you had to do. For him really. He liked her.'

'She liked him.'

'So, maybe . . . I mean, just while I've got a few things to do . . . '

This would be Austin's life from now on, Issy realised. He would always have a few things to do. His phone would always be ringing; his work would always be his priority.

'Of course,' she said. 'I'll need to text it to you when I hang up.'

There was a pause. Neither of them quite knew whether this meant she was about to hang up; and if so, how final it was.

'Issy,' said Austin, eventually.

That was too much. She choked.

'Don't,' she said. 'Don't say it. Please. Just don't. I'll text you the number.'

'No Christmas?' said Darny, gazing at Marian in sheer amazement. 'How can that even be?'

'Don't you do religion at school?' grumbled Marian.

'Yeah,' said Darny. 'We do how all religions are super-great. It's rubbish. And I got kicked out of the class anyway for going on about the Inquisition.'

'They aren't allowed to teach the Inquisition?'

'I brought a book of pictures in,' shrugged Darny. 'Kelise Flaherty threw up all over the whiteboard. Well, she was the *first* one to throw up.'

Marian's lips twitched. 'You remind me of someone,' she said. 'Anyway, we have something much cooler. It's called Hanukkah.'

'Oh yeah. My mate Joel has that. He says it's rubbish.'

'But you get a present every night for eight nights! It's the festival of lights.'

'He says the presents get really rubbish by the end, and him and his sister complained and drew Christmas trees all over the place, so his parents just gave up in the end and had Christmas too. So now he has Hanukkah *and* Christmas.' He glanced up at Marian. 'Maybe I'll do that.'

'Maybe,' said Marian. 'But it's very disrespectful.'

'Good,' said Darny, kicking his chair. His feet didn't quite reach the bottom of the bar stool he was sitting on so he could sip his root beer float.

'Do you like getting into trouble?' asked Marian gently.

Darny shrugged. 'S'all right. If I get into trouble with the teachers, I get into less trouble with the big kids. So, you know. On balance. Teachers hit less.'

Marian smiled. 'I know what you mean. I just used to bunk off all the time.'

'I do that too,' said Darny. 'Only problem is, where we live, everybody knows us. I get spotted by busybodies all the time and they tell Austin and he sighs and makes those big puppy-dog eyes at me. It's rubbish. I wish I lived where nobody knew me. Where did you go when you bunked off?'

'I used to go to the fairground,' said Marian. 'They gave me free goes on the rides.'

'Really?' said Darny. 'That sounds amazing.'

'Well, it had certain . . . consequences,' said Marian. 'I would say I paid for it in the end.'

'Is that a metaphor?' said Darny. 'Or am I meant to understand it right away?'

'You are far too smart for your age,' said Marian. 'If

there was a way of making young people understand any of it, and then actually act on it – ha. Well, I'm sure they'd have discovered it by now. But your mistakes are all yours to make.'

She handed him a small parcel wrapped in brown paper.

'What's this?' said Darny. 'Can I open it now?'

'Have you not been listening to me at all?' said Marian, but with a smile in her croaky voice. 'Of course you can open it.'

Darny did. It was a small square wooden spinning top covered in letters. Marian had expected him to be dismissive of it, but had hoped to explain where it came from and what it meant. She liked this boy. He had something about him.

Instead of casting it aside as a child's toy, though, he picked it up and held it carefully and looked at it from all angles.

'I can't read the letters,' he said. 'They're weird, like something out of *Ben Ten: Alien Force*. Which blows.'

'It's a dreidel,' said Marian. 'You can play games with it.'

Darny spun it in his hands.

'That's right. A long time ago Jewish scholars had to pretend they weren't studying the Talmud – the holy book. So they pretended they were playing a game instead. And tomorrow you'll get another present, and that will be gelt.'

'What's that?'

'You'll see. You'll like it.'

'Can you eat it?'

'In fact, yes. Now, would you like to come for a walk with me?'

'It's freezing outside.'

'To the cinema. It's two blocks – they're showing *Miracle on 34th Street*. I think you'll like it.'

'That sounds like it's for girls,' said Darny dubiously.

'I won't tell a soul,' said Marian.

Chapter Sixteen

Caroline's Turnip Pie Surprise

Chop turnip, mushroom, radishes, Brussels sprouts
and a red onion and put in a dish with a spray of
flax oil. Add cumin (not too much).

Cover with wholemeal pastry. Bake.

Fumigate house. Call out for pizza.

Three days before Christmas, Caroline saw Donald
again. Looking like a very small bear in his footsie pyjamas, he was creeping out of Kate's house. He saw her
looking at him and blinked, his thumb in his mouth.
Caroline gave him a stern look and mounted the impos-
ing stone steps. The house had been remodelled
beautifully by a builder she had had a fling with the year
before. The affair had finished when he'd tried to buy

her a bacon sandwich and they had both realised they had no future together. He was a good builder, though. Immaculate box trees stood either side of the forest-green-painted front door.

'Come on, you,' said Caroline, taking Donald's hand. She rang the bell. No one answered, so she pushed the door open. The nanny was standing exhaustedly over a huge pile of ironing, while the twins charged up and down the stunning stairs, with their freshly painted balustrade and tasteful works of art, hitting each other with sticks.

'Um, missing anyone?' Caroline said. The nanny looked up, a defeated look on her face.

'Oh,' she said. 'Come here. Was he running away again?'

'He's a baby,' said Caroline. 'He's just looking for his mother. Where is she?'

The nanny shrugged. 'In bed. She say she needed lie-in after the jet lag. They just got back from Cyprus.'

'Cyprus?'

Caroline marched up the stairs.

'Kate! KATE!'

A door clicked open.

'Heinke? Could you keep those bloody children quiet for five seconds?'

'Kate?'

Kate was wearing an expensive-looking silk night shirt and yawning widely. Caroline glanced at her watch. It was after eleven; she'd been doing the early shift.

'Good holiday?'

Kate snapped awake. Her eyes went wide.

'Caroline? What on earth are you doing here?'

'Picking your children up off the street. What are *you* doing?'

Kate snorted. 'Oh, thanks for the lecture about children. And who's been doing all the complaining to Richard about school fees?'

Suddenly there was a male voice from behind her in the bedroom. Both women froze.

'Darling, it's no one,' called back Kate, optimistically. But it was too late. Caroline had already recognised the unmistakable tones of her ex-husband. She felt like she'd been punched in the stomach. So this was where the bastard had been hiding! No wonder she and Kate hadn't been getting together so much.

Caroline may have been many things, but she wasn't a coward. She took a deep breath and stood up straight in the face of adversity, just as she'd learned at her hard-ass boarding school.

'Good lord, you do both get around,' she held on to herself long enough to say. 'I hope you used a condom, Richard; remember that time you gave everyone chlamydia?'

Kate went pale and gasped, as Caroline turned on her heel. Downstairs, the nanny was unplugging the iron.

'I quit!' she shouted. 'Is like being slave for crazy woman! I'm going to look for job for non-crazy woman. Bye! Stop losing child!'

The three children started wailing their heads off all over their smart Petit Bateau Breton shirts. Snot was going on the William Morris wallpaper. Donald dropped his juice carton on the pale landing carpet. Caroline carried on out of the house.

'And lock the bloody door behind me for once!' she shouted over her shoulder.

Later, she looked at her handiwork. She had made the children a pie. They were terrified of her cooking; normally she tried to get them to eat raw food. Hermia especially, her daughter, tended, even at the age of nine, to shrink from her mother's highly critical gaze. She consoled herself at school, finishing up the thick stodgy puddings the other girls were already pushing away. It showed.

Caroline added turnip, cabbage, carrot and some pieces of apple for flavouring, and a spray of low-calorie oil. Then she put the pastry over the top. That would cover it up, then she'd suggest that Hermia didn't eat the pastry, just as she herself wouldn't be doing.

Perdita was bustling round the kitchen and looked dubiously at the pie, but a warning look from Caroline soon froze her off. Caroline also fired off an email to her lawyer, demanding additional damages for pain and distress caused by Richard flaunting his infidelity.

Then, at a loose end, with Maya taking the afternoon shift and Issy back, she found herself sitting down with her photo albums. Like many other things in her life, Caroline's photo albums were immaculate. She chose only the best pictures of them all in carefully staged perfect environments – round the fire in the ski chalet, wearing matching jumpers and toasting cups of hot chocolate (Achilles had screamed and refused to touch the snow or go outside; Hermia had been horribly bullied at ski school and woken up with nightmares for five months); on their island getaway (Richard had stayed on the phone to work pretty much the entire time; Caroline had gone mad without childcare and with all the mosquitoes); dressed up for a wedding (Richard had chatted up a bridesmaid, Caroline had burst into tears, the marriage had lasted six months before the bride ran away with the caterer). She smiled ruefully at the expensive albums and the stories they did not tell.

But there were other stories, too, real ones. Hermia putting her nursery angel on the Christmas tree, one branch totally weighed down by decorations (Caroline had immediately tidied the tree up once the children had gone to bed, so it looked nice). She glanced over at this year's tree. It was exquisitely tasteful in silver and white. But it didn't have Hermia's nursery angel on it. Caroline wondered where it had gone.

There was Achilles, in the same kind of footsie baby-gro Donald had been wearing. Her little snuggly boy, who now looked hostile and rebellious if she suggested he change his shirt or put down his DS. He was sitting in Richard's lap; Richard had just unwrapped an enormous, ridiculous puppet he'd brought back from a business trip somewhere. It was a huge gawky parrot with a purple and pink feathered crest and a manic grin. It had been hideous; Caroline had given it to Oxfam the second Christmas was over. In the picture, though, father and son were breathless with laughter and suddenly looked very like each other. It was a beautiful shot.

Caroline swore under her breath. Perdita had left, and the house – secondary glazed, of course, well set back from the road – suddenly seemed very quiet, only the ticking of the beautifully restored pale French grand-father clock in the hall disturbing the silence. Caroline didn't want to look at photo albums any more. She wanted to gather her children close to her, feed them pie, apologise on some level for the family she had put in the photo albums, and the family they had turned out to be.

On impulse, she went to pick them up from school – normally they stayed late for homework hour so she could have some me-time. The other mothers at the gate smiled at her nervously, but didn't engage her in conversation. Obviously they thought divorce was catch-ing, like nits. Caroline ignored them. She also ignored the surprise – and, if she was being completely honest, worry – on the children's faces as they emerged in their smart hats and blazers, marshalled by a teacher who looked suspicious that they were skipping homework club.

'Is anything wrong?' said Achilles.

'Nothing at all, darling,' lied Caroline. 'I just wanted to see you, that's all.'

'Has something happened to Granny?' asked Hermia.

'No, but don't worry, when it does, you're getting a new pony. No, come on, let's all go home together.'

'I made a decoration!' said Achilles, holding up a mis-shapen Santa with a huge head.

Normally Caroline would have smiled politely. Today she picked it up. 'That's fantastic!' she said. 'Shall we put it on the tree?'

The children looked nervous.

'I thought we weren't allowed to touch the tree,' said Achilles.

'I would never say that,' said Caroline. 'Did I? Did I say that?'

The children swapped glances.

'OK, OK, never mind. Today it will be different. And I've made supper! Pie!' She caught Achilles' hand. Unusually, he let her hold it.

'What kind of pie?'

'Surprise pie.'

Their faces fell.

'Now, tell me all about your day.'

And to her surprise, they did. Normally she got Perdita to pick them up for karate or swimming or Kumon maths or whatever it was they were supposed to have scheduled that evening. But just walking along with them, she was amazed when Hermia launched into a long and detailed description of how she and Meghan and Martha and Maud had been best friends, but now they couldn't all be best friends and they had said to her that they would let her be best friends again when they'd got enough space and when she didn't have a tummy any more, and Caroline listened carefully to the saga, which Hermia told in a completely flat tone of voice, as if of course it was the way of things that a group of small girls would turn on you sometimes and explain that you couldn't be in their gang any more. She looked at Hermia's wilfully black, tufty hair, inherited directly from Richard, and mentally contrasted it, as she so often did, with the smooth blonde locks of her friends' daughters. Then she gave Hermia a big hug.

'Are you looking forward to Christmas?' she said.

Hermia shrugged. 'Don't know,' she said. 'I get scared at Grandma Hanford's.' Richard's mother was a terrifying old horsey bag who lived out in the middle of nowhere in a spooky old house that she refused to heat.

'Never mind,' said Caroline. 'We'll have a proper celebration the next day.'

When they arrived home, Achilles unpacked his

school bag. There were mountains of books and home-work.

'I know for a fact that Louis McGregor gets no home-work till he's nine,' said Caroline. 'Do you get this much every night?'

Achilles winced, and suddenly his face, which often seemed discontented and mulish to Caroline, looked simply exhausted. He was such a little boy. Such a small thing to be sitting in rows at old-fashioned desks, com-peting with other children who were also overscheduled and anxious and doing their best to please everyone. Caroline stroked his face. She wondered if it would really be the worst thing in the world if Richard stopped paying the school fees. Maybe if they went to Louis' school, with their black history months and potato cut-outs and . . . No. That would be ridiculous.

A horrible smell was coming from the kitchen.

'Shall we see if this pie is really terrible?' she said. 'And if it is, shall we call out for pizza?'

'Can we eat it in front of the TV?' said Achilles, pouncing on their mother's moment of weakness. Between the Aubusson carpet and the pristine reclaimed oak floors, this was absolutely verboten; no food, shoes, wine or animals were allowed in Caroline's front room. It was, she liked to tell the interviewer in the imaginary *Homes and Gardens* piece she occasionally did in her head, her oasis; a sanctuary from the hustle and bustle of London life. She would add that she often used the room to perform her meditations, even though she'd given up meditating when the divorce had started, because when she wasn't busy doing something, she started thinking about how much she wanted to kill Richard.

Caroline rolled her eyes. 'OK. Just this once.'

She scanned through the Sky TV guide.

'It's Christmas. They must be showing *The Wizard of Oz*.'

They were.

Issy's favourite Christmas song was Sufjan Stevens singing 'Only At Christmas Time'. It was so beautiful, and at the moment she seemed to be hearing it everywhere. It accompanied her as she did a huge food shop (Helena had come with her, then Chadani Imelda had kicked off like a maniac at the selection boxes, so Issy had sent them home), its refrain following her up and down the aisles: 'Only to bring you peace/ Only at Christmas time/ Only the King of Kings ... Only what once was mine'.

She felt as if she was regarding the world from behind a fuzzy mask, or through the wrong end of a telescope; all around her were families – she had none – and children – no – and happy couples giggling and pointing at mistletoe, and here she was piling loads of sprouts into the trolley because Ashok's relatives were vegetarian, and even though Ashok had assured her that they'd bring food, she was hardly going to greet guests with empty plates and a hopeful expression.

She threw in pâté and stuffing and mounds of potatoes and lots of nuts for the nut roast, and tutted loudly at the ingredients in the mince pies, and added an extra four boxes of crackers. Ashok had insisted on paying for the food, but as many of his relatives didn't drink either, she reckoned she'd have to do the booze, or perhaps everyone could contribute. She stood in front of the special seasonal shelves of spirits and liqueurs and lots of things she couldn't imagine people wanting to drink ordinarily, and sighed. She didn't know how she'd feel on the day; whether her awful black mood would bring everyone else down and she'd have to get a bit squiffy to perk herself up. Or the opposite; she'd be able to put a brave face on it until she'd had a couple of glasses, then she'd be a puddle on the floor.

A woman, younger than her, pushed a buggy into her and grimaced apologetically. 'Sorry,' she said. 'It's just so busy.'

'Not at all,' said Issy. 'Not at all. It's me who was ... just standing ...'

The woman smiled. 'Oh, you're so lucky. If I stop moving, he screams the place down.'

Issy smiled politely. She didn't feel lucky.

'So are we going home, or what?' said Darny. They were back in the New York City Cupcake Store. Kelly-Lee was absolutely triumphant when she saw that Issy had gone.

'Will she be back soon?' she asked pointedly. Austin tried to half-smile at her in a distracted way, then forgot about her completely.

'We can't go to Issy's mum's,' said Darny. 'They don't have Christmas.'

Austin bit his lip. He knew Issy wasn't staying at his house. He called the number deep into the night, letting it ring on and on, even though he knew it was stupid, and pointless. Although he guessed she must be at Helena's, he didn't call there. Just dialled his own number, letting it go, letting himself imagine, just for a second, that she'd creep downstairs in that terrible old fleece he had left over from his diving days, complaining about the cold wooden floors, which creaked everywhere, and stand, bouncing up and down on the tips of her toes, telling him off for ringing her so late when she had to get up so early, then immediately forgiving him.

'No,' he said. 'Merv's invited us out with his family. If we want to. He said there'll be millions of them there, we'll fit right in.'

Darny stared glumly at his stale apple and cinnamon muffin.

'We won't,' he said. 'We'll be the weirdo foreigners with the funny accents that everyone wants to pinch.'

'I know,' said Austin. 'But here's the thing . . . '

He remembered last year. Giggling under the duvet. Refusing to get dressed, but wearing their 'formal pyjamas' that Issy packed away the next day and insisted they could only have on special occasions. Playing chicken with the Quality Streets until only the toffee ones were left. And later, when Darny had gone to bed, Issy had lit the candles and put in her new diamond earrings, and her pale skin had glowed in the light . . .

Austin blinked twice, hard. No. It was time to come back to reality. To do what he always did: make the best of it. Which meant it was time to break the news to Darny. He took the letter out of his pocket.

'Here's the thing, Darny. And I know I'm supposed to be cross with you, but I don't really know how, because I think, apart from the fact that you're really, really annoying, that you're doing brilliantly well.'

'Shut up,' said Darny, reading the letter upside down. The swagger left his face and he immediately seemed about two years younger. 'Expulsion? Really?'

Austin shrugged. 'Oh come on, Darny, you've been asking for it.'

'True,' said Darny.

'You really pushed it with them.'

'Hmm.'

'And you hated that school.'

'I hated that school.'

Darny swallowed. He was, Austin saw, genuinely upset.

'I thought ... I kind of hoped ... '

'What?'

Darny kicked the table leg. 'It's stupid ... '

'What?'

Darny grimaced. 'I thought they might kind of come round ... maybe think that kids should have a voice.'

Austin sat back. 'Tell me this isn't about your Children Should Vote campaign.'

'We *should*,' said Darny. 'Nobody listens to us.'

'That's all anybody does,' said Austin. 'Oh, bloody hell. They're going to bring this up when you're bloody prime minister.'

Darny suddenly looked very tiny.

'I didn't mean ... I didn't think it would be a big problem for you.'

Austin took perhaps the deepest breath of his life. 'No,' he said. 'No, you didn't. Because you are eleven, and you can't think like that yet. But oh, Darny. I really wish you had.'

'Am I going to have to go to King's Mount?' said Darny, with a note of panic in his voice. 'They skin kids there, Austin. Especially wee kids. Remember that gang who branded all those year sevens?'

'I do remember,' said Austin sombrely. King's Mount was very rarely out of the local paper. 'And that's why,' he glanced round, 'that's why I think we're just going to stay here, Darny. They have amazing schools here, places you wouldn't believe, that like independent thinkers and do all sorts of amazing, cool things, and you'll get to meet kids from all over the world, and, well, I really think you'd like it . . . '

'We're staying? In New York?'

Darny looked at him. Austin was prepared for tears, shouting, defiance – anything but this.

'All right!' said Darny, punching the air. 'Can't be worse than that shit hole. Cool! I wish Stebson could see me now! Living in New York! Yeah! When's Issy coming back?'

'She . . . she might not be,' said Austin. 'It's hard for her to leave the shop.'

'Don't be stupid,' said Darny. 'Of course she can leave the shop, there's loads of people there.'

'It's not quite that simple,' said Austin. 'It's her business.'

Darny just stared at him. 'She's not coming?'

Kelly-Lee came over. 'Is everything OK over here? And I'm sorry, I couldn't help overhearing – is it true you're staying?'

'Looks like it,' said Austin.

'Oh, that's WUNNERFUL! I'll be your new friend.' She put her hand on his shoulder. 'Show you around. And you, sweetie. I'm sure we're going to be the best of friends.'

Darny looked at her without saying anything and

295

rudely kicked the table. After a while he said quietly, 'I think it was me. I think it was my fault.'

Austin squinted at him. 'What?'

'That Issy's not coming.'

'You think you drove Issy away?'

'I was bad at school, then I was mean to her.' Darny's face was terribly distressed. 'I didn't mean to, Austin. I didn't mean to. I'm sorry. I'm sorry.'

'Ssh, sssh,' said Austin, who suddenly found himself wanting to swear. 'No. Of course not. Of course it wasn't you. She loves you.'

Darny started to cry.

'It was me,' said Austin. 'Being a selfish idiot. And things moving and changing and me thinking, like an idiot, that it would be great and I should just go along with it, and well, here we are ...'

Darny no longer looked like a truculent pre-teen. He looked like an upset, terrified little boy.

'Please make her come back,' he said. 'Please, Austin.'

Austin swallowed hard. He didn't answer.

Chapter Seventeen

Issy had unpacked all the food and drink down in the basement, along with as many small random gifts as she'd been able to grab charging through Boots in a tearing hurry. Upstairs, Maya was still on her rounds, and Pearl and Caroline were bickering happily about what age children should be told the truth about Santa Claus. Caroline felt that if the parents had worked hard for the money, children should appreciate that and learn the cost of things. Pearl did not agree. It was the Saturday before Christmas, and Louis was making a Santa beard for himself out of a huge roll of cotton wool and cardboard and sticky tape. He also had a Santa hat on that Big Louis had given him, and was smiling benignly at other children coming into the shop.

'I'm not the real Santa,' he said helpfully to one little girl. 'Would you like a beard?'

The little girl nodded, and before long Louis had turned his handiwork into a thriving cottage industry. Eventually a small woman who'd come in by herself and ordered only a green tea, then looked around for a long time and started writing furiously in a small notebook, leant over.

'Can I have one?' she said.

'Yes,' said Louis. 'But don't pretend to be Santa Claus. You aren't him.'

'I don't think anyone would ever mistake me for Santa Claus.'

'Or a pleesman. You're not allowed to dress up as a pleesman.'

The woman looked puzzled and assured Louis she had no intention of masquerading as a policeman.

'Sorry,' said Pearl through her thick white beard. 'His dad let him watch *Terminator 2* and it scared him half to death.'

'I'm not surprised,' said the woman. 'It scared me half to death and I'm grown up.'

Louis fixed her with his warm brown eyes.

'It's not real, lady. It just in a film. Go back to sleep.'

The woman suddenly cracked open a huge grin and shut her notebook with a clunk. She turned towards Pearl.

'OK, OK,' she said. 'I give up. I've had enough. It's nearly Christmas and I'm really knackered.' She stepped up to the counter and held out her hand to shake. 'Abigail Lester. *Super Secret London Guide*. Style section.'

Pearl took her hand politely without having the faintest idea why.

'Um, hello.'

Caroline threw herself across the counter like a skinned cat.

'A-BIGAIL!' she screeched, as if they were dearest friends. The woman looked rather nonplussed.

'Um, is this your establishment?' she said.

'No, it belongs to the girl crying downstairs in the basement,' said Pearl. 'Hang on. ISSY!'

'Can I offer you a complimentary cake ... cup of hot chocolate? Glass of wine? We don't serve wine, but we keep some for Friday nights ...' Caroline was babbling, and Pearl still couldn't figure it out.

'No, no thanks. I can tell by the happy punters that everything's just lovely.'

Issy clumped up the stairs feeling red-eyed and dull. It was as if the jet lag she'd brought back from the States had never gone away, but thickened, and deepened, and settled into her skin, as if she wanted to wake up, rouse herself, but couldn't, because she knew that if she was wide awake, she would see the world as it was: a space where Austin was thousands of miles away and always would be.

'Congratulations,' someone was saying. Issy squinted and noticed the slender girl with the blonde hair. 'We'll officially announce it in the next issue, but you win our best-decorated independent shop award.'

Issy blinked.

'It's the little man that swung it,' Abigail said, looking at Louis, who knew he'd done something good and was waiting to find out exactly what. 'Giving free Santa beards away is a level of customer service that just goes above and beyond. Well done, young man.'

'Thank oo very much,' said Louis, without prompting.

'So, we'll send a photographer round ... And there'll be a cheque for five hundred pounds. Congratulations!'

Abigail obviously expected Issy to say something, but Issy couldn't do much more than mumble her thanks.

'Of course, the concept was all mine,' said Caroline, moving in closer. 'I can take you through all my suppliers and my many inspirations in the world of interior design.'

'Well, I would like that,' said Abigail. 'Here's my card. We'll give you a call next week in the doldrums after Christmas – nice and quiet to take the pics.'

Caroline snatched the card before Issy could even raise her hand.

'Will do! Mwah! Mwah!'

As Abigail departed, to a kiss from Louis, wearing her beard, Caroline turned round in triumph.

'What just happened?' asked Issy wearily.

'Best-decorated shop! I KNEW we could win it. I think it was probably my clever *trompe l'oeil* tinsel.'

'I'm sure it was,' said Issy, trying to muster a smile. They'd done well without her after all. This gave her a bittersweet feeling. 'Five hundred pounds, eh? Well, I reckon you should split it as an extra Christmas bonus. I can advance it to you if you like.'

'Well, conceptually speaking it was really my ...' began Caroline, but a quick look from Issy stopped her. Pearl's heart leapt, but she didn't want to be unfair.

'It *was* Caroline's concept,' she said. 'And she did enter us.'

Caroline looked at Pearl, amazed at her generosity.

'No chance,' said Issy. 'It was Louis' beards, she said so herself. If anything, it should be his. Plus, you've been cleaning and dusting all those new decorations every day.'

Caroline couldn't bear anyone being magnanimous without her.

'Of course I wouldn't dream of taking more than my fair share,' she said. 'And, after all, it's not like I need the money.'

Pearl and Issy smiled at one another, and Issy, looking round at the beautiful shop, and the happy punters, felt that surely she ought to be able to squeeze a bit of Christmas spirit out, somewhere.

'I have made your beard for you here,' said Louis seriously, holding up stuck-together cotton wool and cardboard with sellotape loops for her ears.

'Thank you, Louis,' said Issy. And she put it on.

The traditional crate of wine – clearly her mother hadn't realised she'd moved house – arrived at the flat on Christmas Eve. It was kosher, she noticed. She called Marian, but no luck. Anyway, she supposed her mother didn't celebrate Christmas any more. Not that she ever had, not really.

Everything was ready for tomorrow, all the food prepped and covered in cling film, ready to pop into the big industrial ovens at the café. They could peel all the potatoes tomorrow, but there were many hands for the job. All the bits and bobs like cranberry sauce and buttered cabbage Issy had happily outsourced to Marks & Spencer. The kosher wine would join the bottles of champagne contributed by Caroline and the two bottles of whisky given to Ashok by a grateful patient.

She and Helena sat up late, chatting, as they wrapped presents for Chadani Imelda, who didn't know what was happening but knew something was, so was using it as an excuse to stay up late. Ashok was dealing with her. Every so often he would run past the sitting room door pursuing a tiny shrieking girl holding a dirty nappy above her head, and Helena and Issy would ignore it.

They were talking about the future.

'The flat above the café has come up,' Issy was saying. 'He's not sure whether to rent it or sell it. He reckons he'll get more for it because of where it is. So, basically, I've priced myself out of it just by making nice baking smells.'

'Well, see if he'll let you lease it. He already knows you're a good tenant. Then you can decide what you want to do later.'

'Hmm, maybe,' said Issy.

'And we won't be here for much longer,' pointed out Helena. 'As soon as I start working again, we'll get a bigger mortgage and move. We need a garden for Chadani Imelda anyway.'

Chadani Imelda was now riding Ashok like a horse and giggling uncontrollably.

'So you could have this place back.'

'I could,' said Issy, looking at the pink kitchen and the nice old faded floral armchairs, currently completely hidden under mountains and mountains of presents. 'I don't know. Maybe it's time to move on.'

'I've registered,' said Helena. 'With a nursing agency. Look.' She held up a sheaf of forms.

'Wow,' said Issy. 'What did you say when they asked why you wanted to come back?'

'I said, darlings, I can be fabulous simultaneously in many arenas.'

'Like that?'

'Yes, exactly like that. No, don't be stupid. I just reminded them how lucky they'd be to have me, and not to ask such impertinent questions.'

'Heh,' said Issy.

'Now, look away,' said Helena. 'I need to wrap your present.'

'Oh, don't be daft,' said Issy.

'I mean it! Look away, or you're not getting it.'

Grumbling, Issy went and stood in the doorway. Chadani Imelda now had pants on her head. Ashok was growling at her and pretending to be a bear. Issy watched them, smiling. It was a nice sight. Ashok realised she was watching and looked up at her. He stopped growling.

'You could have had this,' he said, seriously.

Issy felt herself stiffen.

'You two. You were very silly.'

'Ashok, STOP THAT THIS INSTANT!' came a voice from the sitting room that brooked no argument.

'I just want Isabel to be happy. Do you not want Isabel to be happy? You want her off renting new flats and opening new shops instead of saying well, Isabel, it was nice when you were happy because your friends were also happy so everyone was happy.'

'I'm warning you,' came the voice again.

Issy choked up. 'It wasn't my fault,' she said. 'I'm not the one who left.'

'Are you sure about that?'

'I'll be fine.'

Ashok gathered Chadani into his arms and nuzzled her soft olive cheek.

'I want you to be better than fine, Isabel.'

Helena stomped through.

'BED. Bed bed bed. For everyone.'

Chapter Eighteen

Figgy Pudding Cupcakes

100g unsalted butter

100g treacle

50g sugar

2 eggs

1 tsp cinnamon

1 tsp ground ginger

½ tsp cardamom

½ tsp ground cloves

250g all-purpose flour

25g unsweetened cocoa powder

½ tsp baking soda

2 tsp baking powder

1 tsp salt

100ml milk

1 tsp brandy
1 tsp vanilla

Preheat oven to 170°C/gas mark 3 and butter cupcake tin.

Combine dry ingredients and sift; set aside.

Cream butter, treacle and sugar on medium-high speed until fluffy. Add eggs, one at a time, beating until each is incorporated, then add vanilla and brandy.

Mix in the dry ingredients in three batches, alternating with two additions of milk, and beating until combined after each.

Bake for about 20–22 minutes. Ice if you like with brandy butter icing.

'HAPPY CWISMAS! HAPPY CWISMAS EVERY-BODY!'

Louis kissed his mother and grandmother hard.

'It's five thirty,' said Pearl. 'Go back to sleep.'

'SANNA CLAUS DID COME.'

Louis was pointing excitedly to the stocking under the little stubby tree they reused every year, and which was covered in his creations. Pearl had kept back his large gift till they got to the café; there was nowhere to hide it where they lived. But he had his little things, all wrapped.

'Can you go back to sleep?' she asked groggily. She felt bone-tired still, and the flat was freezing. She didn't keep the heating on overnight and there'd been a really cold snap.

'NOOO.' Louis shook his head vehemently to show how much he really couldn't. Pearl couldn't begin to imagine how you could get a four-year-old to go back to sleep on Christmas morning.

'All right then,' she said. 'Do you want to open your stocking really quietly . . . '

'I'm cold, Mamma.'

'. . . really quietly in the bed?'

Louis clambered in happily beside her, and proceeded to very noisily unwrap the cheaply sellotaped gifts Pearl had put together late the previous evening.

'MAMMA! A TOOFBRUSH!' he cried out in delight. 'AN I GOT AN ORANGE! AND SOME CHOCOLATES! AND SOCKS! Oh, socks,' he said in a slightly more normal tone.

'Yes, but they're monster garage socks,' said Pearl.

Louis' eyes darted round the room. There was not – could not be – a parcel big enough to be a monster garage. He tried to look nonchalant.

'I doan care about monster garage,' he said quietly.

Pearl was suddenly wide awake, pulsing with adrenalin. She'd sneaked the monster garage in after the shop was closed; rushing down to Argos with Issy's cheque only just deposited, heart in her mouth, clammy with excitement. She knew she had to put some of that money to one side, keep the power key charged and for the inevitable rises in her transport costs which were due in January. Really she ought, she realised as she fought her way through the freezing winds, to buy herself a new winter coat. This one was so thin ... and she'd love some of those cosy-looking sheepskin boots girls seemed to wear these days. But no. She was going to make this one purchase. This one day.

'Do you have a monster garage?' she said, bursting into the shop, wild-eyed. She'd been panicked all day that there would be none left; the most successful toy of the year. There had been a piece in the paper about a fight breaking out in a large toy shop over the last one; apparently they were changing hands on eBay for hundreds of pounds. But she had to try. She had to.

A silence had fallen over the shop, and Pearl registered that it had started to sleet outside and had soaked through her thin coat, then remembered that you didn't ask for what you wanted in Argos, you filled in a piece of paper. Everyone was looking at her. Then the nice girl had smiled. 'You are totally in luck,' she said. 'Our last delivery got delayed. It's only just arrived, far too late for most people. I've had people swearing at me for a week for one of these.'

She paused, dramatically.

'But yes, we have one.'

As Pearl filled in the order slip with shaking hands,

she heard people all round her on their phones –
'They've got them! They've got monster garages' – and
starting to rush their orders in. People began to fill the
store, drawn by the news.

'Whoops,' said the girl as Pearl took hold of the large,
brightly coloured box. 'Looks like you've caused a stam-
pede.'

Pearl had bought a sheet of terribly expensive, unutterably wasteful silver wrapping paper too, and made up
the parcel reverently with a giant red bow, then hidden
it under the oven until the next day.

She was nearly back home when her phone rang.

'Pearl,' Caroline was saying. 'I need some of that
money back.'

'Well,' said Pearl, trying to keep the excitement out of
her voice. 'Remember, Santa knows you go to the
Cupcake Café. I think he might have stopped there.
Remember, they have a real chimney.'

'OH YES,' said Louis, brightening up immediately.
He dived back into his stocking and came up with a
packet of stickers.

'STICKERS!'

'Can you be a bit quieter?'

'Can you tell Santa I didn't really mean it when I said
I din care bout monster garage?'

'I'm sure Santa knows that already.'

'Like Baby Jesus.'

'Exactly.'

'Thank you for the pwesents, Baby Jesus.'

Pearl decided to let that one roll. With a slight groaning noise, she pushed herself off the bed and went to light the Calor gas heater and make a cup of coffee. It was going to be a long day.

⊕

Caroline woke alone in the emperor-sized bed with its pristine Egyptian cotton sheets and numerous rolls, cushions, pillows and bits and bobs (less of a bed, more of a haven for the real me, she liked to think). At first she felt a stab of pain at waking up alone on Christmas morning.

Then she remembered the previous day. Outside, all had been sleet and freezing wind. Nonetheless, violin lessons and rugby were still on – many parents felt it wasn't ideal to give children holidays, as it made them slack. Hermia and Achilles had got up obediently enough and were just getting dressed when Caroline appeared in their bedrooms.

'Well,' she announced, still wearing her long Japanese robe. 'I have decided.'

The children looked at her.

'It is disgusting weather outside. Who wants to stay in all day and not get changed out of their pyjamas?'

The children had roared their approval. So Caroline had turned the heating up (normally she felt a hot house was terribly common and bad for the skin) and they had watched *Mary Poppins*, then played snakes and ladders, then Achilles had had a nap (overscheduled and at a demanding school, he was almost constantly tired, which explained, Caroline realised, why he whined all the time and why Louis almost never did. Caroline had put it down to Louis getting everything he wanted. She was beginning to suspect this might not be the case), and she and Hermia went upstairs and Caroline let her try on all her make-up and clothes and looked at her in the mirror and realised how her beautiful little girl would, any minute now, be turning into a beautiful adolescent (if she could improve her posture, she couldn't help thinking), and that she would need to be armed for that.

Then she had ordered in noodles for supper and cracked open a box of chocolates afterwards, and they had sat round the tree and Caroline had had a glass of champagne and let them both taste it, then they had opened their gifts.

Unlike last year, Caroline wasn't trying to make a point this year. She wasn't trying to hurt Richard by throwing in his face how well she knew the children, or how they were her kids first, or how much of his money she could spend on them. She'd simply thought about them, and got them what she thought they would like, regardless of whether it would clutter up her minimalist space, or whether she thought it would interfere with them getting into good universities.

So Hermia had a Nintendo with a fashion design program on it, and some fashion dolls, and Achilles had a Scalextric, which she even had the time and energy to sit down and piece together with him; and because the children were both getting so much of her attention, she noticed, they didn't bicker and snarl at one another.

This seems remarkably easy, thought Caroline. Perhaps I should write a book on the subject and become an international guru, like that woman in France. Then she looked around the sitting room, which was now an utterly disgusting mess, and burped those noodles she really oughtn't to have eaten, and wondered if Perdita would mind coming in on Christmas Day, and realised perhaps she couldn't be a parenting guru.

But she could do her best.

Richard arrived in the evening, expecting the usual litany of bitter complaints and sullen children and shining resentment, all fermented in the immaculate house whose mortgage he kept up and whose cleaning he paid for.

Instead, the house was a terrible tip, and the children were – were they laughing? Were they all laughing? Was Caroline wearing pyjamas? Pyjamas must have come back in fashion, then; they must be Stella McCartney and had probably cost him a fortune.

'Daddy!' the children had yelled. 'Come and see what we got! And what we've been doing.'

Richard half smiled nervously at Caroline. Kate, as it

turned out, was being just as difficult as Caroline – particularly about money, attention and general attitude. He cursed, yet again, his taste in aerobicised blondes. But Caroline seemed in a mellow mood.

'Well, I have a bottle of champagne open,' she said. 'If you want to come in for five minutes?'

He had. And they had managed to sit and talk, civilly, whilst the children played in the wreckage of the Christmas paper, about finishing off the divorce and finding a way to move forward, and Caroline might have mentioned that she had heard Kate wanted a huge second wedding party, incredibly luxurious, just for the pleasure of seeing him blanch a little, but on the whole she was on her best behaviour and they managed to toast the day like adults.

And for the first time, Caroline on Christmas morning, sitting up in bed looking at the gifts from the children, which she would open when she saw them that evening, didn't feel vengeful, or lonely, or angry. She felt, tentatively . . . OK.

Then she remembered the disgusting mess she was going to have to clean up in the kitchen, and sighed.

Issy woke with Chadani Imelda clambering on her face. Fair enough, she was in her room, although Chadani had insisted on sleeping with her mother since she was born (Ashok pretended he didn't mind; Helena told a barefaced lie to anyone who asked her about it). It was rather nice, actually, the toddler sleigh bed with its brand-new mattress and pristine White Company sheets.

For a second, she almost forgot what was happening.

'GAHAHABAGAGA!' said Chadani Imelda, her little face right up to Issy's, drool dripping from her mouth on to Issy's nose.

'Oh, yes,' said Issy out loud. 'My life is over and yours is just beginning, I remember. Good morning, Chadani Imelda! Merry Christmas!' And she kissed her.

Then she had to stand, clutching her coffee cup, for forty-five minutes whilst Helena and Ashok and Chadani, all dressed in matching red outfits, opened their gifts. They had presents for Issy too, of course, but mostly she took family photographs. Finally, the acres of wrapping paper were cleared away and Chadani Imelda had completely ignored her first computer, her first beauty bag, her miniature car and her new spotty Dalmatian fur coat in favour of trying to consume large quantities of bubble wrap. Then the door rang, and it was Ashok's family, all of them carrying vast tupperware boxes full of fragrant-smelling food and gigantic gifts for Chadani. Issy slipped off and got changed quietly, glancing outside at the grey sky. There was snow coming down; not much, but enough to powder the streets and chimney tops of Stoke Newington; the Victorian terraces and grand villas and occasional tower blocks and big mish-mash of lovely London all silent in the Christmas-morning hush. Issy leaned her head against the window pane.

'I miss you, Gramps,' she said softly. Then she put on the plain navy blue dress she'd bought that looked smart, though also, she realised, not really very festive. Well, that didn't matter, she'd be in a pinny all day. Which was the best way. She glanced out at the quiet city again and didn't voice who else she missed. Love was not a choice. But work was. She rolled up her sleeves.

'OK you lot,' she said to Ashok's family; Chadani's four aunties were cooing vigorously over her, whilst discussing competitively at the top of their lungs the most recent achievements of their own children. It was going to be a noisy day. She could do with a couple of hours to clear her head. 'I'll see you down at the café after you've had breakfast.'

Austin was dreaming. In his dream he was back there, back at the Cupcake Café. Then he woke up with a horrible start, his head throbbing. What had happened last night? Oh God, he remembered. Darny had been staying at Marian's, and Merv had taken Austin out for a couple of drinks, then he'd had a couple more on his own, which was stupid, because American drinks as far as he could tell were made from pure alcohol, then, unsteady on his feet, he'd tried to get back to his hotel and he'd run into that girl from the cupcake shop, almost as if she'd been hanging around waiting for him, and she'd helped him stagger on a little bit, then pushed him backwards in the snow and made what he supposed was meant to be a sexy face at him, then tried to snog him! And he had pushed her away and explained that he had a girlfriend and she'd just laughed and said, well, she didn't appear to be here, and had tried to snog him again. He'd got quite cross with her then, and she'd got really really annoyed and started yelling at him about how nobody understood her problems.

It got quite blurry after that, but he'd made it back to the hotel in one piece. It wasn't an evening he was particularly proud of. Great. Happy Christmas. And here he was, awake at an ungodly hour of the morning and all by himself. Brilliant. Well done, Austin, with your great new successful life and new successful career. It's all working out brilliantly. Well done.

He guessed he'd better go and get Darny. His PA hated him, it was clear; fortunately this was fine by him and he'd already put in for an urgent transfer for Janet, whose only son lived in Buffalo. Still, MacKenzie had asked him if he wanted any Christmas shopping done; apparently this was normal behaviour from support staff. So he'd asked her to get what she thought a fourteen-year-old boy would like (Darny wasn't even twelve yet, but Austin figured this would probably suit him) and she had come back with a pile of gift-wrapped shapes that she had thrown on his desk, so he didn't actually have the faintest clue what Darny was getting for Christmas. But the subways were running all day, so he was heading out to Queens to see Marian. It seemed on the one hand absolutely ludicrous that he was spending Christmas Day with his ex's mother. On the other, she'd assured him that they didn't do Christmas, that they would be eating Chinese food in a restaurant and they were quite welcome to sit on the sofa watching movies in their pyjamas all afternoon, which compared to Merv's exhausting schedule of party games and family in-jokes sounded just the tonic. He hauled himself out of bed and took a very, very long bath.

It was definitely droplets of steam on his face, he told himself. He absolutely and positively wasn't crying.

'Only to bring you peace . . . '

The song was playing again on the radio. Issy had peeled four thousand potatoes and was about to start on three thousand carrots. But she didn't mind really. There was something about the repetition of the work, and the forced bonhomie of the DJ, who was, presumably, at work on Christmas Day all by himself, and the sweet familiarity of the songs – ones you liked (Sufjan) and ones you didn't (Issy was done with travelling space-men). Then she switched channels and listened to the boys singing carols from King's, even though listening to the boys made her think of Darny and even though Darny actually hated to sing anyway.

The turkey was glistening and turning golden in the

oven, along with a beautiful glazed ham; the Brussels sprouts were ready to go, as was the red cabbage. She had tins of goose fat to make the best roast potatoes, and was planning on whipping up a fabulous pavlova for dessert; she liked to get the meringue just right. So everything was ticking over perfectly. Fine. Lovely.

At eleven, everyone started to file in; first Pearl, who had been up for a long time, and who immediately put on her pinny and wanted to clean. Issy tried to stop her. Louis was dancing along in her wake, full of chatter about church and the sweets the minister had given him and the singing and how Caroline had come to pick them up in her BIG CAR ('I like you more now I saw your car,' he had announced, to Pearl's utter horror, but Caroline had, amazingly, laughed it off and rumpled Louis' tight curls); then all Ashok's family had piled in, and Issy regretted immediately making all the vegetarian food, or indeed any food at all given the sheer heft that they had brought, and everything in the kitchen downstairs took on a spicier, more unusual tang and Caroline opened the first bottle of champagne.

Then, first things first, everyone scuffled around quickly under the tree so they could put out each other's gifts. Then everyone went very shy and said you first, no, you first, but actually it was totally obvious that it should be Louis first, so Issy went in and found his packages and hauled them out.

'Well, that's odd,' said Helena.

And it was. Because there were five large square packages, all exactly the same size and shape. Louis' eyes
were like saucers.

'I said Santa would pass by here,' said Pearl, sending
him forward. He ripped into the first one – Pearl's, with
the beautiful silver wrapping and the huge red ribbon.

There was an enormously long pause. Then Louis
turned round to his mother, his eyes huge, shining with
unspilt tears, his mouth hanging open in shock and
amazement.

'SANTA BWOUGHT ME A MONSTER
GARAGE!'

Then everyone looked at the four other, identically
shaped parcels, and realised immediately what had happened.

There was one from Issy, who had spent her lunch hour
running down to Hamleys and paying a fortune for it.
There was one from Ashok and Helena, who had ordered
theirs online months ago. One from Caroline, beautifully
wrapped. Pearl's, of course. And the last one Pearl couldn't
figure out at all. Then it dawned on her. It was from
Doti. She shook her head in disbelief. She thought it was
because everyone loved Louis so much. She didn't realise
that it wasn't only Louis.

'Santa's made a mistake,' she said, cuddling him. 'I'm
sure we can take the others back.' She waggled her eyebrows furiously at the others.

'I believe Santa trades things in for other toys,' said

Issy loudly, digging in her wallet for the receipt. 'No wonder there was such a shortage.'

Louis didn't say anything at all. He was lying down right across the shop, oblivious to everyone else, making all the different monster noises and car noises and monster truck noises and talking to each monster in turn. He was completely in everybody's way. Nobody minded at all.

Pearl slipped off to text Doti. Then she added at the end, 'pop round if you're free xx'. Just as she was about to send it, a movement at the window caught her eye. She glanced up. It was Ben, whom she hadn't seen since that fight. He was looking apologetic, with his hands open.

She went to the door.

'Hey,' she said.

'Hey,' he said, looking at the ground.

'Look,' he said. 'You were right. I shouldn't have had that damn garage. I bought it off a bloke in the pub.'

'*Ben*,' said Pearl, bitterly disappointed.

'But I took it back, all right? I knew it was dodgy. I'm sorry. I've been working late shifts. It's only as a security guard, but it's work, right? Look, I'm still in my uniform.'

She looked at him. He was.

'It suits you, that uniform.'

'Shut up,' he said, running his eyes up and down the curves of Pearl's soft old wool dress, the best thing she owned. It still suited her.

'Anyway,' he said, handing over a package. 'It's not the garage, right. It's what I could afford. Properly.'

'Come in,' said Pearl. She deleted, quickly, the message on her phone. 'Come on in.'

Everyone greeted him cheerily, and Caroline immediately handed him a glass. Louis jumped up, his grin so wide he looked like he could burst.

'SANTA BROUGHT ME A MONSTER GARAGE,' he said.

'And I brought you this,' said Ben.

Louis ripped the package open. Inside was a pair of pyjamas, covered in monster garage characters. They were fluffy and warm and the right size and exactly what Louis actually needed.

'MONSTER GARAGE JAMAS!' said Louis. He started pulling off his clothes. Pearl thought about stopping him – he was wearing a lovely smart shirt and a new pullover – but at the last minute decided against it.

'Merry Christmas,' she said to the room, raising her glass.

'Merry Christmas,' said everyone back.

After that, it was a present free-for-all. Caroline did her best not to wrinkle her nose at the tasteless candles and knick-knacks that headed her way. Chadani Imelda managed to eat an entire rosette. Louis didn't look up from his garage. Issy, hanging back near the kitchen, noticed that she didn't get any presents, but didn't think much of it.

They had lined up all the tables in a row to make one long table with space for everyone, and Ashok's sisters jostled Issy for space in the kitchen, chatting and laughing and sharing jokes and handing out crackers, and Issy felt herself coasting along and letting the shared comfort of happiness and ease carry her with it. Chester from the ironmonger's shop was there, of course, and Mrs Hanowitz, whose children lived in Australia, and all in all they were a very long table by the time they sat down to eat, slightly drunk, carols playing loudly in the background.

The meal was magnificent. Bhajis and ginger beet curry nestled next to the perfectly cooked turkey, acres of chipolatas and the crunchiest roast potatoes, all delicious. Everyone ate and drank themselves to bursting, except Issy, who didn't feel like it, and Caroline, who couldn't, but did her best with the red cabbage.

At the end of the meal, Ashok stood up.

'Now, I just want to say a few words,' he said, swaying a little bit. 'First of all, thank you to Issy for throwing open her shop – her home – for all of us waifs and strays at Christmas time.'

At this there was much stamping of feet and cheering.

'That was a wonderful meal – thanks to everyone who contributed . . .'

'Hear hear,' said Caroline.

'... and Caroline.'

There was a great deal of laughter and banging of forks.

'OK, I have two orders of business. Firstly, Issy, you may have noticed that you didn't get any Christmas presents?'

Issy shrugged, to say it didn't matter.

'Well, aha! That is not the case!' said Ashok. He lifted up an envelope. 'Here is a small token of our esteem. Of all of our esteem. Oh, and we've hired Maya back.'

'Who's Maya?' Ben asked Pearl. His large hand was squeezing her thigh under the table.

'No one,' said Pearl quickly.

Issy, her hands shaking, opened the envelope. Inside was a return ticket to New York.

'Everyone put in,' said Ashok. 'Because ...'

'Because you're an idiot!' hooted Caroline. 'And you can't borrow my coat again.'

Issy looked at Helena, eyes glistening.

'But I've been ... I tried ...'

'Well, you try again, you bloody idiot,' said Helena. 'Are you nuts? I bet he is totally bloody miserable. Your mum said he is.'

'I like the way everyone gets to chat with my mum except me,' said Issy. She glanced down at the date on the ticket.

'You have to be joking.'

'Nope,' said Caroline. 'Cheapest date to fly. And no time like the present; we've got Maya all of next week.'

'I can't even get to the airport.'

323

'Fortunately I treated a cabbie with renal failure,' said Ashok. 'He asked if there was anything he could do. I said could he drive my friend to Heathrow on Christmas Day. He sighed a lot and looked really grumpy, but he's on his way over.'

'And I packed for you!' said Helena. 'Proper clothes this time you'll be pleased to hear.'

Issy didn't know where to look. Her hand flickered to her mouth, shaking.

'Come on,' said Helena. 'Do you really have anything to lose?'

Issy bit her lip. Her pride? Her self-respect? Well, maybe they didn't mean so much. But she had to know. She had to know.

'Th ... th ... thanks,' she stammered. 'Thank you. Thank you so much.'

'I'll make you up a sandwich for the plane,' said Pearl. 'It's not business class this time.'

Caroline had managed to convince Pearl, when she realised how much Pearl needed the money, that the amount everyone was putting in the pot for the ticket was ten pounds. Pearl had only the fuzziest idea of how much flights cost and had chosen to believe her.

❧

There came a honking outside.

'That's your cab,' said Ashok.

Helena handed her her bag and her passport. Issy had

324

no words. They hugged, then Pearl joined in, then Caroline too, and they were all one big ball.

'Do it,' said Helena. 'Or sort it. Or whatever. OK?'

Issy swallowed. 'OK,' she said. 'OK.'

And the table watched her go out into the snow.

'Now,' said Ashok, swallowing very hard, and taking out a small jeweller's box from his pocket. 'Ahem. I have another order of business.'

But there was a cry from Caroline. Coming out of the snow was the tiny figure of Donald, and directly behind him, chasing after him, were Hermia and Achilles. The baby headed straight for the Cupcake Café and everyone crowded round to welcome him.

'He ran away!' said Hermia.

'We ran away too,' said Achilles. 'It's really boring in there.'

Pearl winked at Caroline.

'Well, I'll put on some hot chocolate and then you're heading straight back,' Caroline said.

Caroline called Richard and he agreed that they could stay for afternoon games. Then there was a pause. 'Actually, could we all come over?' said Richard. 'It's dead boring here.'

Caroline thought.

'No,' she said, but not unkindly. 'It isn't my home to invite you. But we'll speak soon.'

Pearl, stacking the big dishwasher downstairs, wrote a text and deleted it, and wrote another and deleted it again. Then, finally, she texted the simple words, 'Thank you. Merry Christmas' and sent it to Doti. What else was there to say?

'What are you doing down there?' came Ben's deep voice.

'Nothing!' said Pearl.

'Good,' said Ben. 'Because I have an idea of a few things we could do.'

Pearl giggled and told him off, and felt the touch of his warm hand on her face and thought after that simply, Merry Christmas. Merry Christmas.

Chapter Nineteen

Galette de Rois, the Cake of the New Year

30g almond paste

30g white sugar

3 tbsp unsalted butter, softened

1 egg

¼ tsp vanilla extract

¼ tsp almond extract

2 tbsp all-purpose flour

1 pinch salt

1 packet of puff pastry

1 egg, beaten

one favour (traditionally a small china – not
    plastic! – figurine)

icing sugar for dusting

one gold party hat

Preheat oven to 220°C/gas mark 7; line baking sheet with baking paper.

Blend almond paste in the food processor with half the sugar, then add the butter and the rest of the sugar, then the egg, vanilla and almond extracts, then flour and salt.

Roll out one sheet of the puff pastry, about 20cm square. Keep the pastry cool; do not knead or stretch. Cut a large circle. Repeat and chill the circles.

Mound the almond filling on to the centre of one of the pastry circles on the baking sheet. Leave a large margin. Press the figurine down into the filling. Place the second sheet of pastry on top, and seal edges.

Egg-wash the top of the pastry and add slits (artistically if you like).

Bake for 15 minutes in the preheated oven. Do not open the oven until the time is up, as the pastry will not fully puff. Remove from the oven and dust with icing sugar. Return to the oven and cook for an additional 12–15 minutes, or until the top is a deep golden brown. Transfer to a wire rack to cool. Crown with gold party hat. Give gold party hat to whoever gets the favour (or Louis).

Austin turned up at Marian's with a bottle of kirsch, even though he wasn't quite sure why. He instantly felt a bit strange, being the only man there without a beard, but everyone seemed very nice – there were about four families, and dumplings were boiling on top of the stove. There were no decorations up, of course, no cards, no television; nothing to indicate that this wasn't just another day. Which of course it was. To everyone else.

Darny was happily sitting chatting to one of the old men in the sitting room over a small, sticky-looking coffee.

'We're discussing the nature of evil,' said Darny. 'It's great.'

'Is that coffee?' said Austin. 'Great. That's all you need.'

He popped his head round the door. 'Hi, Maria ... Miriam. Do you need a hand?'

'No, no,' said Marian, who was rolling out pastry, very badly.

'OK. Listen, is it all right if I give Darny his presents? I realise it's not really ... '

'No, no, that's fine,' said Marian. 'Half of them get secret presents anyway, we're just not supposed to mention it.' She smiled naughtily.

'You seem really happy here, really settled,' said Austin.

Marian grinned and looked out through the kitchen door. In the sitting room, a man in his fifties, with a long beard and beautiful brown eyes, glanced up, caught the gaze and smiled at her.

'It's all right,' said Marian, colouring. 'Though of course everyone here is too smart for me.'

'Are you pretending to be stupid?' asked Austin, affectionately.

'No, that would be you,' said Marian, giving him a look that reminded him inexorably of her daughter. 'Now, give your brother his gifts. He thinks he isn't getting any.'

'Really?'

Austin went back into the room with the large bag of presents.

'Merry Christmas,' he said.

Darny's eyes widened. 'I thought I wasn't getting any presents.'

'What, because you're Jewish now?'

Darny shook his head. 'No,' he said. 'Because I've been so awful.'

Austin felt as though his heart would crack.

'Darny,' he said, kneeling down. 'Darny, whatever happens ... I never, ever think you're awful. I think you're amazing and brilliant and occasionally a bit tricky ...'

'And in the way.'

'Well, that's not your fault, is it?'

Darny hung his head.

'If ... ' he said. 'If I hadn't got chucked out of school, would we still be living in England with Issy?'

'That doesn't matter,' said Austin. 'It's good that we're here. It's good. Isn't it?'

'So you can make lots of money and work all day and I'll never see you?' said Darny. 'Mmm.'

He sat down and started opening his gifts. Austin looked on, as did the other children, fascinated to see what MacKenzie had bought. There was something called an NFL game for the Wii (which Darny didn't have), and a long basketball shirt that came down to his knees and looked like a dress, and a baseball cap with a propeller on the top. Darny looked up at Austin. 'I don't know what any of this is for,' he said quietly. 'Is it to make me American?'

'Don't you like it?' said Austin.

Darny looked down, desperate not to appear ungrateful. He had been on his best behaviour. It was slightly freaking Austin out.

'Yes ... I mean, you need a computer and stuff to work it ... but I suppose ...'

There was a pause.

'Thank you,' said Darny.

A much older boy with an incipient wispy moustache picked up the NFL game. 'I can show you how to work this if you like.'

'Thanks,' said Darny, brightening a bit. 'Cool.'

Marian came in from the kitchen and beckoned Austin over.

'I have a gift for you,' she said. Austin raised his

eyebrows as she brought out an envelope. 'I want you to go see my daughter,' she said. 'No, I insist on it. Just for a day or two. See if you kids can't work something out without distractions around you. We'll keep Darny here; he has fun with the other kids. Just go and see her. She doesn't know it's finished. She doesn't know what's going on. I like you, Austin, but if you make her unhappy and leave her dangling, I will cut off all your fingers. Is that clear?'

Austin opened the envelope, shaking. He stared at it.

'Where did you get the money for this?' he said.

'Oh, a friend who made rather a lot of money in those computer things ... he died,' she said. 'Lovely man. Well, sometimes horrible. Very clever, though.'

Austin raised his eyebrows.

They both looked at the drifting snow in the little garden.

Austin looked at the ticket again.

'This flight leaves in two hours.'

'Lucky you're already in Queens, then, isn't it?'

This time, there was no sleeping on the flight. Full already from Christmas dinner, Issy couldn't face another one. The crew were very jolly and cheerful, but the flight was full of grumpy-looking people who hated Christmas, or plenty of people to whom it didn't mean anything, so their exuberance was slightly lost on them. She clutched her bag fiercely, biting her lip, trying not to think about anything except that for the first time in a fortnight she wasn't crying. And that, one way or another, they'd soon be in the same room again. Beyond that, she wouldn't let herself go, simply looking at the crackling ice over the oval window and staring into space.

Austin found himself on his plane so fast he didn't have time to think at all. He tried to order his thoughts, but he felt too full of gibberish. He drank an extremely large whisky and tried to sleep. He failed.

Their flights crossed over Newfoundland; Issy flying into a New York morning, Austin into a London afternoon, the pure white traces of vapour drawing a large X in the sky.

There was no traffic. Austin didn't stop to think; he knew exactly where she'd be. Where she'd always be. As the taxi driver – chatting animatedly about his recent miraculous recovery from renal failure, Austin barely listening – drew up just by the tiny little alleyway on Church Street, Austin's eye was distracted by the rows of fairy lights outside the Cupcake Café reflecting off the dirty white snow, the steamed-up windows and, inside, the hint of shapes of happy people moving about.

As soon as he saw it, in an instant of clarity, he knew. He would come back. They could start again. He'd try something, anything. They'd figure it out. New York was harsh, a shiny dream. Not for him. He had given up everything once before in his life. He could do it again. Because at the end of the sacrifice was happiness. He knew that. And however much money he made, or however good Darny's school, they couldn't be happy – neither of them – without Issy. And that was that. He paused for a minute as the cab pulled away, the night coming on fast, his long overcoat flapping in the wind, his scarf likewise; paused and took a deep breath full of happiness before marching forward, cheerfully and with an open heart, towards his future. He pulled open the tinging door.

There was a long silence.

'What the *hell*?' said a slightly tipsy Pearl, as, just at the same moment, Louis launched himself at Austin's legs.

'AUSTIN! WEAH'S DARNY! I DID MISS YOU AUSTIN!'

One of Ashok's cousins blew a party hooter. It sounded a low note in the silence.

Snow was still falling. Issy could barely remember a minute of the trip, or the shorter-than-normal line at immigration. Sometimes it felt like the outskirts of London and the outskirts of New York could touch each other, that they were all part of the same metropolis of taxis and restaurants and businesses and people rushing with lots to do.

The cab dropped her at the hotel.

'I'm sorry, ma'am,' said the same lovely woman who'd been there before. 'I'm afraid Mr Tyler's been checked out.'

Issy swallowed. This had never occurred to her. She had no idea where he might be. Had he gone to his boss's house for Christmas? She didn't know how to contact him. And she'd kind of hoped ... she realised this was stupid, daft, but she'd kind of hoped just to meet him; to see him; to see his face – hopefully – break into that wide smile of his; to run into his arms. Not to have to call and have an awkward conversation and sound desperate – or worse, crazy. Much better just to appear and explain later, she thought.

'Do you have a room?' she asked.

'We have one room left,' said the woman, smiling nicely. 'It'll be seven hundred and eighty dollars.'

Issy snatched up her credit card like she'd been stung.

'Oh,' she said. 'Oh, I'll leave it for now.'

The woman looked worried. 'You know, it's quite difficult to find a hotel room in New York at Christmas time,' she said sympathetically.

Issy sighed. 'It's all right,' she said, shaking her head, stunned at how badly her mission was failing, with all the excitement and good intentions her friends had sent her off with. 'I can stay on my mum's couch.'

'Super!' said the friendly receptionist.

It would be best, thought Issy. Stay at her mum's tonight, call Austin tomorrow wherever he was, meet up like civilised adults. That would be best. She could catch up on sleep and have a bath and all of that stuff. She sighed. Sit through her mum's lecture about not relying on men, or in fact anyone. All of that.

First, she wandered the streets. It was a beautiful day; sunny, with the ice crackling. As long as you stayed in the sun, it didn't even seem that cold. There were lots of people out and about, taking a stroll and saying good day to each other; tourists, not quite sure what to do on Christmas Day, hoicking rucksacks and taking photographs; lots of Jewish people noisily cramming into Chinese restaurants. It was … it was nice.

She found herself, eventually, on a familiar back street. The big shops weren't open, of course, but it was amazing how many of the smaller ones were. Even at Christmas time, commerce was everything. She heard, suddenly, a snatch of her favourite Christmas song coming through an open door … and caught a slightly off smell. She went through the door. She was, she noticed with a quick pang, the only customer. Well. He *might* have been there. The sole member of staff was standing red-eyed by the till, and didn't even look up.

'Hello,' said Issy.

Chapter Twenty

Vanilla Cupcake, Courtesy of the Caked Crusader

For the cupcakes

125g unsalted butter, at room temperature

125g caster sugar

2 large eggs, at room temperature

125g self-raising flour, sifted i.e. passed through a
sieve

2 tsp vanilla extract (N.B. 'extract', not 'essence'.
Extract is natural whereas essence contains
chemicals and is nasty)

2 tbsp milk (you can use whole milk or semi-
skimmed but not skimmed, as it tastes horrible)

For the buttercream

125g unsalted butter, at room temperature

250g icing sugar, sifted i.e. passed through a sieve

1 tsp vanilla extract

Splash of milk – by which I mean, start with a
tablespoon, beat that in, see if the buttercream is
the texture you want, if it isn't add a further
tablespoon etc.

How to make

Preheat the oven to 190°C/fan oven 170°C/gas
mark 5.

Line a cupcake pan with paper cases. This
recipe will make 12 cupcakes.

Beat the butter and sugar together until they
are smooth, fluffy and pale. This will take several
minutes even with soft butter. Don't skimp on this
stage, as this is where you get air into the mix.
How you choose to beat the ingredients is up to
you. When I started baking I used a wooden
spoon, then I got handheld electric beaters and
now I use a stand mixer. They will all yield the
same result, however, if you use the wooden spoon,
you will get a rather splendid upper arm
workout . . . who said cake was unhealthy?

Add the eggs, flour, vanilla and milk and beat
until smooth. Some recipes require you to add all
these ingredients separately but, for this recipe, you
don't have to worry about that. You are looking
for what's called 'dropping consistency'; this means
that when you take a spoonful of mixture and

gently tap the spoon, the mixture will drop off. If the mixture doesn't drop off the spoon, mix it some more. If it still won't drop, add a further tablespoon of milk.

Spoon into the paper cases. There is no need to level the batter, as the heat of the oven will do this for you. Place the tray in the upper half of the oven. Do not open the oven door until the cakes have baked for twelve minutes, then check them by inserting a skewer (if you don't have one, use a wooden cocktail stick) into the centre of the sponges – if it comes out clean, the cakes are ready and you can remove them from the oven. If raw batter comes out on the skewer, pop them back in the oven and give them a couple more minutes. Cupcakes, being small, can switch from underdone to overdone quickly so don't get distracted! Don't worry if your cakes take longer than a recipe states – ovens vary.

As soon as the cupcakes come out of the oven, tip them out of the tin on to a wire rack. If you leave them in the tin they will carry on cooking (the tin is very hot) and the paper cases may start to pull away from the sponge, which looks ugly. Once on the wire rack they will cool quickly – about thirty minutes.

Now make the buttercream: beat the butter in a bowl, on its own, until very soft. It will start to look almost like whipped cream. It is this stage in the process that makes your buttercream light and delicious.

Add the icing sugar and beat until light and fluffy. Go gently at first otherwise the icing sugar will cloud up and coat you and your kitchen with white dust! Keep mixing until the butter and sugar are combined and smooth; the best test for this is to place a small amount of the icing on your tongue and press it up against the roof of your mouth. If it feels gritty, it needs more beating. If it's smooth, you can move on to the next step.

Beat in the vanilla and milk. If the buttercream isn't as soft as you would like, then add a tiny bit more milk but be careful – you don't want to make the buttercream sloppy.

Either spread or pipe over the cupcakes. Spreading is easier and requires no additional equipment. However, if you want your cupcakes to look fancy it might be worth buying an icing bag and star-shaped nozzle. You can get disposable icing bags, which cut down on washing-up.

Add any additional decoration you desire – this is where you can be creative. In the past I have used sugar flowers, hundreds and thousands, Maltesers, edible glitter, sprinkles, nuts, crumbled Flake . . . the options are endless.

Bask in glory at the wonderful thing you have made.

Eat.

It was amazing, the capacity for human sympathy, thought Issy. She would honestly not believe that she could sit here and listen to another human being pour out how unfair it was that Issy's boyfriend wouldn't get off with them.

'You'd met me,' she said finally. 'You knew I existed.'

Kelly-Lee kept weeping, big tears pouring off the end of her perfect retroussé nose. 'But you're foreign,' she said. 'So I figured it didn't really matter, know what I mean?'

'No,' said Issy.

'You're from Eurp! Everyone knows everyone has six girlfriends over there.'

'Does everyone know that?'

'Oh yeah,' said Kelly-Lee. 'And you have no idea how hard it is. Now I'm going to lose my job . . . '

'For trying to pull someone?' said Issy. 'Cor, your boss is miles tougher than me.'

'No . . . apparently my cupcakes are no good.'

'They are no good,' agreed Issy. 'They're terrible, in fact.'

'Well, they drop off half, then I'm meant to practise making them fresh, but I never really bothered.'

Issy rolled her eyes.

Kelly-Lee blinked at her. 'Does he really, really love you?'

'I don't know,' said Issy, truthfully.

'Maybe when I'm as old as you I'll know what real love feels like,' said Kelly-Lee, starting to weep again.

'Yes, yes, maybe,' said Issy. 'Show me your kitchen?'

Kelly-Lee showed it to her. The oven wasn't even warm, but the place was amazingly well equipped.

'Look at all this space!' said Issy. 'I work in a bunker! You have windows and everything.'

Kelly-Lee looked around dully. 'Whatever.'

Issy looked in the enormous, state-of-the-art vacuum fridge. 'Wow. I would *love* one of these.'

'You don't have a fridge?'

Issy ignored her, and took out a dozen eggs and some butter. She sniffed at it. 'This butter is very average,' she said. 'It's a bad start. But it will do.' She added milk, then went to the large flour and sugar vats, and started pulling on an apron. Kelly-Lee regarded her in confusion.

'Come on,' said Issy. 'We haven't got all day. Well, we have, because it's Christmas Day and neither of us has any-where better to go. But let's not think about that right now.'

Kelly-Lee listened, at first half-heartedly, then with closer attention, as Issy talked her patiently through the right temperature for creaming the butter and sugar, the importance of not overmixing, the right height for siev-ing the flour, which Kelly-Lee had never heard of.

Twenty minutes later, they put four batches into the oven, and Issy started to unravel the secrets of butter icing.

'Wait for this,' she said. 'You won't believe the other muck you were churning out.'

She whipped the icing into a confection lighter than cream, and made Kelly-Lee taste it. 'If you don't taste, you don't know what you're doing,' she said. 'You have to taste all the time.'

'But I won't fit my jeans!'

'If you don't taste, you won't have a job and you won't be able to buy any jeans.'

The smell – for once, heavenly rather than over-whelmingly of baking soda – rose up in the kitchen, and instantly Issy felt calm and more relaxed. She was here. He was here, somewhere. It would all come good. She picked up the phone to call her mother.

'What the *hell*?' said Marian.

In Queens, the situation became clear. Issy turned up accompanied by two dozen of what her mother insisted on referring to as fairy cakes.

'Darny!' said Issy, as he flew into her arms. She wasn't expecting that.

'I'm sorry,' he muttered. 'I'm sorry. I was grumpy with you and you went away.'

'No,' she said. 'I was bossy and being like a mum and it was wrong and I hurt you. *I'm* sorry.'

Darny mumbled something. Issy crouched down so she could hear. 'I wish you were my mum,' he said.

Issy didn't say anything, just held him tight. Then she remembered.

'You know why my bag is so damn heavy?' she said. Darny shook his head. 'I brought you a present.'

It had been a last-minute idea; a silly one as she was toting it around. But she could get something else for Louis.

Darny's eyes widened when he saw it.

'WOW!' he said. All the other kids rushed towards it too.

'MONSTER GARAGE!'

Issy smiled at her mother. 'He's only little,' she murmured.

'He is,' said her mother. 'Well. Now. This is a mess.'

Issy sat down with a large glass of kosher red, which she was developing a real fondness for. She shook her head.

'I don't think it is,' she said wonderingly. 'I really don't. I can't believe . . . he'd drop everything. Travel all that way. Oh, I wish I was there now. I wish I was.'

Then her phone rang.

'Don't say anything,' said a strong, humorous, familiar voice. 'And I'll text you.'

'OK . . . I . . . I . . .'

But he'd already hung up.

Chapter Twenty-One

Issy had received a text message with a simple street address on it – cryptic, but to the point. When she got there, first thing on Boxing Day morning, it was quiet, but already people were starting to queue. He wasn't there. But if she'd learned anything, Issy thought, it was that she could no longer wait for Austin. Or anyone.

'One, please,' she said politely. She figured out her skate size in American and strapped on the black boots, then, wobbling slightly, walked out on to the ice. Gramps had used to love to skate; they'd built a municipal rink in Manchester in the fifties, and he liked to go round it with his hands insouciantly behind his back, a funny sight in his smart dark suit. Issy used to go with him sometimes, and he would take her by the hand and whirl her round. She loved it.

Slowly she rotated on the ice, the sun glinting off the

surface crystals, 30 Rock towering overhead, people running in, rushing back to work the day after Christmas. She looked around at the pink light glancing off the high buildings. It was, she thought, spectacular. Wonderful. She and New York had had a rocky start, but now ... Lost in thought, she attempted a small spin, failed, then stumbled. A hand reached out and grabbed her.

'Are you all right?'

She turned. For a moment, the sun was so bright she was dazzled and couldn't see. But she could still make out the shape of him, there, in that long coat, back in the green scarf she had bought him which matched the green dress she was wearing.

'Oh,' was all she could say. Now she could see again, she noticed he looked very tired. But apart from that, he looked so very, very happy. 'Oh.'

And then, balancing on their skates, they were completely and utterly wrapped up in one another, and Issy felt as if she was flying; rushing round and round like an ice dancer leaping through snow flurries, or racing down a snowy slope, or flying through the cold air faster than a jet plane.

'My love,' Austin was saying, kissing her again and again. 'I was such an idiot. *Such* an idiot.'

'I was stubborn too,' said Issy. 'Didn't give a thought to what you were up to. So unfair.'

'You weren't! You weren't at all.'

They looked at each other.

'Let's not talk any more,' said Issy, and they stood together in the centre of the rink, as bemused but indulgent skaters continued to weave around them, and the sun melted the ice, which dripped down from the high towers above them like crystal.

They checked back into the hotel and stayed there for a couple of days, then set about making it up to Darny with outings and exhibitions and treats until he begged for mercy. On the third day, Issy took a phone call and came to Austin with a very strange look on her face.

'That was Kelly-Lee,' she said. The flash of guilt that crossed his face reminded her that she hadn't mentioned that she'd met her, and she decided not to tell him what Kelly-Lee had said.

'I ran into her and helped her make some cupcakes ... that's all,' she said firmly. 'Anyway, apparently her boss came in and was totally astounded, and wants to send her to California to open up a new store, and apparently Kelly-Lee feels she's much more suited to California.'

'I think she is too,' said Austin.

'Anyway, there's an opening to run the New York store if I want it, apparently ... '

Austin hadn't spoken to Merv. He looked at her carefully.

'Hmm,' he said. 'But we're going back to London.'

'It's raining in London, though, isn't it?' said Issy carefully. 'And we'd probably make a bit of money renting out your house. And mine, when Ashok and Helena move. Unless he gets her pregnant again, in which case she's going to kill him and *then* they'll split up.'

Austin kept his face completely neutral.

'It would be nice,' said Issy, 'to give Maya a full-time job. Her post office job has gone now, and she's such an asset. And with Pearl and Caroline getting on so well ...'

Austin coughed at that.

'Comparatively speaking ...'

Issy had been doing a lot of thinking over the last few days, now that she was finally rested. A lot.

Austin looked at her. She was lying on the white bed, looking luscious and pale and beautiful, and he didn't think he'd ever seen anything he liked quite as much.

'Mmm,' he said.

Issy looked at him steadily. 'Well, I suppose ... a couple of years in the world's greatest city, with Darny at the world's greatest school ... it might not be *too* bad ...'

Austin's eyes widened. 'We don't have to. I'm ready to go back. Well, I don't care. I just want to be where you are.'

Issy closed her eyes. She could see it in her head. The Cupcake Café. She could hear the jangle of the bell, and Pearl's throaty laugh as she grabbed the mop in the morning; she could see Caroline's taut face complaining about the price of ski holidays these days. She

saw herself dancing to Capital Radio and feeling Louis'
warm arms around her knees as he dashed in with a new
picture for the back wall. She could remember the faces
of so many of her customers; recall the day she'd first
seen the menus back from the printers; how it had
started out as a dream but had become real. Her
Cupcake Café.

But it *was* real. It wasn't a dream. It wouldn't vanish if
she stopped looking at it. It wouldn't suddenly disappear
in a puff of smoke. Pearl was ready – more than ready –
to step into her managerial shoes, and Maya's frantic
practising and obsessive attention to detail boded well for
her recipes. And Caroline would just be Caroline, she
supposed. She couldn't do much about that. But she
could leave now, confident that it could work, it could run
without her. And maybe she could help the person she
loved with his new life too. The café would, she fervently hoped, never change. But they could.

'I want to be here,' she said. 'Where it's best for
Darny. And close to Mum. But mostly ... for us, Austin.
You are us. It's great for us. And it will be great for me. I
believe that. It's all decided. I'll go back once a month or
so, check up on everything, make sure no one's killed
anyone else, but for a couple of years ... we'd be mad not
to try the adventure. I've changed my life once already.
I think I've got a taste for it now.'

Austin took her in his arms. 'I will devote my entire
life to making it amazing for you,' he said.

'You don't have to,' said Issy, glancing towards the window, at the lights and the life and the buzzing, glittery, jittery streets. 'It already is.'

He stopped and thought. Then thought some more.

'You know,' he said. 'You won't be able to work here without a green card.'

Now it was Issy's turn to be surprised.

'Oh no? I thought, maybe in just a caf . . . '

'Nope,' he said. 'And normally they're quite hard to get.'

'Mmm?'

'Unless you're . . . with someone who has one.' He nuzzled her neck. 'You know, in all the madness, I never got you a Christmas present.'

'Oh no, you didn't!' said Issy. 'I forgot! I want one!'

'You know what they sell lots of in New York?'

'Dreams? Ice skates? Pretzels?'

He looked at her pensively. 'Aim higher.'

She looked back at him without saying anything, but her fingers unconsciously strayed to her little diamond earrings.

'That's it,' said Austin. 'You need something to go with those earrings. Definitely. But maybe . . . on your finger?'

And they dressed warmly, and walked out hand in hand into the sharp, bright, exciting future of a honking, buzzing New York morning.

Back in London, Pearl looked at the post-lunch rush happily poking their fingers at the New Year range of apple and raisin cupcakes; rose blossom for the eventual spring; discounted gingerbread for the last few Christmas addicts, beautifully put together by Maya, and smiled.

'Cappuccino's up!' she yelled.

Acknowledgements

Firstly, thanks to everyone who read *Meet Me at the Cupcake Café* and was kind enough to let me know they enjoyed it, or even kinder to review it online and let other people know. I just can't thank you enough. I love hearing from people, especially if you've tried the recipes! And you can get me on Twitter @jennycolgan or my Facebook page is www.facebook.com/thatwriterjennycolgan. If you haven't read *Meet Me at the Cupcake Café*, don't worry; this book should stand alone.

Special thanks to Sufjan Stevens and Lowell Brams for doing their best to let us have a little Christmas miracle . . . Everything lost will be found.

Also, many thanks to Kate Webster for letting me use her wonderful chocolate cola cupcake recipe (see page 270). For more of her delicious recipes check out her food blog: http://thelittleloaf.wordpress.com.

Huge thanks always to Ali Gunn, Rebecca Saunders, Jo Dickinson, Manpreet Grewal, David Shelley, Ursula Mackenzie, Emma Williams, Jo Wickham, Camilla Ferrier, Sarah McFadden, Emma Graves for the lovely cover, Wallace Beaton for the art work, everyone at Little, Brown, the Board, and all our friends and relations. Special hugs and Christmas kisses to Mr B and the three wee bees; I so hope your Christmas memories are magical. Even that time we couldn't get the Scalextric to work.

Baking your first cupcake
by The Caked Crusader

So, you've read this fab novel and, apart from thinking, gosh, I want to read all of Jenny Colgan's other novels, you're also thinking, I want to bake my own cupcakes. Congratulations! You are setting out on a journey that will result in pleasure and great cake!

Firstly, I'll let you into a little secret that no cupcake bakery would want me to share: making cupcakes is easy, quick and cheap. You will create cupcakes in your own home – even on your first attempt, I promise – that taste better and look better than commercially produced cakes.

The great thing about making cupcakes is how little equipment they require. Chances are you already have a cupcake tin (the tray with twelve cavities) knocking about in your kitchen cupboards. It's the same pan you use for making Yorkshire puds and, even if you don't have one, they can be picked up for under £5 in your supermarket's kitchenware aisle. The only other thing to buy before you can get started is a pack of paper cases, which, again, any supermarket sells in the home baking aisle.

Before making cupcakes, it's important to absorb what I think of as the four key principles of baking (this makes them sound rather grander than they are!):

- Bring the ingredients (particularly the butter) to room temperature before you start. Not only will this create the best cupcake but also it's so much easier for you to work with the ingredients . . . and why wouldn't you want to make it easy on yourself?
- Preheat your oven i.e. switch it on to the right temperature setting about 20–30 minutes before the cakes go into the oven. This means that the cake batter receives the correct temperature straight away and all the chemical processes will commence, thus producing a light sponge. Thankfully, in order to bake a great cupcake, you don't need to know what all those chemical processes are!
- Weigh your ingredients on a scale and make sure you don't miss anything out. Baking isn't like any other form of cooking – you can't guess the measurements or make substitutions and expect success. If you're making a casserole that requires two carrots and you decide to put in three, chances are it will be

just as lovely (although perhaps a touch more carroty); if your cake recipe requires, for example, two eggs and you put in three, what would have been an airy fluffy sponge will come out like eggy dough. This may sound restrictive but actually, it's great – all the thinking is done for you in the recipe, yet you'll get all the credit for baking a delicious cupcake.

– Use good-quality ingredients. If you put butter on your bread, why would you put margarine in a cake? If you eat nice chocolate, why would you use cooking chocolate in a cake? A cake can only be as nice as the ingredients going into it.

DON'T MISS THE NEXT IRRESISTIBLE NOVEL FROM

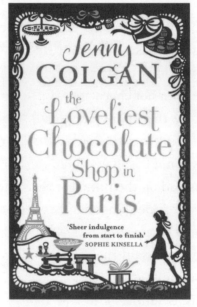

Read on for an exclusive look at the first chapter!

Coming in Spring 2013

A Word From Jenny

There are lots of marvellous artisan chocolate shops in Paris. My favourite is called Paul Rogers on the Rue du Faubourg. I would strongly recommend a visit there, and that you taste their hot chocolate, whichever season you go. They're run by the eponymous Paul, who is, indeed, a curly-haired, twinkly-eyed, roguish-looking chap.

This book is not based on any of those shops in a single detail, but instead on the principle that when people dedicate their lives to one thing that they really really love and learn a lot about it, amazing things can happen.

Somebody once said the reason we love chocolate so much is that it melts at the same temperature as the inside of our mouths. Scientists also talk about releasing endorphins and so on. But the simple truth is that we like chocolate because it is REALLY REALLY NICE. I've put in some really lovely recipes here too. I like to think as I get older I can actually cook with chocolate instead of just, you know, accidentally eating it as soon as it's in the house or sometimes in the car.

When we moved to France a while back (for my husband's work), I was surprised to find they took chocolate as seriously as they take any kind of food. La Maison du Chocolat is a really high-end chain and you'll find one in most towns, where you can chat with the chocolatier about what you want and what else you're going to be eating, just like a wine waiter. But personally I am just as happy with a great big slab of Dairy Milk, or Toblerone or my absolute fave, Fry's Chocolate Cream (plain). Not everything has to be luxury to be enjoyed. Alas, my children have now reached the age where it's becoming obvious who keeps stealing the Kinder bars out of their party bags. Kids, hum, look, I hate to have to tell you this. It was definitely your dad.

Before we start, I wanted to say a word about language. In my experience, learning another language is really bloody difficult, unless you're one of those people who picks things up in two seconds flat, in which case I would say *bllergh* (that's me poking my tongue out) to you because I am extremely jealous.

Traditionally, too, when people in books are speaking a foreign language, it's indicated in *italics*. I've chosen not to do that here. Basically, anyone Anna speaks to in Paris is speaking French back to her unless I've mentioned otherwise. To which you and I would think, cor, that's AMAZING she learned such fantastic French so fast. Obviously she has lots of lessons with Claire, but if you've ever learnt another language you'll know that you can be totally confident in a classroom then turn up in the country and everybody goes 'wabbawabbawabbawabbaWAH?' to you at, like, a million miles an hour, and you panic because you can't understand a single word of it. That's certainly what happened to me.

So, anyway, you need to take it on trust that it's exactly the same for Anna, but for purposes of not repeating myself endlessly and slowing down the story, I've taken out the millions and millions of times she says 'What?' or 'Can you say that again please?' or needs to check her dictionary.

I do hope you enjoy it, and let me know how you get on with the recipes. And Bon Appetit!

Very warmest wishes,

Jenny

Chapter One

The really weird thing about it was that although I knew instantly that something was wrong – very very wrong, something sharp, something very serious, an insult to my entire body – I couldn't stop laughing. Laughing hysterically.

I was lying there covered, drenched, in spilled melted chocolate and I couldn't stop giggling. There were other faces now, looking down at me, some I was sure I even recognised. They weren't laughing. They all looked very serious in fact. This somehow struck me as even funnier and set me off again.

From the periphery I heard someone say, 'Pick them up!' and someone else say, 'No way! You pick them up! Gross!' I heard Flynn, the new stockboy say, 'I'll dial 911,' and someone else say, 'Flynn, don't be stupid, it's 999, you're not American,' and someone else say 'I think you can dial 911 now because there were so many idiots who kept dialling it,' and then someone was taking out their phone and saying something about needing an ambulance, which I thought was hilarious as well, and then someone, who was definitely Del, our old grumpy janitor, saying, 'Well, they're probably going to want to throw this batch away then,' and the idea that they might not throw away the enormous vat of chocolate but try to sell it instead when it had landed all over me actually was funny.

After that, thank God, I don't remember anything, although later, in hospital, a paramedic came over and said I was a total bloody nutter in the ambulance, and that he'd always been told that shock affected people in different ways, but mine was just about the differentest he'd ever seen. Then he saw my face and said, 'Cheer up, love. You'll laugh again.' But at that point I wasn't exactly sure I ever would.

'Oh come off it, Debs, love, it's only a couple of toes. It could have been a lot worse. What if it had been her nose?'

That was my dad, talking to my mum. He liked to look on the bright side.

'Well, they could have given her a new nose. She hates her nose anyway.'

That was definitely my mum. She's not quite as good as my dad at looking on the bright side. In fact, I could hear her sobbing, but somehow my body shied away from the light; I couldn't open my eyes. I didn't think it was a light; it felt like the sun or something. Maybe I was on holiday. I couldn't be at home, the sun never bloody shines in Kidinsborough, my home town, which was voted worst town in England three years in a row before local political pressure got the 'Worst Town' television show taken off the air.

My parents zoned out of earshot, just drifted off like

someone retuning a radio. I had no idea if they were there, or if they ever had been. I knew I wasn't moving, but inside I felt as though I was squirming and wriggling and trapped inside a body-shaped prison someone had buried me in. I could shout but no one could hear me. I tried to move but it wasn't working. The dazzle would turn to black and back again to the sun and none of it made the faintest bit of sense to me as I dreamt – or lived – great big nightmares about toes and feet and parents who spontaneously disappear and whether this was what going crazy felt like and whether I'd actually dreamt my whole other life, the bit about being me, Anna Trent, thirty years old, taster in a chocolate factory.

While I'm here, here are my top ten Taster in a Chocolate Factory jokes that I get at Faces, our local nightclub. It's not very nice, but the rest are really much, much worse:

1. Yes. I will give you some free samples.
2. No, I'm not as fat as you clearly just expected me to be.
3. Yes, it is exactly like *Charlie and the Chocolate Factory*.
4. No, no one has ever done a poo in the chocolate vat.*
5. No, it doesn't actually make me more popular than a normal person as I am thirty, not seven.
6. No, I don't feel sick when confronted with chocolate. I absolutely adore it, but if it makes you feel better about your job to think that I am, feel free.

*Though I wouldn't have put it past Flynn.

7. Oh, that is so interesting that you have something even tastier than chocolate in your underpants, yawn. (NB: I would like to be brave enough to say that but I'm not that brave really. I normally just grimace and look at something else for a while. My best mate Cath soon takes care of them anyway. Or, occasionally, she kisses them).

8. Yes, I will suggest your peanut/beer/vodka/jam-flavoured chocolate idea, but I doubt we'll be as rich as you think.

9. Yes, I can make actual real chocolate, although at Brader's Family Chocolates they're all processed automatically in a huge vat and I'm more of a supervisor really. I wish I did more complex work, but according to the bosses nobody wants their chocolates messed about with; they want them tasting exactly the same, and lasting a long time. So it's quite a synthetic process.

10. No, it's not the best job in the world. But it's mine and I like it. Or at least I did, until I ended up in here.

And a rum and Coke, thanks for asking.

'Anna.'

A man was sitting on the end of my bed. I couldn't focus on him. He knew my name but I didn't know his. That seemed unfair.

I tried to open my mouth. It was full of sand. Someone had put sand in my mouth. Why would anyone do that?

'Anna?'

The voice came again. It was definitely real, it was definitely connected to the shadow at the end of my bed.

'Can you hear me?'

Well, of course I can hear you. You're sitting on the end of my bed shouting at me, was what I wanted to say, but all that came out was a kind of dry croak.

'That's great, that's great, very good. Would you like a drink of water?'

I nodded. It seemed easiest.

'Good, good. Don't nod too much, you'll dislodge the wires. NURSE!'

I don't know whether the nurse came or not, I was suddenly gone again. my last conscious thought was that I hoped she or he didn't mind being yelled at by people who sat on other people's beds, shouting.

'Here she is.'

It was the same voice, but how much later I couldn't tell. The light seemed different. A sudden shock of pain travelled through me like a lightning bolt and I gasped.

'There you go, she's going to be great.'

Dad.

'Oh, I don't like the look of this.'

Mum.

'Uhm ... can I have that water?' I asked, but it came out like, 'Ca ha wa?'

Thankfully someone spoke desert sand, because instantly a plastic cup was put to my lips. That small cup of tepid chalky tap water was the single best thing I had ever put in my mouth in my entire life, and that includes the first time I tasted a Creme Egg.

I slurped it down and asked for another, but someone said no, and that was that. Maybe I was in prison.

'Can you open your eyes for us?' came the commanding voice.

'Course she can.'

'Oh, Pete, I don't know. I just don't know.'

Oddly, it was slightly to spite my mother's lack of ambition for me in the eye-opening department that really made me try. I flickered and, suddenly, hazing into view was the shape sitting on the end of my bed I'd been aware of before – I wished he'd stop that – and two shapes that were as familiar as my own hands. I could see my mother's reddish hair that she coloured at home even though my best mate Cath had offered to do it down at the salon for next to nothing, but my mother thought that was extravagant and that Cath was loose (that last bit was true, though that had nothing to do with how good she was at hair. Which, admittedly, wasn't very), so now my mum had this kind of odd, henna-like fringe round the top of her forehead where she hadn't wiped the dye off properly. And my dad was in his best shirt, which really made me worry. He didn't dress like that for anything but weddings and funerals and I was pretty much a hundred per cent sure I wasn't getting married, unless Chris had suddenly regenerated into a completely different physical and personality type, which was unlikely.

'Hello?' I said, feeling as I did so a rush as though the desert sands were retreating, that the division between what was real and what was a writhing ball of confusion and pain was retreating, that Anna was back, that the skin I was wearing was mine after all.

'Darling!'

My mum burst into tears. My dad, not prone to huge out-bursts of affection, gently squeezed my hand – the hand, I noticed, that didn't have a big tube going into it. My other hand did have one. It was the grossest thing I'd ever seen in my life.

'Ugh, gah,' I said. 'What's this? It's disgusting.'

The figure at the end of my bed smiled in a rather patro-nising way.

'I think you'd find things a lot more disgusting if it wasn't there,' he said. 'It's giving you painkillers and medication.'

'Well, can I have some more?' I said. The lightning-sharp pain flashed through me again, from the toes of my left foot upwards.

I suddenly became aware of other tubes on me, some going in and out of places I didn't really want to discuss in front of my dad. I went quiet. I felt really really weird.

'Is your head spinning?' said the bedsitter. 'That's quite normal.'

My mum was still sniffing.

'It's all right, Mum.'

What she said next chilled me to the bone.

'It's not all right, love. It's not all right at all.'

Over the next few days – I seemed to fall asleep on and off at completely random moments. The bedsitter is Dr Ed – yes, really, that's how he referred to himself. Yeah, all right I know he was a doctor and everything, tra la la, but you can be Ed or you can be Dr Smith or something. Anything else is just showing off, like you're a doctor on telly or something.

I think Dr Ed would have *loved* to have been a doctor on the telly, looking at people who've got two bumholes and things. He was always very smartly turned out and did things like sit on the end of the bed, which other doctors didn't do, and look you in the eye, as if he was making a huge effort to be with you as a person. I actually already knew I was a person. I think I preferred the snotty consultant who came round once a week, barely looked at me and asked his medical students embarrassing questions.

Anyway, Dr Ed shouldn't have been so chummy because it was kind of his fault that I was even there. I had slipped at the factory – everyone had got very excited wondering if there was some health and safety rule that hadn't been followed and we were all about to become millionaires, but actually it turned out to be completely my fault. It was an unusually warm spring day and I'd decided to try out my new shoes, which turned out to be hilariously inappropriate for the factory floor and I'd skidded and, in a total freak, hit a vat ladder and upended the entire thing. The ladder joist had sliced straight through the fourth toe of my right foot.

Someone had packed the toe in ice and brought it to the hospital – they would be getting a big bunch of flowers from me when I found out who had done that, I vowed – but before they had a chance to sew it back on I'd contracted one of those disgusting hospital diseases and it had nearly killed me, and now it was too late.

'A bug tried to eat me?' I asked Dr Ed.

'Well, yes, that's about right,' he said, smiling to show overtly white teeth that he must have got whitened somewhere. Maybe he just liked to practise for going on television. 'Not a big bug like a spider, Anna.'

'Spiders aren't bugs,' I said crossly.

'Ha! No.' He flicked his hair. 'Well, these things are very very tiny, so small you couldn't see a thousand of them even if they were sitting right here on my finger!'

Perhaps there was something misprinted on my medical notes that said instead of being nearly thirty-one I was in fact eight.

'I don't care what size they are,' I said. 'They make me feel like total crap.'

'And that's why we're fighting them with every weapon we have!' said Dr Ed, like he was Spiderman or something. I didn't mention that if everyone had cleaned up with every brush they had, I probably wouldn't have caught it in the first place.

And anyway, oh Lord, I just felt so rough. I didn't feel like eating or drinking anything like water (Dad brought me some marshmallows and Mum practically whacked him because she was a hundred per cent certain they'd get trapped in my throat and I'd totally die right there in front of him) and I slept a lot. When I wasn't sleeping I didn't feel well enough to watch telly or read or speak to people or anything. I had a lot of messages on Facebook, according to my phone, which someone – Cath I was guessing – had plugged in beside my bed, but I wasn't really fussed about reading any of them.

I felt different, as if I'd woken up foreign, or in a strange land where nobody spoke my language – not Mum, not Dad, not my friends. They didn't speak the language of strange hazy days where nothing made much sense, they weren't constantly aching, or dealing with the idea of moving even just an arm across the bed being too difficult to contemplate. The country of the sick seemed a very different place, where you were fed and moved and everyone spoke to you like a child and you were always, always hot.

I was dozing off again, when I heard a noise. Something familiar, I was sure of it, but I couldn't tell from when. I was at school. School figured a lot in my fever dreams. I had hated it. Mum had always said she wasn't academic so I wouldn't be either, and that had pretty much sealed the deal, which in retrospect seemed absolutely stupid. So for ages when I hallucinated my old teachers' faces in front of me, I didn't take it too seriously. Then one day I woke up very early, when the hospital was still cool, and as quiet as it ever got, which wasn't very, and I turned my head carefully to the side, and there, not a dream or a hallucination, was Mrs Shawcourt, my old French teacher, gazing at me calmly.

I blinked in case she would go away. She didn't.

It was a small four-bed side ward I'd been put on, a few days or a couple of weeks ago – it was hard to tell precisely – which seemed a bit strange; either I was infectious or I wasn't, surely. The other two beds were empty, and over the days that followed, had a fairly speedy turnover of extremely old ladies who didn't seem to do much but cry.

'Hello,' she said. 'I know you, don't I?'

I suddenly felt a flush, like I hadn't done my homework.

I had never done my homework. Cath and I used to bunk off – French, it was totally useless, who could possibly need that? – and go sit round the back field where the teachers couldn't see you and speak with fake Mancunian accents about how crap Kidinsborough was and how we were going to leave the first chance we got.

'Anna Trent.'

I nodded.

'I had you for two years.'

I peered at her more closely. She'd always stood out in the school. She was by far the best dressed teacher, most of them were a right bunch of slobs. She used to wear these really nicely fitted dresses that made her look a bit different, you could tell she hadn't got them down at Matalan. She'd had blonde hair then—

I realised with a bit of a shock that she didn't have any hair at all. She was very thin, but then she always had been thin, but now she was really really thin.

I said the stupidest thing I could think of; in my defence, I really wasn't well.

'Are you sick then?'

'No,' said Mrs Shawcourt. 'I'm on holiday.'

There was a pause, then I grinned. I remembered that, actually, she was a really good teacher.

'I'm sorry to hear about your toes,' she said briskly.

I glanced down at the bandage covering my right foot.

'Ah, they'll be all right, just had a bit of a fall,' I said. Then

I saw her face. And I realised that all the time people had been talking about my fever and my illness and my accident, nobody had thought to tell me the truth.

It couldn't be though. I could feel them.

I stared at her, and she unblinkingly held my gaze.

'I can feel them,' I said.

'I can't believe nobody told you,' she said. 'Bloody hospitals. My darling, I heard them discuss it.'

I stared at the bandage again. I wanted to be sick. Then I was sick in a big cardboard bedpan, which they left a supply of by the side of my bed, for every time I wanted to be sick.

Dr Ed came by later and sat on my bed. I scowled at him.

'Now ...' he checked his notes, '... Anna. I'm sorry you weren't aware of the full gravity of the situation.'

'Because you kept talking about "accidents" and "regrettable incidents",' I said crossly. 'I didn't realise they'd gone altogether. AND I can feel them. They really hurt.'

He nodded.

'That's quite common, I'm afraid.'

'Why didn't anyone tell me? Everyone kept banging on about fever and bugs and things.'

'Well, that's what we were worried about. Losing a couple of toes was a lot less likely to kill you.'

'Well, that's good to know. And it's not "a couple of toes". It's *my toes*.'

As we spoke, a nurse was gently unwrapping the bandages from my foot. I gulped, worried I was going to throw up again.

Did you ever play that game at school where you lie on your front with your eyes closed and someone pulls your arms taut above your head, then very slowly lowers them so it feels like your arms are going down a hole? That was what this was like. My brain couldn't compute what it was seeing; what it could feel and knew to be true. My toes were there. They were there. But in front of my eyes was a curious diagonal slicing; two tiny stumps taken off in a descending line, very sharp, like it had been done on purpose with a razor.

'Now,' Dr Ed was saying, 'you know you are actually very lucky, because if you'd lost your big toe or your little one, you'd have had real problems with balance.'

I looked at him like he had horns growing out of his head.

'I absolutely and definitely do not feel lucky,' I said.

'Try being me,' came a voice from behind the next curtain, where Mrs Shawcourt was waiting for her next round of chemotherapy.

Suddenly, without warning, we both started to laugh.

I was in hospital for another three weeks. Loads of my mates came by and said I'd been in the paper, and could they have a look (no, apart from getting my dressing changed I couldn't bear to look at them) and keeping me up to date on social events that, suddenly, I really found I'd lost interest in. In fact, the only person I could talk to was Mrs Shawcourt, except of course she told me to call her Claire, which took a bit of getting used to and made me feel a bit too grown up. She had two sons who came to visit, who always looked a bit short for time, and her daughters-in-law, who were dead nice and used to give me their gossip mags because Claire couldn't be bothered with them, and once they brought some little girls in, both of whom got completely freaked out by the wires and the smell and the beeping. It was the only time I saw Claire really truly sad.

The rest of the time we talked. Well, I talked. Mostly about how bored I was, and how I was going to walk; physio was rubbish. For two things I had *never* ever thought about, except when I was getting a pedicure and not really even then, toes were annoyingly useful when it came to getting about. Even more embarrassing, I had to use the same physio lab as people who had really horrible traumatic injuries and were in wheelchairs and stuff and I felt like the most horrendous fraud marching up and down parallel bars with an injury most people thought was quite amusing, if anything.

Claire understood though. She was such easy company and sometimes, when she was very ill, I'd read to her. Most of her books, though, were in French.

'I can't read this,' I said.

'You ought to be able to,' she said. 'You had me.'

'Yeah, kind of,' I muttered.

'You were a good student,' said Claire. 'You showed a real aptitutde, I remember.'

Suddenly I flashed back to my first year report card. Among the 'doesn't apply herself' and 'could do betters' I suddenly remembered my French mark had been good. Why hadn't I applied myself?

'I don't know,' I said. 'I thought school was stupid.'

Claire shook her head. 'But I've met your parents, they're lovely. You're from such a nice family.'

'You don't have to live with them,' I said, then felt guilty that I'd been mean about them. They'd been in every single day even if, as Dad complained almost constantly, the parking charges were appalling.

'You still live at home?' she asked, surprised, and I felt a bit defensive.

'Neh. I lived with my boyfriend for a bit, but he turned out to be a pillock, so I moved back in, that's all.'

'I see,' said Claire. She looked at her watch. It was only nine-thirty in the morning. We'd already been up for three hours and lunch wasn't till twelve.

'If you like . . .' she began, 'I'm bored too. If I taught you some French, you could read to me. And I would feel less like a big sick bored bald plum who does nothing but dwell on the past and feel old and stupid and useless. Would you like that?'

I looked down at the magazine I was holding that had an enormous picture of Kim Kardashian's arse on it. And she had ten toes.

'Yeah, all right,' I said.

1973

'Don't cry,' the man was saying, shouting to be heard over the stiff sea breeze and the honking of the ferries and the rattle of the trains.

'It is a tiny ... look, la Manche. We can swim it if we have to.' He was trying to make a weak joke but it did nothing

This did nothing to stem the tide of tears rolling down the girl's cheeks. He wiped one away tenderly with his thumb.

'I would,' she said. 'I will swim it for you.'

'You,' he said, his voice cracking, 'will go back and finish school and do wonderful things and be happy.'

'I don't want to,' she groaned. 'I want to stay here with you.'

The man grimaced and attempted to stop her tears with kisses. They were dripping on his long-collared shirt.

'Ssh, bout-chou. Ssssh. We will be together again, you'll see.'

'I love you,' said the girl. 'I will never love anyone so much in my entire life.'

'I love you too,' said the man. 'I care for you and I love you and I shall see you again and I shall write you letters and you shall finish school and you shall see, all will be well.'

The girl's sobs started to quiet.

'I can't ... I can't bear it,' she said.

'Ah, love,' said the man, his accent strong. 'That is what it is; the need to bear things.' He buried his face in her hair. 'Alors. My love. Come back. Soon.'

'I will,' said the girl. 'Of course I will come back soon.'

Life is sweet with

Jenny
COLGAN

WELCOME TO ROSIE HOPKINS' SWEETSHOP OF DREAMS

Jenny Colgan

Were you a sherbet lemon or chocolate lime fan? Penny chews or hard-boiled sweeties (you do get more for your money that way)? The jangle of your pocket money . . . the rustle of the pink and green striped paper bag . . .

Rosie Hopkins thinks leaving her busy London life, and her boyfriend Gerard, to sort out her elderly Aunt Lilian's sweetshop in a small country village is going to be dull. Boy, is she wrong.

Lilian Hopkins has spent her life running Lipton's sweetshop, through wartime and family feuds. As she struggles with the idea that it might finally be the time to settle up, she also wrestles with the secret history hidden behind the jars of beautifully coloured sweets.

'This funny, sweet story is Jenny Colgan at her absolute best'
Heat

978-0-7515-4454-1

MEET ME AT THE CUPCAKE CAFÉ

Jenny Colgan

Come and meet Issy Randall, proud owner of
The Cupcake Café.

Issy Randall can bake. No, more than that – Issy can create
stunning, mouth-wateringly divine cakes. After a childhood
spent in her beloved Grampa Joe's bakery, she has undoubtedly
inherited his talent.

When she's made redundant from her safe but dull City job,
Issy decides to seize the moment. Armed with recipes from
Grampa, and with her best friends and local bank manager
fighting her corner, The Cupcake Café opens its doors. But Issy
has absolutely no idea what she's let herself in for. It will take all
her courage – and confectionery – to avert disaster . . .

'Sheer indulgence from start to finish'
Sophie Kinsella

978-0-7515-4449-7

WEST END GIRLS

Jenny Colgan

They may be twin sisters, but Lizzie and Penny Berry are complete opposites – Penny is blonde, thin and outrageous; Lizzie quiet, thoughtful and definitely not thin. The one trait they do share is a desire to DO something with their lives and, as far as they're concerned, the place to get noticed is London.

Out of the blue they discover they have a grandmother living in Chelsea – and when she has to go into hospital, they find themselves flat-sitting on the King's Road. But, as they discover, it's not as easy to become It Girls as they'd imagined, and West End Boys aren't at all like Hugh Grant . . .

'A brilliant novel from the mistress of chick-lit'
Eve

978-0-7515-4332-2

OPERATION SUNSHINE

Jenny Colgan

Evie needs a good holiday. Not just because she's been working all hours in her job, but also because every holiday she has ever been on has involved sunburn, arguments and projectile vomiting – sometimes all three at once. Why can't she have a normal holiday, like other people seem to have – some sun, sand, sea and (hopefully) sex?

So when her employers invite her to attend a conference with them in the South of France, she can't believe her luck. It's certainly going to be the holiday of a lifetime – but not quite in the way Evie imagines!

'Colgan at her warm, down-to-earth best'
Cosmopolitan

978-0-7515-3762-8

DIAMONDS ARE A GIRL'S BEST FRIEND

Jenny Colgan

Sophie Chesterton has been living the high life of glamorous
parties, men and new clothes, never thinking about tomorrow.
But after one shocking evening, she comes back down to earth
with the cruellest of bumps. Facing up to life in the real world
for the first time, Sophie quickly realises that when you've
hit rock bottom, the only way is up.

Join her as she starts life all over again: from cleaning toilets for
a living to the joys of bring-your-own-booze parties; from
squeezing out that last piece of lip gloss from the
tube to bargaining with bus drivers.

For anyone who's ever been scared of losing it all, this book is
here to show you money can't buy you love, and best friends are
so much more fun than diamonds . . .

'Jenny Colgan always writes an unputdownable, page-turning
bestseller – she's the queen of modern chick-lit'
Louise Bagshawe

978-0-7515-4031-4

THE GOOD, THE BAD AND THE DUMPED

Jenny Colgan

Now, you obviously, would never, ever look up your exes on Facebook. Nooo. And even if you did, you most certainly wouldn't run off trying to track them down, risking your job, family and happiness in the process. Posy Fairweather, on the other hand . . .

Posy is delighted when Matt proposes – on top of a mountain, in a gale, in full-on romantic mode. But a few days later disaster strikes: he backs out of the engagement. Crushed and humiliated, Posy starts thinking. Why has her love life always ended in total disaster? Determined to discover how she got to this point, Posy resolves to get online and track down her exes. Can she learn from past mistakes? And what if she has let Mr Right slip through her fingers on the way?

'A Jenny Colgan novel is as essential for a week in the sun as Alka Seltzer, aftersun and far too many pairs of sandals'
Heat

978-0-7515-4030-7

Keep in touch with

Jenny

www.jennycolgan.com

For more information on all Jenny's books, latest news and mouth-watering recipes